Meet You Under the Stars

A MORGAN'S GROVE NOVEL

TRACI BORUM

Meet You Under the Stars
A Morgan's Grove™ Novel
Red Adept Publishing, LLC
104 Bugenfield Court
Garner, NC 27529
http://RedAdeptPublishing.com/

---

1. http://StreetlightGraphics.com

Chapter One

Chaynie Mayfield tapped down the staircase of her childhood home, still experiencing the haze of a post-holiday fog, and continued the frantic search for her purse. She had assumed she would be ready to return to work in the new year, but now, after rushing through her morning with one eye on the clock, she wasn't so sure. One more day spent lounging around the house in pajamas while eating leftover gingerbread would've been nice.

"Max, have you seen my purse?"

The fat gray cat sauntered across the hardwood floor, his shoulder blades rising and falling with each fluid step. He replied with an unsympathetic "meow" and kept walking.

"You're no help," Chaynie mumbled, brushing a loose chestnut-colored curl from her cheek. "It's here somewhere..."

She moved past the hallway and into the cozy living room, still decked out with Christmas décor—nutcrackers and garland and her mother's Texas-shaped-ornament collection. Chaynie and her mother had made at least *some* progress dismantling the Christmas tree last night. The ornaments had been gingerly removed, and the next step would be to unwind and store away the white lights without tangling them.

As she scanned the room, Chaynie realized that if she left the house in the next few minutes, she might still have time to get coffee on the way to work.

"Ah-*ha*!" She spied her taupe leather bag in the other room, slung over a chair at the breakfast table. The corner of a Sue Grafton paperback peeked out through the zipper.

As she flipped on the light and hurried toward her bag, Chaynie noticed the three empty champagne flutes near the kitchen sink—a reminder of the quiet New Year's Eve she and her mom had spent together two nights before. The third flute had been for her father. Her mother had poured champagne into it then clinked the glass against her own.

"Happy New Year, Danny. We miss you," she had whispered.

Chaynie had followed suit, clinking her glass too. It was their second New Year's without him. This year had started out a little brighter, a little happier than the last one, but even as the edges of grief had begun to dull, the memory of him was still vivid, leaving a vacancy inside the house.

Chaynie abandoned her purse and moved to the sink, dumping out her father's portion of flat champagne then rinsing the flute carefully.

"Did you see the illustration?"

Chaynie shut off the faucet and turned to see her mother blustering into the room, juggling her keys and purse and leather case in her typical panicked before-class routine—she was *always* late for school.

"I couldn't sleep last night," her mother explained, "so I went back to the sketch and added some color. What do you think?" Abby Mayfield reached for the cardstock that sat on the breakfast table and tilted her head. "I'm not sure about the chartreuse for his scarf. It might be too bold." She looked up, her crystal-blue eyes shining, caught in the ray of sunlight streaming through the kitchen window.

Chaynie walked to the table and peered at the sketch she had doodled before Christmas. In the span of those next few evenings, Abby had transformed the doodle into a pencil-sketched masterpiece.

For the last couple of years, the seed of an idea for a children's story had batted around Chaynie's consciousness, a story involving a mouse who runs away from his family and makes a home in the local library. She'd finally committed to writing the story early last year, months after her father had passed away.

The story idea had soon become a team project when Chaynie had gathered enough courage to show her mother the text—half-written, with one doodle penciled in on the last page. Chaynie was no artist, but she had a specific vision in her head for the story's illustrations. Her mother—an art teacher at the high school—had adored the library-mouse idea, and they'd decided to work on the project together. Chaynie had spent months revising and polishing the story then creating mediocre drawings, which her mother had brought to life with her vibrant colors and creative ideas.

Chaynie smiled at the newest sketch, where Martin the Mouse was discovered by his mouse family. She realized it was the final drawing and the story would soon be complete.

"Not too bold at all," Chaynie said. "I like it. The color really pops."

Her mother nudged her daughter's shoulder and nodded. "Well, good. Maybe we can decide on the other details tonight, if you're up for it."

Chaynie gave a gentle nudge back with her elbow. At five foot nine, she stood a few inches taller than her mother. "Absolutely. And I'll make us some brownies for our work session."

"Mm, brownies. A nice change from the candy-cane-flavored everything we've been having the last few weeks."

"That's what I was thinking."

"I'll buy some milk on my way home. We can't have brownies without milk." Her mother set down the cardstock then slipped her other hand into her jacket sleeve. "Gotta go. I'm late! See you tonight."

Chaynie watched her leave through the garage door and heard Max meow goodbye from the living room.

On the verge of being late herself, Chaynie grabbed her purse and flicked the light off. She headed for the front door, planning to walk to the library, as she always did. Her mother's house was only a block behind the town square, so it seemed silly to drive the short distance to work. Besides, the quirky town laws forbade parking inside the square, so a brisk walk was her only choice.

Chaynie stepped out into the chilly January day. As she craned her neck to observe the bare tree branches cutting into a gray sky, she wondered if their small Texas town would see snow again soon. The week before, on Christmas Eve, Morgan's Grove had received a rare dusting, but the snowfall had been short-lived. The sun had melted all of it by the next evening.

Along her walk, Chaynie waved to Mrs. Butterfield, bringing her trash bin out to the curb, then said a quick hello to Marcy Turner as she jogged past, huffing and puffing, on her usual morning run.

Chaynie approached the familiar town square, expecting it to be mostly empty—shops didn't open until nine, and some might still be closed for the holidays. But as she rounded the corner, she saw men on ladders reaching high above to remove giant garland wreaths from lampposts and long strands of ivy hanging on each store front. Even though a part of Chaynie was glad to see that life would return to normal in Morgan's Grove, she felt a pinch of sadness at watching the decorations come down to be packed away until the next year.

Tourists and residents usually flooded the town square during the holidays, but immediately afterward, the sidewalks became quite ghost townish, with people returning to their families and hometowns, their jobs, their lives. Chaynie walked down the crisscross brick sidewalk that lined the square, admiring the variety of colored awnings and unique storefronts made of either brick or stone. Having lived in Morgan's Grove most of her life, she sometimes took for granted how well-kept and pristine the town was. No wonder it had recently been dubbed "A Tourist's #1 Texas Destination" in an online article. With its quaint shops, friendly residents, and clean streets, it was small-town America at its best.

As she crossed the street inside the square, she heard barking nearby and saw Lucille Wright, a seventy-something resident, walking her two corgis. Their eager, stumpy legs carried them forward, tongues wagging all the way.

"Good morning," Chaynie told Lucille as they approached. She stopped at the curb to let the corgis sniff her pants leg. "They probably smell Max, our cat."

The corgis plopped down on the pavement, tongues still hanging out, as they watched the conversation going on above their heads.

"How was your New Year's?" Lucille asked.

"Nice. Quiet. How was yours?"

"The same. My favorite kind actually."

"Mine too."

Chaynie had known Lucille for most of her life—Lucille had taught Sunday School when Chaynie was a little girl, and she was a vibrant part of the Morgan's Grove community. In fact, she and her grandson, Rick, had recently begun plans to open a new bakery inside the square, where Lucille would sell her famous gingerbread cookies and other sweet treats.

"How's the bakery coming along?" Chaynie asked even as part of her brain nagged at her. *You don't have* time *for a chat...*

Lucille shook her head. "It's actually hard to tell. Right now, it's nothing but dust and noise and debris on the floors. But Rick assures me it will all be beautiful in the end. We should be opening in a few weeks!"

"That's wonderful news. I'll be one of your first customers." Chaynie peered down to see one of the corgis stand and stretch. "Looks like they're ready for the rest of their walk. I guess I'd better get going too. Have a lovely day."

"You too!"

Chaynie continued on her usual trek past the kitchen supply shop then the novelties store to reach her favorite coffee shop, Top Roast. The Open sign was visible, so she pushed the door forward and breathed in the lovely rich scent of fresh-brewed coffee.

Only one other customer stood in line at the counter, and Chaynie waited impatiently as he gave his long and complicated order to the barista.

"Next?" said the young employee, who Chaynie didn't recognize. He must be a new hire.

"A black coffee, please." She fished some dollar bills from her bag as he scribbled her order.

His pencil paused as he looked up, tilting his youthful teenaged face. "That's it?"

"Yep, black, straight up." Chaynie held out her bills, ready to pay, ready to rush out and move on with her day.

"But won't you try our...?" His eyes darted toward a cheat-sheet menu beside his pad. "Warm and spicy hot chocolate? Or maybe a..." His eyes dipped downward again. "Sweet berry frappuccino?"

Chaynie suppressed a giggle and said in the politest possible tone, "No thanks. Just a coffee, black."

The teenager shrugged. "You're missing out. We've got some cool specials."

"That's okay. I don't like fancy coffees. I'm sort of—"

"Old-school?" he offered.

"Well, I was going to say traditional."

Before she'd turned thirty last year, Chaynie had never been particularly bothered by conversations like this one. But more and more, her interactions with younger people—their fancy new technologies, their choices in music, their confusing vernacular—were starting to make her *feel* thirty.

The young man tapped the order into the register, then Chaynie paid for her plain, boring, old-school coffee. She moved to the other counter for sugar packets while she waited.

Thankfully, the teenager wasn't as slow in making her coffee as he was at taking her order, and soon, Chaynie was on her way out the door.

A tapping sound caught her attention before she could cross the street. Chaynie paused to see that Mindy's Boutique next door had some commotion going on inside the front window. Mindy herself was on a ladder, stretched high to attach something to the glass. Chaynie squinted as the "something" came into view—pink and red paper hearts flanked by Cupids.

Mindy fastened the decoration to the window then caught Chaynie's gaze below and waved. Chaynie used her free hand to wave back then crossed the street as she caught the paradox. Christmas decorations still lingered on one side of the town square while pink hearts and Cupids were being erected on the other side. Seeing them in their vivid glory, Chaynie felt the painfully fresh sting of last year's Valentine's.

Blake, her boyfriend of almost a year, had broken up with her *on* Valentine's Day. Even worse, he'd taken the coward's way out and had done it by text. Chaynie had read the message several times before it sank in: *Been doing a lot of thinking this week. Not sure this is working anymore. Us. Please understand. Sorry.*

Granted, the final few months of their relationship had been conducted mostly by text or video chats because of the distance between them—Chaynie had temporarily moved back to Morgan's Grove after her father died in order to help her mother through the transition process. However, Blake had remained in west Austin, a fifty-minute drive. When Chaynie had made her decision to move, she'd had faith in their communication skills and in the strength of their relationship, and she'd thought Blake had too. So his break-up text had come as a particular shock.

That Valentine's morning, Chaynie had stared hard at the text, at the word "sorry," for several seconds afterward, until it became a nonsense word to her brain. *Sorry.* Such a brief word to end a year-long relationship. She'd thought about texting him back, but it would've been pointless. It was over. He'd later apologized—again, by text—for breaking up with her on that particular day, saying he'd completely forgotten about Valentine's. Whether he was lying or not didn't matter. The damage had already been done.

Ironically, Valentine's had always been one of Chaynie's favorite holidays. Until last year's breakup, she had believed in its magical properties—a breathless hope, an enchanted promise that love still existed in such an unpredictable world. But since Blake's text, the magic had disappeared, and the only thing Chaynie felt about Valentine's was jaded.

Stepping onto the curb of the town square's centerpiece—the courthouse and library buildings—Chaynie decided to brush off Valentine's completely. She couldn't avoid the décor, the ads, or the mushy music, but she could divert her eyes, change the channel, and focus on other things until the holiday had passed. If she pretended Valentine's didn't exist, perhaps, somehow, it wouldn't.

Chaynie searched for her keys as she approached the library—the familiar, imposing structure covered with smooth honey-colored stone blocks. The historic hundred-year-old building usually drew just as many tourists as the charming town square did, and it had been Chaynie's favorite building since she was a child.

She jiggled the key into the old lock and pushed open the tall, thick oak door. It always reminded her of a castle door. As she did every morning, Chaynie hesitated at the threshold to run her fingers over the bronze plaque embedded near the doorframe that greeted each newcomer. The plaque held an engraved quote by Jorge Luis Borges that compared libraries to paradise.

Chaynie shut the door and set her coffee on a table inside the narrow alcove, then removed her coat to reveal her tailored navy jacket. Although her boss didn't require a specific dress code, Chaynie usually wore blazers with slacks or sweaters with long skirts to the library. Since the building she worked in was formal and immaculate, she felt a strong urge to dress accordingly.

The heater hummed, and the warmth touched Chaynie's cheeks as she took her coffee farther into the main room, which opened widely before her, then paused to smile. After one week off, she'd missed this place, as she always did. She missed the dark, ornate woodwork on each wall, floor to ceiling. She missed the high vaulted ceilings and the crown molding. She missed the thick Oriental carpeting beneath her feet and the spaces carved out for readers, comfy chairs in corners and sturdy desks for studying. She missed the stained glass windows that lined the walls, each one dedicated to a famous scene from literature: *Romeo and Juliet, Little Women, Wuthering Heights, Pride and Prejudice.*

And she missed the books. Rows and rows of them in perfect alignment, thousands and thousands of titles lovingly shelved and dusted and cared for. Mary Richards, the head librarian, took great pride in appearances. "We want the library to look its finest" was always her motto, and it showed.

"Chaynie?"

Britney Atkins rounded the corner and offered a bright expression to match her brassy-blond hair, which always contained streaks of another color—today, the streaks were purple. She was a waif of a girl, weighing barely a hundred pounds, but her happy spirit always filled the room before she entered it. An eighteen-year-old senior in high school hired by Mary before the holidays as an assistant, Britney was still learning the ropes, figuring out what her many roles and duties would be.

"Hi. I didn't expect you in today. I thought you had school," Chaynie noted.

"Oh, it's a teacher in-service day. Tomorrow too. Mary's already here. She let me in."

"How was your holiday?"

"Good. Busy." Britney held up a stack of note cards and smirked. "And now I'm trying to learn this stuff before tomorrow. Mary gave me the script over the holidays. She's put me on 'tour guide' duty. There's a whole class of kids coming tomorrow morning."

"You'll do great."

Chaynie remembered those days. She, too, had worked at the library as a teenager, memorizing the history of the building, ushering groups of tourists or students through the structure, and answering their questions.

"Well, I'll leave you to your notecards," she told Britney. "If you need a study partner, I might have a few extra minutes this afternoon."

"I'll probably take you up on it."

Chaynie took a sharp left then climbed the stairs to her second-floor office. As she went, she could hear Britney's voice drifting, rattling off the facts that Chaynie knew so well. She mouthed along with Britney, "The founder of Morgan's Grove... lovingly built the library for his daughter... also named Morgan. Took three years to build, finished in 1912... architecturally influenced by European libraries... stained glass designed by Frederick Mendel... Italian wood panels shipped from overseas..."

Mary hadn't changed the script in all those years, and Chaynie felt something oddly comforting in that.

Upstairs, Chaynie walked the length of the floor toward her office at the back. Sunlight pierced through the stained glass windows on the east side, and Chaynie remembered when, as a child, she had noticed a tiny kaleidoscope of colors sometimes appearing on her hand from the nearby window as she read in the Children's Corner. She would pause her reading and tilt her hand, fascinated by her own personal rainbow.

In her youth, Chaynie had spent countless hours in the Children's Corner, a space designed by Mary when she first took on the position of head librarian nearly forty years ago. Mary's singular goal had been to create a cozy, inviting space where children would wish to stay indefinitely—and, in doing so, to develop a lifelong comfort and ease with books. It had worked. In fact, Chaynie had chosen to spend nearly an entire night in that very corner when she was nine years old.

That evening, she had been jealous of her older brother over something she couldn't even remember anymore, something her parents had allowed him to do that little Chaynie couldn't. *He's their favorite child*, she told herself, knowing it wasn't really true. Still, she let her hurt feelings fester and, after an early supper, made plans to run away. She sneaked out a first-floor window with a backpack full of coloring books, markers, half an apple, a flashlight, and a peanut butter sandwich.

In that moment, sliding the window shut with a quiet *click*, little Chaynie had no clear idea of where she was running *to*, but when she ventured toward the town square, she had the answer in sight. The library. It was her favorite place in the world aside from her bedroom. She would often beg her mother to take her there, where she would linger for hours in the Children's Corner, selecting new books, slouching in comfortable bean bag chairs, and reading the afternoon away.

Chaynie approached the enormous library door and tapped the bronze quote with her fingers before entering. Then she walked upstairs with her backpack and found a place tucked deep inside the corner where nobody would discover her. Half an hour later, it was closing time, and Chaynie held her breath when she saw the lights clicking off and heard people down below telling each other, "Good night! See you in the morning!"

She had done it. She had run away, and no one had known.

When it was safe, Chaynie peeked her head around the corner, eyed the open space of the second floor, and saw the glow of night lights coming from various corners. She had the library all to herself, and it felt deliciously adventurous, much like the siblings who'd spent several nights in the Metropolitan Museum in *From the Mixed-Up Files of Mrs. Basil E. Frankweiler*. The empty library looked entirely different at this hour, in this lighting. Chaynie imagined the books coming to life while people were gone, their pages opening to reveal various characters who might throw a gregarious party together or partake in exciting adventures.

But instead, everything was still and quiet, and for a moment, Chaynie's new adventure shifted into something spooky. The hush of the library grew louder in her ears until she craved a diversion.

She returned to the safety of her corner and selected from the shelves her favorite, most comforting book, *Anne of Green Gables*. Finding her flashlight and settling deep into the bean bag chair, Chaynie munched on the crisp apple as she started to read.

Before long, reading gave way to yawns, and Chaynie splayed the book on her chest as she leaned back and closed her eyes.

"Hello? Honey, are you okay?"

Chaynie blinked her eyes open and wondered how long she'd been asleep. She saw a middle-aged man crouched down, staring back at her. She recognized him as a worker in the library. *The library*. She remembered—she had run away.

"You're the Mayfields' girl, aren't you?"

"I'm Chaynie Mayfield," she confirmed, suppressing a yawn. "And you're... Sam. The janitor?"

He chuckled and scratched at his chin. "Well, I guess that's my official title, but I like to think of myself as 'Keeper of the Library.' I do all sorts of things—make repairs, dust off the highest shelves, replace lightbulbs in the tallest chandeliers. I'm also the first to open and the last to close every day. I take care of her, the old girl."

"Her?"

"The library. She's a special place, isn't she?"

Chaynie nodded and shifted, catching her book before it could slide off her chest and fall to the ground. She realized the flashlight was still on—it was probably what had drawn Sam over to her corner in the first place.

"What are you doing here all alone at this time of night?" Sam asked. "Did you get locked in or somethin'?"

Chaynie shook her head, feeling suddenly ashamed. Her parents were probably worried. "I ran away from home," she whispered.

"Oh, I see." Sam raised his eyebrows slightly. "Well, you came to a good location, at least. No place safer than being surrounded by books, eh?" He reached toward her copy of *Anne of Green Gables* and tilted it. "Hey, I know this one. My granddaughter reads this series." He stood up and searched a nearby shelf. "How about this one?" Sam slid the book from its slot and handed it to Chaynie. "Have you read it?"

"*Emily of New Moon*," she read from the cover. "I don't think so."

"It's one I mailed to my granddaughter for her birthday last week. She lives all the way in Kentucky."

Chaynie sensed a sadness in his tone.

"Here. Why don't you take it?" Sam offered. "You can return it to me when you finish. It will be our secret."

Chaynie took the book and slid it into her backpack. "Thanks." She rose to her feet and reshelved *Anne of Green Gables*, then gathered up the flashlight and apple core, dumped them into her backpack, and zipped it shut.

"Are you ready to go home? See your parents? I'm sure they're worried 'bout you."

As Sam escorted her home, all Chaynie could focus on was her impending punishment—surely her parents would be furious with her. But when her mother opened the door, she gasped and leaned in to clutch her daughter in an embrace so tight that Chaynie could hardly breathe. Her father had shaken Sam's hand vigorously, thanking him over and over.

Passing by the Children's Corner now, Chaynie shook her head at the memory of a dreamy, wide-eyed little girl seeking comfort and solace while surrounded by books. In hindsight, it seemed she had been living that same philosophy clear through adulthood, with her library science degree from UT, a job as library technician, and the goal of becoming a head librarian.

Chaynie had essentially arranged her life, her entire career, so she would always be surrounded by books.

Chaynie glanced toward Mary's office next door but saw no sign of her. She was likely downstairs running through her routine of clicking on the study-desk lights, turning on computers and making sure they were in working order, rearranging items on the circulation desk, and scanning the entire floor for any issues or mishaps to address before the doors opened. Those menial duties easily should have been Britney's or even Chaynie's to perform, but Mary took pride in preparing the library for each new opening day. It was her ritual.

Settling at her own office desk, Chaynie sipped her coffee and warmed up the laptop, eager to check her email. She'd only sent in her applications two days ago, but the wait was already excruciating. On January first, she'd decided it was time. New year, new plan. She loved being back home in Morgan's Grove, living with her mother and working at the library, but it had never been her long-term goal. Since getting her master's degree, Chaynie had dreamed of being hired as head librarian at some prestigious university or big-city library, and she was willing to travel for it—Boston, New York, Denver, wherever the job took her. But her father's sudden illness had postponed that goal, as her family became her main priority.

But with a fresh, shiny new year, it felt like time to try again. To revisit those old dreams and see where they might take her. Chaynie hadn't told her mother about the applications yet—no use telling her when they might not even pan out. The odds of getting her dream job, especially two days after submitting resumes and applications, was insanely slim.

Clicking open her email, Chaynie only saw a couple of spam letters, a chatty note from her aunt in Dallas, and a reminder of a dentist appointment coming up next month.

"Knock, knock!" Mary's cheerful face appeared in the doorway, and Chaynie shifted her focus toward it.

"Hi, come in! How was your holiday?" Chaynie was genuinely interested but secretly wondered how many times she would either ask that question or *be* asked that question today.

"Really good. My daughter and granddaughters visited. They left yesterday and took a few pieces of my heart right along with them." She put her hands to her chest and winced.

Mary was in her early seventies but could easily pass for late fifties. Her dark hair was always impeccable, her makeup perfect, and her outfits tidy and professional. She had hardly aged a day from Chaynie's little-girl memories of her.

"How was your holiday?" Mary asked.

"My brother was here over Christmas with his family," Chaynie said. "We had a nice visit too."

"I'm glad." Mary came closer to Chaynie's desk and clasped her hands together. "I need to call a brief meeting before we open today. Can you come to my office in, say, ten minutes?"

"Of course." Chaynie had fully expected a meeting that morning. They usually held once-a-week meetings anyway, so it was no surprise.

"Good. I have something... exciting to tell you."

"Sounds mysterious. I'll wrap this up and be right in."

Mary disappeared while Chaynie sipped her coffee and consulted her calendar to see what the week held—children's story times, two lectures to high school students about research and citations, and a meeting with a new book distributor. At the end of the week, she had a couple of reports to write up, and she needed to phone Steve about the computer downstairs that had poor connection issues.

Usually, the duties of a library technician were quite clerical in nature, but Mary knew of Chaynie's overqualification for the position and trusted her, more and more, with crucial and sensitive tasks. If she didn't know better, Chaynie would've believed Mary was grooming her to take over the head-librarian position someday. But since Mary hadn't even hinted at retirement—in fact, the running joke was that she intended to stay in the position forever—Chaynie didn't let herself hope that she could take Mary's place in the near future.

Taking a final sip of coffee, Chaynie tossed the paper cup into the trash can and quickly touched up her full lips with a mauve gloss. In junior high, she'd been teased for her plump lips, so she'd never added color to them, trying desperately to tone them down, wishing they were thinner, less noticeable. She had rarely smiled in class pictures because of the teasing. But somewhere along the way, Chaynie's face had matured to fit the size of her mouth, and as an adult, she had discovered the truth—most women envied her lips and even spent money to obtain that plumped-up look from doctors. So, she'd finally learned, after years of feeling self-conscious, to embrace them just as they were.

She stood to smooth out her jacket then carried her notepad into Mary's office for the meeting. Chaynie paused in the doorway when she saw the circle of chairs—Britney and Sam sat side by side, and two empty chairs remained, while Mary sat on the other side of her desk.

"Just in time." Mary gestured toward an empty chair.

Chaynie sat beside Sam, still a faithful keeper of the library. She saw him every day, somewhere in the library, as he cleaned or repaired or adjusted, and she would usually make time for a chat, asking about his granddaughters and three great-grandsons. He would always reciprocate by asking how her mother was doing. Chaynie hadn't seen Sam since before Christmas, so they whispered their brief "How were your holidays?" before Mary began the meeting.

Chaynie wasn't sure why a fourth chair stood empty next to hers. *Who else are we expecting?*

Mary cleared her throat and shuffled some papers on her desk then stacked them neatly aside. "Welcome back! It's a new year at the Morgan's Grove Library, and I anticipate a wonderful one. Chaynie and I can meet again this week to go over budgets and projections and our regular agenda, but this is a special meeting today. I wanted to invite Britney and Sam to let them hear the news firsthand." She laced her fingers together, preparing to make the big announcement. "The Morgan's Grove Library has been given an extremely generous and unexpected gift. A sort of... Christmas present. Lucille Wright's grandson, Rick, has made a sizeable donation to our library."

"Rick, the head of Quantum Software?" Britney asked. "I've heard he's loaded."

Mary suppressed a chuckle. "Well, that's one way of putting it. He's been blessed with enormous wealth, yes, and he's worked hard for it. He built his company from the ground up. In any case, he's in the process of moving back to Morgan's Grove and has expressed his desire to invest some of his wealth into the town. 'Giving back,' he called it. Over the holidays, we had a couple of meetings where he asked about the library's greatest needs. As you know, we've had our funding cut significantly over the past year or two. But even more dire, this beautiful building is in great disrepair. The infrastructure is in need of renovations, and Rick has generously offered to fund them all." Mary paused expectantly and let the news soak in.

"That's incredible," Chaynie said. "But... I'm a bit confused, honestly. The building, at least cosmetically, looks good. You've kept it in excellent shape over the years, Mary."

"Well, thank you. But I can only do so much. As you said, the cosmetics have been attended to, but it's things we can't see—the basement's musty areas and the outdated electricity and plumbing—that need the most care. They're becoming safety hazards. The elevator system is archaic and possibly dangerous, and the roof needs retiling. That hailstorm we had a few weeks ago caused significant damage. Much of that cost will be covered by insurance, thankfully, but Rick's generosity can now be factored in. Renovations will begin next week. I've already spoken to an architect who will oversee the project. He should be here any moment, in fact." Mary checked her watch.

That explained the empty chair.

"Sorry I'm late," someone said in a deep voice behind Chaynie. A tall man with jet-black hair and light-blue eyes stood in the doorframe. He wore a tan suede jacket, jeans, and boots. "The truck wouldn't start. I had to jump the battery."

That, for some reason, did not inspire confidence in Chaynie. *This guy is the expert in charge of carefully, lovingly renovating a hundred-year-old historic building?*

"It's fine," Mary reassured him. "Just take a seat, and I'll start the introductions."

The man slid into the chair beside Chaynie with a shy nod. His face was so familiar.

"Everyone, this is Greg—"

"Peterson," Chaynie added, turning toward him. "We went to high school together, didn't we?"

The pieces fell immediately into place as her memory filled in the gaps. Greg Peterson had been a scrawny teenager, shy and quiet, skating on the fringes of the high school social scene. She hadn't known much about him back then, and they'd never exchanged more than a passing hello. From what she recalled, he hadn't been involved in athletics or music or much of anything else. In fact, she thought his family owned a ranch or farm, so he had probably been involved in 4-H, showing cattle and sheep on weekends, a world Chaynie knew nothing about. The only class she recalled having with him was chemistry—*or was it algebra?*—where he'd sat in the back row and never made a sound.

But *this* Greg Peterson, sitting in front of her years later, was nearly unrecognizable. Age had been kind to him. His gawkiness had disappeared, replaced by a rugged, masculine demeanor and an air of deeper confidence. Still, a hint of timidity remained.

"That's right," Greg confirmed with a half smile. "We were in the same high school—junior high and elementary too. You're Chaynie Mayfield."

"Well, this is off to a good start," Mary said. "Chaynie is my right hand, and here are Britney and Sam, two of our other library employees."

Chaynie peeled her eyes away from Greg and tried to focus on the rest of the meeting.

"In the spirit of full disclosure," Mary admitted, "Greg happens to be my godson. I've known him his entire life, and he's the best person to oversee this renovation." In order to prove it, Mary rattled off a list of details from his resume, which she held in front of her. "Received a master's in conservation architecture from the University of Virginia... worked at the Penter and Nichols firm for the past six years... specialty is restoring historic buildings." She set down the resume, her face beaming. "And lucky for us, he's decided to move back to Morgan's Grove to open his own firm! The timing couldn't be better."

Chaynie had to admit, his credentials sounded impressive. She marveled at his decision to return to his hometown, when he could probably have chosen any metropolitan city in the country to open a new firm.

Greg dipped his head, likely embarrassed by all the flattery. "Well, I'm honored to be asked. The library will be in good hands. I've loved this building all my life. It's probably what got me interested in architecture in the first place. It's an amazing structure with a deep history."

Chaynie wondered how she could've missed Greg at the library all those years, growing up in Morgan's Grove. He'd probably spent countless hours there during childhood, too, with his godmother, gazing up at the architecture, while Chaynie gazed eye level at all the books. They'd been rotating in separate orbits nearby all that time.

Mary checked her watch again then glanced up. "I have more exciting news. I'm putting Chaynie in charge of this year's Valentine's event. We do something each year—decorate the library, choose a romantic book for the book club—small efforts, barely noticeable. But I see this year as a greater opportunity. Bluntly, we're losing our patrons to digital books, and I want to draw them back into the library, pique their curiosity again. So, Chaynie, your mission is to brainstorm an event that encompasses romance, fun, and a bit of whimsy that will bring people of all ages to the library this year. Are you in?"

With everyone staring, including her boss, Chaynie had no choice *but* to be "in," even as her heart crumpled at the thought of being handed a Valentine-centered project—in her face, every day, for the next six weeks.

"Yes. Count me in," she agreed, forcing an affable smile.

"Good. Well, there's much more to go over, but it will have to wait. It's time to open the library. We can set up another meeting soon. Chaynie, Sam, and Britney, if you can think of any questions about the renovations for Greg in the meantime, email them to me, and we'll bring them up in the next meeting. I want everyone to feel like they're a significant part of this project. Okay, let's have a great day!"

Mary rose, indicating the meeting was over, and they all followed suit. As Chaynie stood, she watched Greg bend to reach for his chair and hers, moving them back in place against the wall. When he returned to her side, Chaynie realized he was at least six inches taller than she was. She'd been so used to wearing flats and subconsciously slouching around shorter men all her life that it was refreshing to stand near someone as tall as Greg.

"What is it?" Greg asked. "You're smiling."

"Am I? Oh. Well, I'm just glad about this project. You know, with the library. I guess it needed a good face-lift."

"That's one way of putting it."

Chaynie said goodbye to Greg then followed the others out the door.

"WHY AM I ALWAYS SO caught off guard by the exhaustion that floods my entire body after the first day back to school?" Chaynie's mother stretched her back with a wince then poured a second glass of milk while standing at the kitchen island. "Those faculty meetings are brutal. I think they steal away small pieces of my soul every time."

Chaynie snickered at her mother's melodramatic description.

"I mean, I've done this 'first day back to school' how many times? At least..." She stared at the ceiling to do the math. "Fifty-two? If I'm counting individual semesters."

"Sounds exhausting when you put it like that." Chaynie licked the swirl of fudgy frosting from the tip of her finger. She had been too tired after work to make brownies from scratch, as intended, so she'd taken the easy way out and made a quick stop at The Pit, a popular barbecue restaurant in the square, for spareribs and their famous dessert called Mississippi Mud—a fudge-covered concoction made of devil's food cake and marshmallow filling. Gooey and rich and insanely fattening.

"Let's eat it by the fireplace," her mother suggested as Max followed them into the living room with a loud "meow."

"No, Max. Go eat your food," Chaynie ordered, but he disobeyed and sprang to the arm of the couch as Chaynie took a seat. When food was involved, he usually remained at a respectful distance, licking his paw, so she would let him stay.

"I've told you about my day. How was yours?"

Chaynie sank her fork into the first delectable bite of Mississippi Mud. "Pretty standard. Busy. Mary's put me in charge of the big Valentine's project this year. I have to be creative, draw extra patrons into the library using more than hearts and Cupids. I have no idea how I'll accomplish that."

"You'll think of something. You're great at that sort of thing."

Her mom had a sweet-but-annoying habit of shifting into encourager mode anytime Chaynie expressed self-doubt.

Chaynie let the first bite of dessert dissolve on her tongue and contemplated how many walks around the square she would need to take tomorrow to neutralize the calories. "And the library is getting a makeover."

"What do you mean?" her mother asked before taking a gulp of milk.

"Well, Mary has hired an architect to oversee some renovation projects. It seems the hundred-year-old building is in desperate need of some repairs. Rick, Lucille's grandson, has donated the money."

"How wonderful. A Christmas gift to the library."

"That's exactly what Mary said."

Chaynie wasn't sure why she didn't mention more details about "the architect," Greg—that she'd known him at school, that he was more handsome than she remembered, that he had kind eyes and a gentle spirit. Maybe she needed to hold those observations internally for the time being. She barely knew anything about him, and it would probably stay that way, in the scheme of things. She imagined their paths would only cross here and there.

Chaynie and her mother ate the rest of their desserts in peaceful silence, watching the fire crackle and pop—the ideal way to end a hectic first day back to real life.

Chapter Two

"We have two copies of that book, actually. I can pull one and hold it for you at the front desk." Chaynie hovered a finger over the keyboard, waiting for Mrs. Thompson's answer.

"Thank you, dear. I'll pick it up this afternoon."

Chaynie clicked the Checked Out button, told Mrs. Thompson goodbye, then snapped a photo of the computer screen, which displayed the cover, book title, and shelf location. As she turned to retrieve the book, *Needlepoint Techniques for Beginners*, Chaynie nearly ran right into Mary, who had approached quietly from behind sometime during the phone call.

"Sorry for startling you. I have a question." Mary tugged at the nape of her turtleneck sweater. "I meant to approach you yesterday, but time got away from me because of the renovations and Greg's arrival and so forth."

Chaynie held her breath and wondered which task Mary was about to dump onto her already-full plate. Mary had been doing that a lot lately, adding new duties to her agenda at a moment's notice.

"It's about the book club." Mary clasped her hands together.

"Which one?"

"The Sassy Ladies."

The library hosted several different book clubs each month, from children's literature to mysteries-only to classic novels. Something for everyone, but by far the most enduring and active one remained the Sassy Ladies Book Club. Friends for decades, the ladies were raucous and animated, even known to dress up occasionally as characters from whatever book they were reading that month. They always met inside the library's second-floor conference room so they wouldn't disturb the other patrons with their noise.

Mary continued. "I forgot to mention yesterday that I need your help with them. Actually, I'm putting you in charge of the group, at least for this month, so I can clear my desk for some other pertinent things."

Chaynie was already in charge of two other book clubs, which were thankfully quite self-contained and self-directed. Hopefully this one would be too. She shrugged. "Sure, I can handle that. What's involved?"

"Well, the ladies always look to me for book suggestions, so that would be your first order of business, to find the perfect Valentine's-themed title. And they always want me to attend their meetings. I mostly stay quiet and sit in the corner, but when they want an 'expert literary opinion'—that's what they call it—then they'll ask for my input about the history of the book or literary terms, symbolism, that sort of thing. So, once a book is selected, you'll probably need to read it through."

Being told to read and study a book wasn't a problem for Chaynie, depending on what book it was. She remembered having to read *Moby Dick* in her junior year at UT. She'd hated every single page. Being forced to read a Valentine's book when she was trying so hard to avoid the holiday seemed as torturous as reading *Moby Dick*.

"Oh! And this is a special anniversary for the Sassy Ladies. They want to celebrate it with a party, maybe near Valentine's. You'd be handling that too. They'll have been together for thirty years in February. Imagine that," Mary said wistfully. "They've been through so many life events together—marriages and children, deaths of spouses, divorces, new grandchildren, great-grandchildren. I believe most of them are widows now, with family members living far away. This is more than a book club. They've built a family of friends over the years."

In that split second, Chaynie's jaded attitude softened. Friends for *thirty years*, a group formed solely on a mutual love of books. Chaynie would do well to learn from the ladies and their long-lasting friendships. Her own generation, maybe because of the coldness and distance of social media, didn't seem able to make friends easily—or to keep them. The one exception for Chaynie, thankfully, was Savannah, her dearest friend since third grade. In fact, they had made lunch plans for later that afternoon.

Mary added, "The Sassy Ladies have lost a couple of their members inside the thirty years, with some moving outside of Morgan's Grove, or even passing away. But I think Lucille joined them recently, so their numbers remain fairly steady. Well, that's about it. They'll arrive in thirty minutes."

"That soon? I guess I should shuffle some things around..." Chaynie mumbled.

Mary placed a grateful hand on Chaynie's arm. "Thank you. I know they will love whatever book you suggest. And trust me, you'll get something out of it too. When those ladies get together, it's a hoot!"

"I'll bet." Chaynie had often heard them cackling and commiserating, even through the thick conference room windows.

As Mary swiveled to leave, Chaynie's phone pinged, and she drew it out of her pocket to see a text from Savannah. *Still on for lunch? I can come get you at noon.*

Perfect, Chaynie tapped out then slipped her phone back into her pocket.

On her way to retrieve Mrs. Thompson's book, Chaynie ran through a quick list of possible romance titles for the Sassy Ladies, but she wasn't sure if they might prefer classic or contemporary, tragic or happy, sweet or spicy.

She found the needlepoint book within seconds then trotted upstairs to her office, where she had just enough time to check her email—still no responses to any of her applications—and grab a notepad. It wasn't until she walked briskly to the conference room and reached for the doorknob that she remembered she still held Mrs. Thompson's book. She could deliver it to the circulation desk after the meeting.

Chaynie scanned the ample room with its elongated, glossy conference table, pristine as always thanks to Sam's tender care, and moved one of the chairs to the corner of the room so she could be a mostly invisible bystander for the first meeting.

Before she could set down her materials and take a seat, someone opened the door mid bluster. Doris Johnson entered the room, leaning on her cane with each step, and Sam followed, holding an enormous plastic-wrapped platter. He and Doris were discussing the unseasonably cold Texas weather.

"Well, Chaynie's here." Doris interrupted herself. "Mary told me you'd be takin' over for her this month. Welcome!" Doris's thick and charming Texas drawl embedded itself into every syllable. She was born and raised in Morgan's Grove, and it showed.

Chaynie and Doris had only ever had a couple of conversations in passing, nothing too personal in nature. She knew that Doris was a widow, a choir member at the Baptist church, the head of practically every social committee in town, and the founding member of the Sassy Ladies.

Sam set the tray in the center of the table then gave Chaynie a nod. "Mornin.'"

"Hi, Sam. Thanks for helping out."

"No trouble at all."

Sam probably would've exited then, except that a cluster of ladies had made their way toward the open door, each carrying something brunch related—casseroles, fruit trays, croissants, plastic cups and plates, a jug marked "Sweet Tea," and a stack of snowman napkins. Sam remained at the door and collected the items from the ladies as they entered, setting them down on the table as Doris arranged everything and greeted the members.

It took several minutes for the ladies to remove coats, drape handbags over chairs, unwrap food, and begin filling plates. Individual conversations overlapped as they chattered about the holidays, family gatherings, hobbies, and of course, books.

"Chaynie!" Lucille was the first to notice her quietly scribbling down book titles on a notepad from her corner spot. Lucille motioned her toward the table. "Come. Have some food. This all looks so delicious." She handed Chaynie a plate.

"Thank you. I will."

She abandoned her notepad for the plate, then squeezed in beside Lucille to cut out a sliver of hash-brown casserole. Chaynie wasn't much of a brunch eater, but the succulent mixture of home-made scents that filled the conference room as the ladies peeled back the plastic wrap made her stomach growl.

"Oh, Lucille. I heard about your grandson's gift to the library." Chaynie reached for a croissant. "We'll be able to pay for much-needed renovations. It was incredibly generous of him."

Lucille beamed. "I'm so proud of Rick. That was all his idea. He loves this town and wanted to give back. Did you know he's moving to Morgan's Grove permanently? I'm so thrilled about it. And... something else has enticed him to stay."

"You mean Jill?" Chaynie offered. "I noticed the two of them holding hands around town during the holidays. I'm so glad she's making a home here too."

Several weeks ago, Jill McCallister had come to Morgan's Grove as a tourist from Denver. But when she'd revealed the actual reason for her visit—that she'd recently discovered she was the great-great-great-granddaughter of Alfred J. Stout, the town's original founder—Jill had become quite the celebrity. When she'd entered the library looking for research on her ancestors, Chaynie had easily bonded with her over their mutual love of books. It had also helped that Jill happened to be a bestselling mystery author, which had intrigued Chaynie, along with most of the town.

"Yes, I'm excited about Jill staying in Morgan's Grove permanently. She'll be helping me out at the bakery from time to time." Lucille's expression turned wistful. "It was a treat to watch her romance with Rick blossom. They're a perfect match. I'm so glad they found each other."

Is that how it happens? Chaynie wondered as she spooned strawberries and grapes onto her plate. *Simple as that, just a matter of finding each other? What about complications like fate or poor timing or crisscrossed destinations? Or what about glitches and wrong turns and insecurities that could keep two people from staying together, even if they did find each other? And why does one person experience pure happiness in love while another struggles to have it at all?*

None of it made much sense to Chaynie in the scheme of things, but still, she told Lucille, "I'm happy for them," and meant it.

The ladies settled in at the table, where Lucille made a place for Chaynie, and the room quieted down as they ate.

Soon, Doris tapped the end of her fork against the table. She sat at the head, naturally. "Let's call this first meeting of the year to order, ladies. Happy New Year!"

"Happy New Year!" they all chimed in.

"First, let's welcome Chaynie Mayfield. She's subbing for Mary and will help us figure out the next book selection. Plus, she'll come to all the meetings and become our literary expert. No pressure." Doris winked.

"I'm glad to be here. I'll help out in any way I can," Chaynie assured her.

"Before we get started," Doris added, "I thought we could give Chaynie an inkling of this group's history. As you can see, we're all of a certain age. Thirty years ago, my Dave and Sharlene left for college, and I was an empty nester with time on my hands. I loved a good read to pass the time, and I knew that Ginger did too."

Ginger nodded from her seat.

"And so, we hatched an idea for a book club. She brought in some of her friends. I brought in some of mine—all empty nesters, too—and soon, we were meetin' in our houses once a month. What was that very first book?" Doris scanned the faces at the table. "*Sense and Sensibility?*"

"No, that was our second novel," someone corrected. "The first was more modern, suspenseful. John le Carré?"

"That was it. *Tinker, Tailor*—" Doris added.

"*Soldier, Spy!*" Ginger finished.

Doris grinned. "I had so much trouble with that darned title, but the book was a page-turner, and we were hooked." She turned her attention back to Chaynie. "In any case, the book club kept going, steady through all the years, though we've moved our meetings to the library, and here we are today. Our highest number of members was fifteen. We're down to nine, but we're still carrying on."

"Where did the name come from?" Chaynie wondered.

Ginger raised her hand. "That one's on me. Well, my husband, to be exact. We hosted one of the early meetings in my home, and my husband walked in during a rigorous debate over one of the characters. I thought we'd disrupted him watching the ball game in the other room, so I asked if we were being too loud. He paused and stared at us with this serious face, then broke into a smile. 'Nope,' he told us. 'Y'all are being too sassy.' And the name stuck."

"It's incredible," Chaynie admitted. "Strong friendships built on a mutual love of books. Here's to your thirty years together." She held up her Styrofoam cup of sweet tea, and the ladies followed suit.

"Thirty years!" they exclaimed in one collective voice.

Doris moved the meeting along to the most important point, choosing the monthly book. She looked to Chaynie, who had suddenly lost confidence in her brief list of titles. None of them felt quite right for this group, so she tossed out some basic questions first. "I need to know what sort of tone you want. I mean, love stories can be tragic or sweet, light or passionate. That will help to steer me in the right direction."

The ladies mumbled amongst themselves. "What did we pick last Valentine's?" "Do we want a classic or contemporary?" "Chick lit?" "Steamy?" "Happy or sad?"

Doris cleared her throat and tapped her fork again. "What's the consensus, ladies?" She referred to her spiral notebook. "Last year's Valentine's selection was *The Thorn Birds*." She flipped several pages backward. "And the year before was *Pride and Prejudice*."

"A classic," Chaynie noted.

"We may be sassy, but we're also classy!" Ginger piped in.

After the giggles and chuckles subsided, Doris told Chaynie, "Our tastes can run pretty eclectic. Maybe this year, we could go contemporary. Light and fluffy with humor? A feel-good novel." She raised her eyebrows and scoured the room.

The ladies nodded in unison.

"It's settled," Doris said. "Chaynie, find us a sweet and romantic book, and give us a happy ending."

Chaynie wrote down Doris's adjectives on her note pad. "Can I have a couple of days to compile a good list, then you can choose?"

"Sounds like a plan," Doris confirmed. "I'll give you my cell number, and you can text me the list. Ginger, why don't you add Chaynie to our social media group, so she can see our posts there too."

Texting? Social media? Chaynie was ashamed of herself for initially assuming these ladies weren't tech savvy, just because of their ages. They were surprising her more with each minute.

Doris rattled off her cell number to Chaynie, who spent the rest of the time quietly considering book titles while Doris finished off the meeting with details about the group's social and benevolence funds, the minutes from the previous meeting, and some possible theme ideas for the Valentine's party.

Sam returned, right on cue, to help discard the ladies' plates and cups and to help them carry the leftover food and containers.

"Don't bother," he told Chaynie, watching her wipe away crumbs. "I'll clean the table and straighten up the chairs in a bit. No trouble."

"Thanks, Sam." Alone in the conference room, gathering up her things, Chaynie realized she *still* held Mrs. Thompson's needlepoint book. Darting out of the conference room, she noticed a group of children on a library tour, Britney confidently walking backward while giving her talking points about the library's architecture. Chaynie ducked into a nearby aisle of tall shelves, planning to wait it out then sneak downstairs. She didn't want Britney to think she was spying on her.

As she rounded the corner, Chaynie gasped, stopping inches away from a ladder that stood in the middle of the aisle. Looking upward, she saw Greg Peterson grasping the highest rung, peering down at her.

"Sorry. I'm in your way," he called down.

Yes, you are, she wanted to admit, but instead, she politely shrugged and lied. "No problem."

Greg edged down the ladder then stood directly in front of her. When he did, she realized how close the quarters between the bookcases had become. She could still hear Britney's voice floating through the stacks nearby, inching closer. Chaynie and Greg seemed temporarily trapped.

"Why the ladder?" she whispered, staring up at the beautiful, ornate ceiling.

"Checking for damage. We've done a basic inspection, but I wanted to get a closer look myself at some spots of concern before we started the work."

"Ahh." Chaynie returned her gaze to him and noticed something. He had either forgotten to shave or was purposely experimenting with a light beard—thankfully, not some patchy thing that only covered parts of his face, as some men had. The beard suited him and emphasized his strong jaw.

"Sorry about all the chaos we're about to inflict." He pushed his fingers into his jeans pockets. "I mean, we have to bring in a *certain* level of noise and dust, can't help that, but this library is sort of a sacred place. So I promise we'll always have that in mind. We'll be as unobtrusive as we can. I've even got the guys working nights on the loudest jobs, whenever possible."

Chaynie wasn't crazy about the idea of renovations going on for endless weeks in her precious library, but she knew it was ultimately for the benefit of the building. Greg was one of the good guys, on her side, helping to save the library's infrastructure. And the fact that he was sensitive to the library's patrons and employees, well, perhaps Mary had made the right choice after all.

"It's okay. I can deal with chaos. Well, not a *lot* of chaos, but some." She attempted an awkward smile and turned Mrs. Thompson's book over in her hands.

Greg shifted his weight, clearly in no hurry to leave or carry on with his work. The situation became oddly intimate—two people trapped inside a narrow aisle of books, speaking in hushed tones.

"I meant to say this yesterday... I was sorry to hear about your dad," Greg offered. "I wanted to attend the funeral, but I was out of state when I got the news. He was a great man."

The unexpected mention of her father, there in the middle of the library with a guy she barely knew, knocked Chaynie completely off center. She hadn't planned on talking about her dad today, a topic so personal, so close to her core.

"I didn't realize you knew my dad," she whispered.

"I worked at his hardware store a few summers in a row during high school. He was really good to me. I don't know if he fully understood his impact on me. He gave me some much-needed confidence in those days, trusting me to close up the shop, take the deposits to the bank, handle customer questions all on my own. We'd sometimes sit at the back of the shop on a slow day, pop a couple of root beers—"

"He loved root beer! It was his favorite drink." Chaynie hadn't thought about her dad's root beer obsession in ages.

"We'd just shoot the breeze. Sometimes he'd tell these long, wandering jokes. Then when it was over, he'd laugh before I even had a chance to. Man, he had a great laugh."

"He did! It was this huge, hearty chuckle. It came from deep in his chest." Chaynie could sense the echo of it in her memory. She ached to hear that laugh one more time.

"And sometimes we'd talk about baseball or politics or history. He was a well-rounded guy. Seemed to know something about everything."

Chaynie felt hot tears sting her eyes. "Yes. That's exactly how I used to describe him to people. He didn't go to college, but he read *a lot* and soaked up information like a sponge. It's interesting that you picked up on that too."

Greg tilted his head. "I didn't mean to make you sad."

Chaynie brushed a tear from the corner of her eye. "You didn't. The opposite, actually. You've created these new memories for me, of Daddy. All I have left are my old memories, so hearing you talk about him is special. It almost feels like he's still here."

"He is, really." Greg pointed to his chest. "In here, right? Always."

The truth of it hit her at once, and all she could do was nod before the tears came again.

Chaynie's phone jingled in her pocket, and she shifted her attention to it, glad for the distraction. Her head was starting to pound from the busy morning and unexpected encounters.

The screen showed a text from Savannah. *Got out early. Ready for lunch? I'm here, first floor. Can't find you.*

Chaynie texted back, *Second floor*, then took a breath, trying to shift into Savannah mode. She looked up into Greg's rugged face. "Thank you."

"What for?"

"For sharing your stories with me. They were... a gift. Seeing my dad through someone else's eyes, a fresh perspective—it's hard to explain. I had him back, just for a minute."

"I'm glad."

"*There* you are!" Savannah appeared behind Chaynie, fresh and bright, as she always did. She wore a Wedgwood-blue coat, and her dark, sleek hair touched the tip of her collar. Savannah was petite and a natural beauty. Her heritage was a quarter Japanese, which accounted for her exotic dark eyes and hair. The only makeup she ever wore was a bit of mascara and a hint of colored lip gloss.

"Hey." Chaynie swiveled between them. "Have y'all met? Savannah, this is Greg."

Savannah squinted and pointed toward him. "Peterson. Yeah. We went to school together, I think. You were in my algebra class, weren't you?"

"Good memory," Greg noted.

"Did you move back to Morgan's Grove?" She inched closer, and Chaynie suddenly became a third wheel, scrunched between them in the narrow aisle.

"Yeah." Greg grasped the ladder's rung. "I'm renovating the library, starting my own architecture firm. It's pretty permanent."

Savannah's face lit up. "I actually teach at the high school. English. Writing and literature to be exact." After a beat, she added,

"Well, it's good to see you again," then turned awkwardly to Chaynie. "Ready for lunch? Maybe Christine's?"

"Do you have time for that?"

Christine's was a quaint bistro tucked behind the square. It had excellent food but was known for its sometimes-slow service.

"Yeah, Amy's taking over my study hall today."

Chaynie gave Greg a wave. "Guess I'll see you around. Thanks again for the talk."

"Anytime." He offered a reassuring smile.

"SO. GREG PETERSON," Savannah mused as she and Chaynie left the library and entered the town square. "From nerdy kid to hunky architect."

"That sounds like the basis of a new reality show."

"Well, really—who knew? Have you *seen* some of the guys from our class lately? I didn't even recognize Steve Adams when he came home for the holidays. He's lost most of his hair and gained a bunch of weight. And he was the gorgeous quarterback in high school. Every girl wanted him, including me. And now, here's Gorgeous Greg, former shy guy, working in your library. I can't believe you get to see him every day. Lucky you."

Chaynie grinned and rolled her eyes. "It's not like that. We're both professionals, and that's how things will stay."

"Mm-hmm."

The square hummed with activity as shoppers and lunch-goers threaded in and out of stores or paused at benches to rest and chat. Moving along the route to Christine's, Chaynie noticed the bookstore's new décor.

"I can't escape it." She nodded toward the window, where someone was placing copies of *Bridget Jones* and *Wuthering Heights* near a giant paper heart that read, "Valentine's Love Stories."

"Will it be hard for you this year because of Blake?" Savannah asked.

"I'm trying not to let it be."

They continued on past the bookstore, past the new bakery, where men hammered away at renovations, then toward the bed-and-breakfast at the end of the block.

Chaynie reconsidered Savannah's question and elaborated. "I mean, it's been a year, and most of my feelings for him are gone. I never really think about him, but it's not easy watching everyone else celebrate love. It's in my face constantly, the reminder that I'm alone again."

"Well, you're not the only one. My last memorable date was, oh, a couple of years ago. And I've spent this entire school year pining over a guy who barely knows my name."

When they reached the restaurant, half a block behind the square, Chaynie opened the door to a European-style space with photos of France and Italy on the walls and a stone fireplace in the corner. Within seconds, a gregarious server seated them at the last vacant booth in the corner, where they shrugged out of their coats and studied the menu.

"So, how's that going? With Lucas?" Chaynie asked.

"It's not going at all. He's this untouchable crush. And since he's the new teacher, everyone swarms him, especially the other single teachers. I actually tried to approach him during a faculty meeting yesterday, but he was too busy talking to someone else, so I shrank back. He barely knows who I am, even though we're in the same department. I'm too short. That's it. I'm completely invisible."

Chaynie chuckled. "You're not too short or invisible. You're not too anything. You're perfect, and he will turn around and notice that someday."

"At least you have your own crush to view on a daily basis, and he knows your name."

"Greg is not my crush. He's my coworker, sort of. A guy I barely remember from high school. That's it. In fact, I've hardly spoken to him since he got here yesterday. He's busy, and I'm busy. That's probably how it will stay."

Savannah lifted an eyebrow. "I saw that little exchange between you before we left the library."

"What exchange?" Chaynie abandoned her menu and looked across at Savannah.

"Like you were sharing a secret. This *thing* passed between you. I can't describe it."

Chaynie thought of her dad, of the root beer and the joke telling. "Well, we were just catching up. He's a nice guy, and we had a nice, brief talk. Nothing more. Now, what are we eating today?"

The server appeared right in time for the subject to be permanently changed, and Chaynie and Savannah spent the rest of the meal talking about their individual holidays. Savannah recounted her cornbread-dressing fiasco in great detail—she'd forgotten to remove the dish from the oven in time and had filled the entire kitchen with smoke. And as her friend spoke with lively gestures, Chaynie recalled the cheerful chatter of the book club ladies. She was grateful that, twenty years later, she still had a lifelong friend of her own in Savannah, the sister she'd never had.

Chapter Three

Chaynie frowned at the screen as she reread the final paragraph. *Not good enough. It needs more... impact.*

She reached for her cocoa and sipped the steaming liquid, hoping it would offer some inspiration. Setting down the mug, she patted Max's arched furry back before returning to the keyboard.

She should be working on the big Valentine's project Mary had assigned four days ago, but every time she forced ideas, Chaynie would run dry. Nothing came, so tonight, she decided to focus on her children's story. But even *that* wasn't going smoothly. The ending of any book was so crucial. Chaynie felt a unique pressure to find the right words, the perfect images to wrap up the story. It deserved a strong ending, but she hadn't discovered it yet.

The soft clanking of pots and pans drifted from the kitchen as her mother finished the dishes. It had been Chaynie's night to cook—spaghetti and garlic bread, simple but hearty for a cold winter's night—and her mother had taken on the cleaning duties afterward. That had been their pattern since her father had passed away. When they weren't buying takeout, Chaynie and her mother took turns cooking and cleaning. It had become a comforting routine.

Her mother appeared in the doorway and wiped her hands on a dish towel. "Honey, did you want to save the bread? There's half a slice left."

"No thanks. Unless you want it." Chaynie returned to the screen and puffed out a sigh.

"What's wrong?" Her mother walked farther into the room, which elicited a tiny "meow" from Max, who lay against Chaynie's thigh on the sofa near the crackling fire.

"I'm having trouble with the ending. I have confidence in every page of this story except the very last one. Why can't I get this right?"

Her mother came to sit on the coffee table a foot away. "Want me to take a look?"

"Sure. I could use a fresh perspective." Chaynie swiveled the laptop so her mother could place it on her own knees.

Her mother removed her reading glasses from the nape of her blouse and put them on. The screen's brightness reflected in the glass. Her eyes darted back and forth, reading the text, then she removed her glasses. "It's... good."

"But not great. I need it to be a 'wow' ending—or at least a satisfying one. The perfect way to wrap it up, that's what I'm going for."

"I know what you mean." Her mother pursed her lips. "I have an idea. Maybe you just need some inspiration. There's that collection of old children's books upstairs—the ones you used to pore over with your dad and beg him to read a thousand times. Maybe if you flipped through some of those, studied how other authors handled their endings, you could figure out yours."

"Great idea. I haven't looked at those books in years. You kept them?"

"Of course!" Her mother handed the laptop back to Chaynie. "They're in your bedroom closet, tucked away in some dark corner, I think. Try the highest shelf first, a cardboard box."

Newly inspired, Chaynie swiftly made her way upstairs. Years ago, her childhood bedroom had been transformed into a guest room, tastefully decorated with a burgundy-and-forest-green comforter, matching drapes, and a petite rolltop desk. When Chaynie had moved back into the house as an adult, over a year ago, it had become her room again, and even though the décor was completely different and the bed had been repositioned, the space was immediately familiar, comfortable. It had felt like home.

Inside the closet, Chaynie found two boxes right where her mother had said they would be. She was tall enough to reach them on her tiptoes, without a stool, so she lifted each one gingerly down and placed them on her bed with a small bounce.

She sat down next to the boxes and crossed her legs, eager to sort through the treasures. As she opened a box, Chaynie saw the first book. *The Lion, the Witch, and the Wardrobe*—the young children's version, a glossy hardback with illustrations. And below that, *The Tales of Peter Rabbit*. And still further down, *Winnie the Pooh*. She leaned in to sniff the aging, worn pages then flipped through them delicately, remembering her father pulling her into the crook of his arm to read to her until she fell fast asleep.

She had assumed it would be easy, perusing books from her childhood as "research" for her own book, but what she hadn't anticipated were the strong emotions attached to them. The images and words held a magical quality, directly connected to her father across time. Those early memories were precious, still alive and vivid, and sometimes painful. He had left them too soon.

Forcing herself back to her task, Chaynie selected four possible titles for inspiration—books whose endings had worked beautifully, endings she knew by heart and had loved as a child. When her father had read the last words and closed the book, young Chaynie had experienced a happy satisfaction, though she would always reopen the book and plead, "Again, again!" and her father would usually give in.

Closing the box and setting aside the stack of selected books, she remembered the second box she'd pulled down, marked "Memories," scribbled in her own handwriting.

She opened the lid and gasped lightly as she sifted through items she hadn't set eyes on in fifteen or twenty years. First-place ribbons from a roller-skating contest. Her graduation invitation from kindergarten. Handmade crafts—a paper-plate turkey made with feathers and tongue depressors, a palm-sized clay owl baked in an oven in the second grade, a ballpoint pen topped with a fuzzy-haired troll.

Reaching the bottom of the box, Chaynie found an envelope, worn and crinkled with age. Inside it, she touched something cold and metallic, a piece of jewelry. She drew it out and placed it in her palm for a better look.

"I remember this," she whispered aloud.

Before she could fully inspect the silver bracelet, she heard a quiet tap at the door. Her mother peeked in. "Did you find what you needed?"

Chaynie patted the empty space beside her on the bed. "Yes! And more. I found the books and also this other box. Lots of awards and crafty things. And *this*! Do you remember?"

Her mother sat beside her and leaned closer. "The charm bracelet. Of course! You got a new charm every Valentine's Day at school. It was such a mystery for so many years. Your secret admirer."

"This bracelet caused quite a stir. Other girls in my class were so jealous, and every boy in the class was a possible suspect." She touched one of the charms, a silver book, with her fingertip. "I think I got this first one—and the bracelet—in third grade? I can't remember."

Her mother nodded. "It was shortly after we moved here."

"And then every year after that for—" Chaynie counted out the rest of the charms, a Snoopy figure, an angel, a rabbit, and a moon. "Five years."

"Didn't you find them in your desk each Valentine's?"

"It was always on my seat when I got to school, inside a tiny box with my name," Chaynie remembered. She draped the delicate bracelet, child sized, on top of her wrist. "I looked so forward to it. I remember trying to arrive early a couple of years, to see if I could catch the giver in the act. I thought I would never find out."

"Until Dean."

Dean had been Chaynie's first real boyfriend, *if* a boyfriend in the seventh grade could count as "real." And when Chaynie had point-blank asked him about the charm bracelet, he had dipped his head and confessed. It had been him all those years. But theirs had been a short-lived romance, and by the next Valentine's, they'd gone their separate ways, and the charms had stopped coming.

Her mother's phone buzzed, and Chaynie, not meaning to pry or spy, caught the texter's name on the screen.

"Mitch?" she asked, raising her eyebrows. Her mother rarely received texts, especially so late in the evening.

"Yeah, we've been put on this committee together at school."

"A coach and an art teacher on the same committee?"

"Mitch is a history teacher too."

"Oh, that's right. I always forget."

"The principal wanted to create 'random pairs of faculty,' so we could brainstorm across the curriculum for some new program coming down the pipeline next year. Something about goals and assessments and rubrics. Doesn't that sound fun?" She smirked.

"Sounds dry and horrible. At least Mitch could make it fun."

Mitch Turner was the head athletic coach at Morgan's Grove High and had been her father's best friend for twenty years. He'd lost his wife to an accident five years ago, so when Chaynie's father had died, Mitch had offered support to both Chaynie and her mother. He knew what it was like, that kind of sudden, piercing loss. Though talking about feelings wasn't particularly his strong suit, Mitch had helped in other more practical ways around the house now and again—repairing the occasional dripping faucet or broken doorknob or even changing Chaynie's flat tire before Thanksgiving. Chaynie suspected he did it out of genuine kindness but also out of a sense of duty to his best friend, looking out for his widow and daughter when he couldn't.

Chaynie's mother drew the screen closer to her face then tapped out her reply to Mitch. "I'm so bad at this texting thing," she muttered. "Oh no!"

"What?"

Her mother bit her lip and glanced sheepishly toward Chaynie. "I just sent him the word 'thong' instead of 'thing.' I was in too big of a hurry."

Chaynie stifled a giggle and laid the charm bracelet in her lap. "Here." She took her mother's phone and deftly texted, *Oops, wrong word. I meant THING.* Then she added a smiley face and handed the phone back to her mother. "All fixed."

Her mother's crimson cheeks started to regain their natural color as she took the phone. "Thanks for the save. How embarrassing."

"Don't worry. It happens all the time to people. He'll understand."

And it seemed Mitch had, as he sent a matching smiley face to her mother's phone, making her smile too. She lowered the phone and turned to Chaynie. "Talking about the committee reminds me of something. After today's meeting, I stopped by the office supply store and ran into Greg Peterson. He's your age, I think. He was in your class at school? He's moved back to Morgan's Grove, and he says he's renovating the library. I'm surprised you didn't mention it. Do you remember him?"

"Oh. Yeah. Things have been so busy this first week after the holidays. I guess I forgot to tell you. Mary hired him last week." Chaynie lifted the charm bracelet from her lap and dangled it above her palm, then dropped it into the center. "I do remember Greg a little from school. He was super quiet, so we hardly ever talked. In fact, I don't remember having a single conversation with him back then."

"He was a sweet kid, very shy. He worked for your father for a few summers at the store. I believe Greg had a severe stutter as a child, which probably explains why he was so quiet. Well, quiet around everyone except your father, who said he was a chatterbox."

"I had no idea." Chaynie pictured a young Greg in school, nervous and uncomfortable, and felt badly for never reaching out to him, for virtually ignoring him like everyone else had. She thought back on their conversation between the library shelves two days ago. "He doesn't seem to stutter anymore."

"His mother enrolled him in speech therapy early on. He worked hard to overcome it, but the stigma remained for years, I'm sure. The kids were probably cruel, so he learned to keep to himself. But your dad took a special shine to him, brought him under his wing."

"I'm so glad Greg had someone back then, and I'm glad it was Daddy."

"Me too." Her mother stretched an arm around Chaynie's shoulders and gave her a squeeze. "Do you want some help with those books?" She gestured toward the stack on the bed.

"Naw, I might keep them up here awhile, flip through them."

"Okay. I'll head downstairs. I wanted to work more on the illustration." Her mother disappeared through the doorframe.

Chaynie remained at the bed, gathering the items she'd pulled out of her Memories box and placing them carefully back inside. She decided to keep the charm bracelet out for some reason. She wasn't ready to let it go yet. Maybe it was a reminder of happier Valentine's, innocent ones, before broken hearts and disillusioned expectations. And maybe it could give her the inspiration she needed for Mary's project.

She laid the bracelet on top of Thoreau's *Walden* on the nightstand then tucked the box of memories back where it belonged, high on the top shelf.

CHAYNIE SHIFTED THE glossy hardback in her hands, turning the page so that the children could see the illustration. "See?" she said. "The monster isn't scary at all."

"He's *so* cute!" Amanda shrieked.

"He's got green fur!" Mikey added.

Chaynie paused, giving all nine children enough time to fill their wide eyes with the colorful picture before moving on. She loved having six- to eight-year-olds in a reading group. Their little brains still held a curiosity for books that older kids seemed not to possess. They were too busy scrolling and tapping their gadgets. Chaynie had tried to form an older chapter book reading club, but it had dwindled quickly, and the kids who'd attended had been restless and unresponsive to her many clever character voices. But *this* age, the younger children, still had an interest in physical books, in turning pages, in running their stubby fingers over vivid pictures of monsters or bears or insects. Chaynie still had a chance with these children, to make a difference, to cultivate their love of reading.

She finished the last page, revealed the final illustration, then announced to the children and their awaiting parents that refreshments were available outside the alcove.

As Chaynie closed the book and rose from her seat, she heard a *Snap!* followed by a wailing cry. Looking out at the group, she saw Tommy, his red face scrunched up, tears streaming down as he pointed at the chair. It lay on its side with one of the legs pitifully separated from the rest of the chair.

Chaynie rushed to the little boy's side, squatting to his level. "Are you hurt?" She examined his pudgy arms and legs but saw no evidence of injury.

As his mother approached, equally concerned, Tommy shook his head and wiped his cheeks with balled-up fists. "No. But look! I broke it!" He pointed to the chair and started to cry again.

Relieved, his mother patted his back. "Tommy, it's fine. Chairs can be fixed. I'm just glad you're okay." She clutched his hand to leave then mouthed "Sorry" to Chaynie, who was already reaching toward the chair to assess the damage.

"Bye, Tommy. See you next week," Chaynie called as they left the Children's Corner.

As she picked up the broken chair leg, a shadow fell across her bare arm. She glanced up to see Greg.

He crouched beside her. "What happened?"

"It broke when Tommy got up. He's okay. This chair, though... it's a goner."

"I can fix this," Greg assured her. "No problem. The screw came loose. Let me grab a tool from one of the guys. Be right back."

"The guys" had been at it all morning—draping enormous blue tarps over sections of the library then drilling, banging, hammering, and stirring up a good amount of dust. Chaynie knew it was all part of the process, necessary for the renovations. And as promised, Greg *had* kept the noise down to a minimum. She had expected much worse, truth be told.

Chaynie's phone buzzed in her pocket, and she stood to view a text from Doris.

Perfect choice. That's the one. Will order the books today. Thank you!

Chaynie clicked off her phone, relieved that her suggestion for the book club had been so happily received. Yesterday, she had scoured some titles online, seeking the perfect contemporary, romantic, happy-ending book the ladies were hoping for. When that search hadn't yielded much, she'd sorted through her personal book collection at home and found *Julie and Romeo*, by Jeanne Ray. It was a book Savannah had given her a few years before, a modern-day retelling of the famous Shakespearean play, but told with older main characters and lots of quirky humor—and most importantly, a happy ending. Since the book was a short one, Chaynie had suggested that the ladies also tack on the sequel, equally short, to complete their February book club selection.

She had been so confident in her choice that it was the only suggestion she'd made. Thankfully, her gamble had paid off, as evidenced by Doris's text.

Greg entered the Children's Corner with a cordless screwdriver then knelt beside the broken chair. By then, all the children and their mothers had left the area, and Greg had apparently given the workers a break as well. All Chaynie could hear at the moment was blissful silence, the silence she was accustomed to most days at the library.

She watched Greg's capable hands move fluidly—deftly flipping over the tiny chair, replacing the leg, and securing the screw. The entire repair only took a handful of seconds. Making sure that the job was done right, Greg tested the strength of the repair with his hands, rotated the chair back to its sitting position, and declared it "good as new."

"Thanks," Chaynie said. "I think you've done this before."

Greg set the drill down then stood up to meet Chaynie. "Yeah, my dad is a woodworker. He has this shed in back of the ranch where he makes these cool ballpoint pens, all wood. Some furniture too. I guess it rubbed off on me." Greg was clean-shaven today, displaying the dimple in his chin. "Your hair is different," he noticed.

She'd been in a rush that morning and had twisted her hair up into a semi-messy knot with a couple of wavy strands still hanging near her cheek.

Clearing his throat, Greg surveyed the area. "So, this is a nice space for kids. Seems like it gets a lot of use."

"It does. Reading clubs, holiday parties, other events. I've always wanted to fancy it up a bit. It's a good area, but it's sort of plain."

"What would you do if you had the chance to dress it up?"

She'd never been asked that question before. When she had first moved back to Morgan's Grove and taken the library technician position, Chaynie had wanted to approach Mary with her ideas but had assumed the library wouldn't possibly have the funding for them, so she'd stayed quiet, making the best of things.

She stepped out toward the middle of the space, where a colorful ABC rug lay beneath a circle of small chairs, and remembered her original vision. "I would love to create a forest theme with a huge fake tree over there, leaves hanging down." She pointed toward the chair at one end of the alcove where she usually sat to read her stories. "And maybe some different, sturdier chairs—these are so old and rickety—painted in forest colors. Then maybe a special reading corner in that area." She turned and pointed to the other end of the alcove, beyond a series of bookshelves. "And continue the forest theme with some sort of mural on the wall—you know, fairies, deer, a stream, that sort of thing."

Greg followed along as she spoke. He rubbed his chin, and for a moment, she thought he might laugh or shake his head at her outrageous ideas. Instead, his eyes contained a glimmer as he said, "I think it's very doable."

Chaynie blinked. "What do you mean, doable?"

"I think I can make your vision a reality. I have some ideas for materials that could do the job. Plus, there's new money with Rick's donation."

"But that money is allocated for specific repairs. I'd feel weird asking Mary about this. I mean, my forest idea is just a daydream, a luxury and not a necessity."

Greg raised an eyebrow. "We'll see about that. I have an in with Mary, you know. Being her godson and all. Plus, I could save money by doing the work myself. Get my dad to help out. He could build new chairs, even a table."

"You're serious."

"I am."

Chaynie's smile broadened. "It's a real possibility?"

"Absolutely."

"But you don't have time for all this. I mean, with the big renovations on top of trying to open your new architecture office."

"I can make time. I'm my own boss, and I like this type of project. It gives me a chance to create something new." He scanned the room then pointed toward the opposite corner. "The mural. That's one thing I have no talent for. I can't draw a stick figure to save my life."

"Same as me." Chaynie paused then snapped her fingers. "My mother! She's an artist, and she teaches at the school. She's also been working on this project..." Chaynie drifted away, not ready to talk about her children's book with anyone yet. "Anyway, I think she'd still have time for the mural, maybe even painting the chairs too. Let me ask her tonight. That is, if you're sure."

"About the funding? Yeah. We can maneuver some things around if we have to, and my labor is free. So is my dad's. He's in between projects. I think this would be good for him."

"What's the possible timeline?"

"Probably a few weeks."

Chaynie suddenly remembered what *could* be happening in her life over the next few weeks or months.

"Your smile disappeared." Greg studied her face. "Is it Mary? Don't worry. I can pretend the idea for the alcove funding is mine if you want. I'll leave your name out of it."

"It's not that." Chaynie shook her head and walked toward the only stained glass window in the alcove, a colorful image of Mother Goose reading to a group of children. "I might not be here much longer." Pivoting, she grimaced as he moved closer. "It's sort of a secret."

"You can tell me."

Chaynie confessed to him in a whisper, "I've sent some applications to other libraries for a head librarian position. Some are out of state. Mary doesn't know anything about it yet."

"I see." Greg crossed his arms. The sunshine through the stained glass created a colorful rainbow on his skin.

"I'm keeping it quiet because I'm not sure I'll get any bites. Library positions are hard to come by, so my odds are slim, especially for the libraries I've applied to. I already got my rejection email from UT this morning."

"I won't tell anyone. But even if you get a new position, it doesn't have to change the alcove's plans, does it? I mean, the whole job-getting process would still take a lot of time, including your two weeks' notice to Mary. You'd be here for most of the renovations."

"That's true." Chaynie tsked. "I'm being selfish. This isn't about me anyway. It's about the library, about the kids and the Children's Corner." She walked toward the alcove's center and remembered her enthusiasm over Greg's initial suggestion. "Let's do this."

"That's the spirit." Greg joined her on the ABC carpet.

"Well, this has been a productive day, and it's not even noon. I finally found the perfect book for the Sassy Ladies. And now you've come along and fixed my chair and given me this realistic vision for the alcove." Chaynie smirked. "I only wish you could wave your magic wand and rescue me from my Valentine's project. I've been procrastinating that one." Mary had scheduled a meeting for Monday, in fact, to discuss Chaynie's ideas. But at the moment, all she could share with Mary was a blank page. "I want to avoid all the cheesy, ridiculous, clichéd ideas that are probably expected. Mary put the wrong person in charge. I should've told her how much I hate Valentine's."

"Why?"

"Long story. Bad breakup on Valentine's last year. It's given me a sour taste for the holiday. I'd love to fast-forward to February fifteenth this year."

"Sorry. That stinks."

"Yeah. Anyway, here I am, rambling away when you've got work to do. Thanks for all your help today."

"Sure. And if I think up any cool ideas for your Valentine's project..."

"Definitely. Let me know! I'll be outsourcing, asking friends, family, everyone, for their ideas. I'll take all the help I can get."

Greg leaned down to grab his drill. "Well, have a good weekend."

"You too."

She watched him leave then spun around to examine the Children's Corner with brand-new eyes. An enchanted forest, a mural, a total redesign. She imagined herself as a little girl in such a place—the excitement and joy it might've brought to her. Then she imagined future children enjoying the renovated space, discovering books and characters that would hopefully stay with them for a lifetime. She couldn't wait to get started.

Chapter Four

airy tale themes.
Sleeping Beauty?
Snow White?

Chaynie chuckled at her screen, watching her friend's texts roll in. Savannah often texted in quick fragments, one after the other, instead of one long block. Chaynie always tried to wait until Savannah was finished before responding.

Scary witches. Not very Valentine-y.

Oooh! How about the classics?

Romeo and Juliet?
Jane Eyre?
Hmm. Ending in death and tragedy. Okay, scratch that too.

Chaynie rolled onto her side in bed—ten a.m. on a Saturday, her sleep-in day—and hovered her thumbs above the screen, thinking Savannah had finished her train of thought.

As she started to type her reply, Savannah's next text came through. *I give up. I'm terrible at this. Sorry!*

Chaynie began her response with a smiley face. *No worries. This helps, bouncing ideas around.*

Actually, it *did* help. Savannah's brainstorming efforts, as well as her mom's, which had been pretty cheesy, had proved to Chaynie that a good idea was hard to find. It wasn't just her own distaste for Valentine's that had her struggling with Mary's project.

As Chaynie sent her response to Savannah, a call came through from a local number she didn't recognize. She'd learned from experience never to answer an unknown number, which usually turned out to be some annoying sales pitch she had trouble wriggling out of gracefully.

She let the call go, and a minute later, the voicemail notification popped up. Chaynie clicked to hear the message.

"Hey. This is Greg. Peterson. Mary gave me your number. I hope that's okay. You told me to brainstorm ideas for your Valentine's project thing, and, well... I came up with a couple of half-decent ideas. At least, I *think* they're half-decent. So, call me back when you get a chance. Thanks." His voice sounded even deeper over the phone. He had one of those soothing, late-night-DJ type voices that could make his listeners happily drowsy.

Chaynie readjusted the pillows behind her and sat up in bed, forcing Max to find a different spot than on top of her feet. She dialed Greg's number, wondering where he was right then, on a Saturday. Probably at the library, which was open—Britney wanted the extra hours, so she and Mary had agreed to handle the library on Saturdays, giving Chaynie the day off.

The phone only rang twice before Greg picked up. "Hello?"

"Hey. This is Chaynie. I got your voicemail. Are you at the library?"

"Nope, I'm at my new office, in the square."

"Prime location. Where exactly?"

"The block that has the burger place. I'm next door."

"Next to Mindy's? So, you're in the optometrist's old space."

"That's the one, but I don't know how he stood it—the burger-and-fries smell next door starts early and permeates everything nearby. I'm always hungry when I get here to open."

Chaynie knew exactly what he meant. The minute someone at the library made coffee and filled up every crevice with that roasted scent, it was all Chaynie could think about. "So, you've got some project ideas for me?"

"Well, two. Maybe just one. The second one's kind of lame. Maybe they both are."

"They've *got* to be better than what I've come up with."

"So," Greg continued, "I remember you mentioned hating Valentine's, and it got me thinking. You can't be the only one, right? If someone's not totally in love, or part of a solid couple, Valentine's has got to be a hard day—watching all the ads, the hand-holding, the hearts and flowers."

"Exactly."

"Well, why not make this event broader, more inclusive?"

"Broader how?"

"Like, not focused so much on romance but on love in general. The love of friends, family, community. I mean, almost everyone has some love in their life, hopefully. Why not celebrate that? Why does it have to be about romance?"

Chaynie's heart beat faster, the same way it did whenever she felt an idea nudging at the edge of her mind while writing her children's book, when she was onto something good, when the Muse seemed to take over.

Of course. Why does *Valentine's have to be exclusionary? Why does it only have to celebrate one certain kind of love that only a certain percentage of the population is experiencing, leaving everyone else completely out?* In fact, the origins of Valentine's Day supported Greg's idea. If Chaynie remembered correctly from a literary course she'd taken on the Middle Ages at UT, the notion of St. Valentine hadn't been attached to romantic love until Chaucer introduced it into one of his poems. So, Chaucer had been responsible for forcing romance onto Valentine's Day.

Greg was right. Chaynie might not have romantic love in her life at the moment, but she did have love—her mother, her best friend, her cat, even the library and Morgan's Grove itself. She felt a deep love and affection for each of those.

"That's genius," she told Greg. "I absolutely love it."

"Really? Well, that was easy. Glad I don't have to pitch that second idea."

"But how do we put this into motion, make it tangible, connect it directly to the library?"

"I hadn't thought that far," Greg admitted.

"Well, it's a huge start, all the same. You've given me an idea to work with. Thank you!"

"My pleasure."

"I owe you. Big. I mean, first the Children's Corner, and now this. Can you think of anything I could help you with?"

Greg paused then said, "Well, I can think of one thing. I'm standing here in the middle of my half-furnished office, staring at paint swatches and fabrics, and I can't make any sense of it. I have to make some decisions by Monday, but I'm slightly color blind, so I don't trust my own instincts. I could accidentally be pairing orange with red and not even know it."

"I can totally help you with that. Not to brag, but I've got an eye for color." In fact, years ago at UT, word had spread around the dorms that Chaynie had decorated her room with such style that she'd gotten requests from other students to decorate theirs. It had almost made her switch her major to interior design, but she'd known she could only be happy inside a library. "How about I bring over a late breakfast?" she offered. "Bagels or donuts?"

"Definitely donuts. Chocolate, if they've got them."

"And coffee?"

"Straight black."

"We're kindred spirits. See you soon."

Infused with new energy, Chaynie clicked off the phone, tossed the covers aside, which accidentally covered Max's head, then swiveled to get out of bed. It would only take her a few minutes to slip on some jeans and a casual sweater.

"KNOCK, KNOCK." CHAYNIE stepped hesitantly through the open door of Greg's new office, but Greg was nowhere in sight.

She set the box of donuts and coffee holder on a large oak desk next to some paint swatches then wriggled out of her coat. She almost hadn't needed a coat—even though the winds held a strong January chill, the bright Texas sun beamed down its heat, making the weather equal parts warm and cold. She hadn't planned on any outings that day, but after breathing in the fresh, clean air and watching squirrels rummage for nuts in the dry grass as she walked to a donut shop behind the square, she'd been glad for an excuse to get outside.

Chaynie popped the top off her coffee and was tapping a sugar packet over its surface when Greg walked in from the back room.

"Oh. Hey. I didn't hear you." He held a drill and set it down on the desk. He wore a black sweater, which made his hair seem even darker than usual. "I was out back, fixing a broken door hinge."

"You're always renovating something."

"Story of my life." Greg grasped the other cup and eyed the donut box. "Thanks for this. I'm starved, actually."

"I got a dozen. All chocolate." Chaynie opened the box to reveal the donuts stacked together in neat rows. She could smell their sugary goodness wafting upward.

"Here." Greg reached toward his back pocket. "Let me pay for these."

"Absolutely not." She swatted the air. "These are on me. Remember? I owe you."

Greg shrugged and selected a donut. "Well, okay. But after this, you don't owe me anymore. Paid in full with donuts."

Chaynie selected one from the box and folded it into a napkin, then leaned against the desk. "I told my mom about the mural in the Children's Corner, and she's all in. She's already been sketching ideas."

"Great. My dad's in too. He ordered the lumber for the chairs and took some measurements the other day."

"This is really happening."

"Yep."

"And so is the Valentine's project." Chaynie shifted her weight against the desk. "I couldn't stop thinking about your idea as I walked over here—mostly, how I could incorporate this 'inclusive' Valentine's idea into a real project. And then it hit me. Movie night."

Greg chomped on his donut, finishing the last bite, and raised his eyebrows. "Movie night?"

"When I was a little girl, and even a teenager on dateless weekends, my parents would rent movies every Friday night, and we'd watch them as a family. But not just any movies. Musicals. You know, the classics—*Singin' in the Rain*, *Seven Brides for Seven Brothers*, *Gentlemen Prefer Blondes*."

"Sure. My mom used to love those old movies. Still does."

"Right. They're popular, even now. And for those who haven't been exposed to them, we could introduce them to the classics with a movie night for the whole town."

"It's a good idea, but..." Greg grimaced then took a sip of coffee.

"What? You can say it."

"Well, I don't exactly see the connection to the library. Or even to Valentine's, actually. How will it all fit together?"

"So, your all-inclusive idea would culminate in this movie night, on Valentine's night, inside the library. There's plenty of space on the main floor, and we could move a few things to make more room. It's entirely feasible. That would bring people into the library. Coupled, not coupled, it doesn't matter—all are welcome. We could advertise it around town with fliers, radio promos, even a billboard."

"I see where you're going with this. It would be a big town event, where people can spend a fun night, even if they don't have a Valentine's date."

"Exactly! We Morgan's Grove residents love our big town events, but there's not one for Valentine's. I mean, we've always had a Christmas festival, a St. Patrick's parade, and even an egg hunt for Easter, but never anything special for Valentine's."

"I like it." Greg set down his coffee and paced the floor, gesturing as he spoke. "But what if you made it even bigger?"

"Bigger how?"

"Spread it out. Move the event to the lawn."

"Outside the library?"

"Sure. There's that huge patch of grass on the side of the library that's always empty."

Greg pointed out the window, and Chaynie pivoted to see the space he meant, right across the street in the middle of the square. She passed by that spot nearly every day but hadn't noticed before how vast the lawn was.

She turned back toward Greg. "So how would this work? Where would we show the movie?"

"On the side of the library. That wall. We could rent a huge screen, even a real projector system, and set it all up the day of. I can get some of my guys to help out."

Chaynie shifted her gaze through the window toward the empty lawn and envisioned all the details. They could block the street off to give the projector enough room, and maybe provide a popcorn stand and a cotton candy machine. A peerless February night with stars shining overhead. The buzz of excitement before the projector rolled. And people. Young and old, coupled and uncoupled, friends and family members, maybe even beloved pets. The entire town coming together on a day which usually excluded many of them, unified to enjoy a communal evening and to celebrate all kinds of love.

At some point during Chaynie's daydream, Greg had joined her at the window, probably imagining the very same details.

Chaynie placed her fingertips on her cheeks with a happy gasp. "I love it," she whispered. "What a perfect idea."

She looked up toward Greg, who was still staring out at the lawn, nodding. "It is. Perfect." He smiled, revealing his straight white teeth. "This could totally work."

"Mary will love it too. I almost want to tell her today instead of waiting for Monday."

"You should! Especially while the idea is fresh."

Chaynie went to grab her coat but suddenly remembered why she was at Greg's new office in the first place. "But I have a higher priority. We need to make some color selections first. I *really* owe you now."

"Naw. I was just bouncing off your original movie idea. This is all you. But I'll be here to help. I can give you the manpower for the screen, maybe even locate a projector."

"That would be amazing." Chaynie caught a sudden whiff of chocolate. In all the excitement, she hadn't touched her donut. "Brainstorming makes me hungry." She picked up the donut and pinched off a section. "So, show me these colors. We can make this space fantastic."

MARY *had* loved the idea. In fact, she'd so loved it that she had immediately asked whether they could do a movie night every Valentine's, make it a new Morgan's Grove tradition.

"Well, let's make sure this one is successful first," Chaynie had replied. "I'm hoping it will all go as planned, but the turnout might not be as high as we want." Though she suspected it would be. She could already smell success.

Immediately after leaving the library with Mary's blessing to "get going!" on the project, Chaynie had called Savannah to let her know about the new idea, purposely failing to mention that Greg had been the one who'd helped her come up with it. She didn't need Savannah's further teasing about having a crush.

Then she'd returned home to scribble out some more ideas for Movie Night—advertising, food choices, possible movie titles to show. She had so many decisions to make and so little time to implement them.

CHAYNIE RECROSSED HER feet, which were propped up on the desk, and flipped another page. That morning, entering the library, it had dawned on her that she'd completely neglected her homework for the book club—to read the first two chapters of *Julie and Romeo*. So, after rushing through her morning library duties, she had shut her office door upstairs and settled in to read, hoping Mary wouldn't catch her and think she was slacking off.

Reaching the last page of chapter two, Chaynie heard a light tap at the door. She slammed the book shut, covered it with some papers on her desk, and placed her feet on the floor, all in one swift, fluid movement. "Come in!"

Mary opened the door and entered. Her expression was unreadable as she approached Chaynie's desk.

"Is anything wrong?" Chaynie asked.

"You're in trouble, young lady."

Chaynie hoped Mary was joking, but when her serious expression remained serious, Chaynie rifled through any possible infractions she could have committed. *Did I fail to return an important customer call? Get an order of books wrong? Miss a crucial deadline?*

Mary continued, "Greg told me about the Children's Corner, about your plans to renovate it."

"I'm so sorry." Chaynie rose to her feet. "I should've been the one to tell you. It was a total oversight. Greg and I were talking about it last week, and one thing led to another, and before I knew it, we were planning the renovation. But it's actually more of a... sprucing up. I promise I didn't hide it from you on purpose. I was so busy with the Valentine's project—"

Mary put her hand up to silence Chaynie, and that was when she broke into a smile. "No, you're misunderstanding me. I'm upset that you didn't come to me *sooner* with this idea, months ago. Greg let it slip that you've been wanting to do this for a while but thought there wasn't money. We could've scraped together a small budget for your new vision of the alcove. I'm just sorry you didn't feel comfortable coming to me with your idea."

Chaynie's shoulders relaxed. "Oh. Well, I wish I had, in hindsight."

"In any case, there's no better person to helm the project than Greg. He told me all about it—the huge tree, the forest theme, the mural. It sounds like you were mutually inspired. You make a good team."

"Yeah, we seem to be on the same page about a lot of things. I'm so relieved you approve of the alcove. We've got a lot on our plates these days, don't we? I mean, with the library renovations, the Valentine's project, the Children's Corner."

"But isn't it exciting? This place is brimming with activity, with people. We're giving an old building new life."

"That's a nice way to look at it," Chaynie agreed.

Mary said goodbye and turned on her heel, giving Chaynie enough time to read the last two paragraphs of her chapter before heading down to see the Sassy Ladies.

"OH, THAT WAS MY FAVORITE scene. I can't *believe* she said that to him!" Ginger was smiling from ear to ear, as were all the ladies discussing the book selection. It had been ninety minutes of raucous laughter coupled with sincere character analysis.

Chaynie had sat in the corner for their session, wishing to be an observer, speaking only if needed, as had been Mary's role. She didn't want to inject her opinion. It was their club, not hers.

As the ladies gathered their plastic-wrapped goodies and began to leave, Chaynie saw the top of Greg's head in the doorframe, coming her way. He held the door open for Doris and Lucille, who both looked at him wide-eyed behind his back then whispered together, twittering like a pair of junior high girls. Chaynie imagined they were admiring Greg's handsome face—and speculating on the reason he had come in search of Chaynie. Even older ladies weren't immune to his charms.

"Do you have a sec?" Greg asked as Chaynie gathered her book and notepad.

"Sure."

She hadn't seen Greg since Saturday, when they'd met at his office. He'd been busy working in other parts of the library the past two days, but he had texted her a couple more ideas about the alcove.

Greg wore a jacket, so he was either just arriving or about to leave. He shoved his hands into his pockets. "So, I've got a lead on a projector and possibly a screen."

"That's fantastic. So soon?"

"Yeah, one of my guys has a friend of a friend of a friend who specializes in vintage movie stuff. Pete Burrows. He owns a place somewhere in North Austin. I'll probably make a trip there later in the week. I spoke with the guy over the phone. Sounds like he's a hundred years old, but he thinks he can help us out, so it's worth a shot."

"It's good to have an early lead. I mean, everything else hinges on this part—the movie projector, the screen. I'd love to advertise the event as 'on the lawn,' but I can't until we've secured the equipment."

"You're welcome to come along to Austin. I mean, this is your project."

"That's a good idea, actually. I need to meet this man in person, ask him some questions, secure the deposit. And having you there will be great since you'll know more about the labor side of things."

"What's your schedule on Friday?"

Chaynie tried to picture that date on her office calendar but couldn't recall. "I'll have to check, but I think it's pretty clear. And since this is library business, I could take part of the workday for it."

"Sounds good."

"I've made some headway with the poster graphics and popcorn machines. I'm stuck on something, though. It's pretty important."

"What's that?"

"Which movie to show. There are too many choices."

"It'll come to you. Don't worry." Greg's phone buzzed inside his pocket. He pulled it out and glanced at the screen. "Sorry, I need to get this. We can confirm the details about Austin soon."

Chaynie agreed then watched Greg wave and leave the room. She hoped her calendar for Friday was clear, but even if it wasn't, she would make room. She hadn't been to Austin, her second home, in months. As much as she adored Morgan's Grove, she sometimes missed the bustle and activity of a huge city—which was why she'd applied for head librarian positions in major cities across the country. She hadn't given up hope yet.

Chapter Five

*V*ALENTINE'S UNDER THE STARS. *Watch a classic film on the library's lawn. A magical evening of entertainment, food, door prizes, and more. <u>All are welcome</u> (including pets and children). FREE to the public. Blankets not provided.*

Chaynie held the freshly printed flyer and examined the font—she'd changed her mind three times before printing it. *This is it.* And once she received confirmation from Mr. Burrows about the projector and screen, she could send the flyers off to the printers and distribute them all around town.

Over the past few days, she had worked and reworked all the details of the event. The biggest change was that she would hold the first part of the evening *inside* the library before the movie began out on the lawn. Chaynie hoped to remind the townspeople of the beautiful interior and to coax them to browse and take in the books, the ornate ceilings, the stained glass. She and Britney would have a table for library card sign-ups then raffle off some free books and maybe even one of Greg's father's specially crafted pens, if he was willing. They could even move the popcorn and cotton candy machines inside. Chaynie was willing to risk the mess—well worth the price of luring people back to the library, which was the whole point of Mary's project to begin with.

As well, Chaynie had decided that Movie Night didn't sound particularly enchanting, so she'd replaced it with Under the Stars, hoping the stars would actually *be* out that night, with clear skies. The weather was one thing she had no control over. But she had a contingency plan in place. They could move the projector inside the library and set up a large sheet across the ends of the stacks if necessary. Still, she had hope that even the weather would cooperate on that special night.

Special. For the first time since last year's breakup fiasco, Chaynie was actually looking forward to Valentine's. As soon as Greg had helped her remove the romance stigma from the day, she'd begun to see it through entirely different eyes. A day to celebrate love—all kinds of love. It would be a good day. She would make it so.

Chaynie clicked off her laptop, left the flyer on top of her desk, then draped her coat across her arm. Mary had locked up the library an hour ago, leaving Chaynie to finish some necessary tasks, including the flyer.

She shut her office door and realized there was no tapping, no drilling that night. Greg must've given his guys the night off. She peered out onto the open, empty floor with an odd satisfaction about being the only one there. Some people might have become uneasy, standing in such a grand old space after hours alone, but not Chaynie. Maybe her fears had been conquered decades before, when she'd run away from home and burrowed herself in the Children's Corner. The library had become hers that day, and it still felt that way.

As she walked toward the staircase, Chaynie heard soft male voices coming from the alcove. Sam sometimes cleaned or repaired after hours, but she wondered who the second voice belonged to. Chaynie approached the Children's Corner and peeked around the wall where Greg stood, hands on hips, with an older man beside him, pointing at Chaynie's chair, the one she always sat in to read books to the children.

Chaynie cleared her throat, and the men swiveled around together. She could immediately see the resemblance—the shape of the jaw, the tall frame, the blue eyes. This was Greg's father.

"Sorry to interrupt," Chaynie said, moving forward.

Greg flashed a smile. "Hey. I didn't know you were still here." He motioned to the man beside him. "This is my dad, Buck."

Buck extended a hand to Chaynie, and she shook it, ignoring how rough and calloused it was, likely from his woodworking.

"So nice to meet you," she said. "I can't thank you enough for helping out with the alcove. It will mean the world to the children. And to me."

"Glad to do it. I got time on my hands, and this is a worthy project."

"We were taking measurements for the tree," Greg explained. "I'm glad you're here. You can help us out."

Chaynie draped her coat and purse over the nearest child-sized chair and joined them in the space.

"So, how exactly do you envision the tree?" Greg asked. "When you described it, I pictured it climbing clear to the ceiling then draping down with fake leaves and branches to about... here." He reached up high to show the tip of where the leaves might fall above Chaynie's chair.

"I should probably test it. I'm pretty tall, and I don't want leaves in my face every time I stand up."

Greg chuckled as she moved between him and his father to sit in the chair. Greg's hand remained high in the air as Chaynie imagined the leaves above her. To make sure the leaves would hang high enough, she stood to her normal height, and Greg's hand stayed at least six inches above her head.

"That's perfect," she confirmed.

"Good." Greg dropped his hand then scribbled the measurements into his notepad. "I'm doing some research on the trunk to make it look as realistic as possible with grooves and divots. As for the leaves, I know some craft shops that might be able to help out. Fake greenery nowadays looks pretty real."

"I can't wait." Chaynie clasped her hands together. "I never thought this would become a reality."

"It'll become reality pretty soon," Buck noted. "I've already constructed two chairs, and once we get all the details and measurements worked out for the tree, we can start on it. Might be three, four weeks until completion, give or take."

"The children will be ecstatic." She grabbed her belongings from the chair. "Well, I don't want to keep interrupting your work. Thank you again for everything."

"Are we still on for Friday?" Greg asked. "Austin, I mean. To see Pete."

"I cleared it with Mary, and she's ecstatic. We're all set."

"We could take my truck. I've already mapped out the way to Pete's place."

"Sure. Text me the details for when you want to leave. I'll be ready." Chaynie turned to go as she heard the men return to their project.

Bundled up for the walk home, Chaynie texted her mom to see if she wanted some takeout, but after getting no response, she decided on leftovers from the fridge. When she arrived on their block, she noticed a car at the curb and recognized it as Mitch's.

She hadn't seen him since before New Year's, when he'd brought them a holiday pie from Christine's. Her mother had grabbed three forks, and they'd eaten slices at the kitchen table together, reminiscing about their Christmas holidays. Mitch's daughter and grandson had come to Morgan's Grove for the holidays, so he hadn't been alone.

Chaynie pushed the front door open and heard laughter as Max darted in from the living room to greet her. She shut the door and leaned over to scratch his head. He purred with great satisfaction and rubbed his back against her calf, hoping for more affection. But Chaynie was suddenly hungry, tired, and cold, and the fire crackling in the next room sounded extremely appealing. She rounded the corner to see her mother sitting on the floor, leaning back against the sofa, with Mitch beside her, a couple of feet away. Their easy laughter continued until her mother looked up.

"Chaynie. You're home! Are you hungry? We have some leftover Chinese."

Chaynie saw the half-empty containers spread out on the coffee table. "Sure. Fried rice?"

"I saved some extra, just for you." Her mother struggled to her feet with a grunt. "We're finishing up, but I'll get you a plate and a soda."

When her mother left the room, Chaynie moved toward the other side of the table to set her things on the sofa. Mitch stood, nearly reaching her height, and reached out for a quick hug.

"Hey, Mitch," she said as they separated. "Nice to see you."

He wore a green sweater with gray slacks. She'd always thought he was classically handsome for a man her parents' age—rugged features, graying hair—a "silver fox," Savannah had once called him. Of course, Chaynie only saw Mitch as a member of the family, but she could understand how some might find him attractive. She wondered if her mother did too.

"Your mom told me how things are going at the library. They must be keeping you busy." Mitch slipped his hands into his pockets and rocked back on his heels a little.

"Yeah, between the renovations and the projects Mary has me doing, I don't have much time for anything else these days. How are things with you?"

"Oh, fine. School's good. The team's good. No complaints."

"I'm glad."

"Well, I'd better take off. Tell your mom I'll text her about those numbers for the committee meeting." He pointed down at the table, and that was when Chaynie saw the folders and paperwork. It had been a working dinner.

"Will do. Have a good night," she called as he crossed the room to grab his jacket, pat Max's head, and leave.

"Did I hear the door?" Chaynie's mother entered the room and offered a glass and plate.

"Mitch had to go. He said he'd text you. About the numbers."

"Okay, good."

Chaynie spooned some fried rice onto her plate then sank onto a sofa cushion. Her feet throbbed, so she kicked off her pumps and stretched out her toes.

"So, y'all were working on committee stuff? You and Mitch?" Chaynie brought the first forkful of rice to her lips.

Taking a seat across from Chaynie, her mother teased, "Don't make it sound so suspect."

"I wasn't! I just didn't know he was coming over tonight."

"I didn't either. The principal called a special meeting tomorrow, so Mitch suggested we meet briefly to go over our proposal, and when he arrived, he had two bags of Chinese food."

"It's been a while since I've seen him. He seems good."

"He is." Her mother nodded.

"I'm glad you have him. For company, I mean." Chaynie paused her fork. "Just to talk to, I mean."

"There you go, sounding suspect again."

"I'm not trying to. You seem... happy when you're with him lately. You laugh a lot. I like hearing you laugh."

"Well, Mitch is a very good friend, an old friend. I'm comfortable with him."

"Is that all you see him as? Just a friend?" It slipped out before Chaynie could eat her words, and she looked across at her mother with a wince. "Okay. That *did* sound suspect. Sorry. None of my business."

Her mother shrugged. "I don't mind the question, and the answer is yes. He's just a friend."

"Mom, do you think he sees you that way too? Or maybe as more than a friend?"

"Certainly not. He knows where I stand. Where are all these questions coming from?" She busied herself collecting empty containers and wadded-up napkins. "You know Mitch has been a godsend to us—*both* of us—since your father died. And because we're on this new committee together, we have to spend extra time with each other. That's all it is. Can we leave it alone?"

"Sure. Sorry. I didn't mean to pry."

"It's fine. Now, how's the rice?" Her mother was always adept at changing the subject swiftly, and it worked to her advantage at times like these.

"Perfect, thanks. I was ravenous."

Dropping the Mitch topic altogether, Chaynie deliberately spent the rest of the meal discussing the newest Valentine's project details while Max sat at her feet and stared longingly at her rice, hoping a grain or two would fall to the floor.

DARK, MENACING CLOUDS with sharp, cold winds and occasional claps of thunder grew in the distance—not an especially good day for traveling, but Chaynie wasn't about to alter her plans. She'd been looking forward to that afternoon's Austin trip.

Peering through the blinds in the living room, Chaynie watched Greg's green pickup pull forward and halt at the curb. She said goodbye to Max, grabbed her things, paused to find an umbrella in the entryway, and left through the front door.

Greg had exited the truck and was on his way up the path. He'd dressed appropriately for the trip—jeans, boots, and a light windbreaker.

"You didn't have to get out," she said, meeting him halfway.

"What's all this?" He saw Chaynie's load, which included her purse, umbrella, leather tote, and a bulging grocery bag.

"Supplies! Umbrella for the rain contingency, tote containing mock-up fliers for Pete, and a goody bag filled with snacks. It's tradition with any road trip. Plus, you won't let me pay for gas, so it's the least I can do."

"I'm not sure this qualifies as a road trip. Pete's place is only forty-one miles from Morgan's Grove. Still, who am I to argue with tradition?" He walked the few steps ahead of Chaynie and opened her door then offered a hand. "I can take some of this."

Chaynie had thought ahead to how awkward it would be, fumbling with all her items while trying to step up into the truck's cab. She'd thankfully worn jeans and a sweater, which would make the entire journey more comfortable and would also make entering the cab much easier than if she'd worn a skirt. But she still wouldn't turn down offered help.

"Thanks." She handed over the tote and goody bag then climbed inside.

He gave her back the items then shut the door.

When Greg rounded the truck, a sharp crack of thunder made Chaynie jump in her seat. As she settled in, she saw that his truck was old but well cared for, and the heater hummed at her ankles, giving off a soothing warmth. The truck's interior was neat—no wrappers crumpled on the floor, no dust on the dashboard. Her eyes fell onto the Tom Clancy paperback, worn and earmarked, lying inconspicuously inside the dashboard's far corner.

It wasn't until Greg opened his door and shut it again that she noticed the music playing softly in the cab's background. She hummed along to the familiar acoustic melody.

Greg clicked his seat belt and looked at her. "Did you leave something behind?"

"Why do you ask?"

"You're sort of... frowning."

"I think it's because I'm confused." She turned up the volume. "I know this song. I didn't figure you for the indie music type."

"You figured me for, what, the twangy country type? Because of the boots or the old, battered pickup?" He grinned then shifted the truck into gear and pulled away from the curb.

"Sorry. That came out wrong."

"It's fine. My tastes are all over the place—jazz, rock, eighties, classical, and even some country." He glanced at her and winked, putting her gently in her place.

Chaynie had been told before, by both her mother and Savannah, that she was a snob when it came to seeking out compatible men. Although she lived in the heart of Texas and was fiercely loyal to her state, and to her hometown and its people, Chaynie always felt a bit like an outsider, with her wide and varying tastes in music or food or movies. Maybe it was from all that book reading throughout her life. It had seemed to expand her world beyond the Texas borders. She had been introduced, through the pages, to various cultures, different people, other ways of living. And that notion had filtered down to her choices in men. She'd always avoided the stereotypical cowboy types, gravitating instead toward men with broader interests, which was why she adored the city of Austin—a cultured, liberal, educated center of Texas. And it was why she'd first been attracted to Blake. He was a business-suit type, worked in a corporate world, took her to expensive restaurants, and read the *New York Times* every Sunday. But she'd realized over the past year, as she'd reflected on their disintegrated relationship, that she had possibly sacrificed intimacy for compatibility. That their similar tastes weren't enough to forge a genuine relationship, the deeper one she had longed for. Their relationship had a coldness, a formality that had probably killed the relationship faster than Chaynie's move to Morgan's Grove.

"You need to toss out that mental checklist of yours," Savannah had once told Chaynie bluntly, "and let the guy be the guy, be himself, be whoever he is. If you have limited expectations of a man, you'll *always* be disappointed. He'll never meet them."

Wise words. Chaynie had finally understood them after Blake had dumped her and she'd had time to analyze things. But she still didn't know how to translate that wisdom into a real, substantive relationship—or how to stop seeing *all* men through that narrow filter of hers.

Still feeling badly about her music quip to Greg, Chaynie rifled through her goody bag and drew out handfuls of cookies, chips, and chocolate.

"What's your pleasure?"

Greg gave a quick glance and raised his eyebrows. "You were serious."

"About the goody bag? Of course. It's not a road trip without snacks." She dropped the items back into the bag and sorted through the lot to give him better details so he could keep his eyes firmly on the road. It had started to rain. "I've got Snickers, Oreos, Junior Mints, corn chips, Doritos, and sunflower seeds."

Greg chewed at his cheek to make his decision then extended his hand between them. "I'll take them Snickers," he said with a lazy fake drawl. "Ma'am."

With a grin, Chaynie found the Snickers, unwrapped the top, then handed it over. "Here ya go, cowboy."

Greg took a generous bite and clicked on the windshield wipers, which squeaked in rhythm with a new song.

"I enjoyed meeting your dad the other night." Chaynie opened a bag of Doritos but kept her eyes focused on the wet roadway as Greg turned to exit Morgan's Grove.

"He's excited to be working on a project with purpose. He needs the distraction."

"Oh?"

"Yeah, he's going through a 'life change.' That's what my mother calls it. They've decided to sell their ranch. They're getting older and can't manage the property anymore. It's partly why I came back home, to Morgan's Grove. I didn't want them shouldering this alone."

Chaynie munched on a chip then asked, "How long have they had the ranch?"

"Since before I was born. I grew up there."

"With horses, goats, chickens, all that?"

"Yeah, all that. Cows too. Although, in the past year, my folks sold off most of the livestock. They only have a couple of horses left, and no more chickens. Dad doesn't mind losing the animals as much as he'll mind losing his woodworking shop. It's been his lifeline lately. He and Mama have searched a few houses in town, but none of them has the right space for his hobby."

"Do your parents have a realtor, or are they selling it themselves?"

"No realtor. My dad thinks he can handle the sale, even though I advised against it. He's pretty stubborn."

"Well, I have a recommendation!" Chaynie shifted in the seat and faced him. "Savannah has a real estate license."

"I thought she was a teacher." Greg entered the highway carefully, watching for a clear opening, and took it. The rain continued to pound the windshield.

"She is. But she always has to take side jobs—you know how pathetic teachers' salaries are—and a couple of summers ago, she took the test and got licensed. She only practices in the summer, but she'd make an exception for your folks. And I'll bet she could find your dad a woodworking space. She loves a good challenge." Before he could say no, Chaynie pulled out her phone. "Here. I'll text you her info."

"Okay. It's good to have options. I'll talk to my dad."

Chaynie was peering down to finish sending the info when suddenly, the brakes locked, and her body lurched forward. Her phone slipped out of her hand and clattered onto the truck's floor. In the few seconds that Greg tried to control his truck on the slick road, Chaynie glanced up to see what was happening. A tiny Kia had whizzed in front of Greg, cutting him off on a major highway with impending standstill traffic before them.

Still braking, Greg clutched the steering wheel with one hand and reached out with his other hand to shield Chaynie as they skidded forward. She grabbed his jacket sleeve as she gasped, heart in her throat, hoping they weren't about to crash into the eighteen-wheeler in front of them. Greg somehow managed to control his vehicle just in time, coming to a careful stop only inches from the back of the truck. It took several seconds before Chaynie could catch her breath.

"Are you okay?" Greg stared over at her, his eyes intense, and she realized she was still grasping his arm.

"I think so." She released his sleeve then pushed out a purposeful breath. "Still processing what happened. I can't believe that jerk cut you off. He could've killed someone. Could've killed us."

"Yeah, he's gonna cause a wreck farther down, probably some young college kid who thinks he's invincible." Greg returned both hands to the steering wheel and followed the eighteen-wheeler as it inched along again.

"You stayed so calm." Chaynie immediately thought of Blake, how completely opposite he would've handled the situation—in fact, *had* handled similar situations in heavy Austin traffic—yelling at the other driver, spewing a couple of profanities, even tailing the driver closely for a few miles to "give it back to him" while Chaynie begged him to drop the whole matter.

But Greg hadn't done any of those things. His first instinct was to protect Chaynie, offer a steadying hand, make sure she was okay. It was something her dad might have done.

"I know a back road or two," Greg said. "It'll be safer that way, and it won't cost us much time."

Chaynie's heart rate had returned to normal by the time Greg found his way to a small two-lane road that took them toward the city. She hunched toward the cab's floor to feel around for her phone then settled in for the rest of the drive, knowing she was in excellent hands with Greg.

Chapter Six

Somewhere along the drive between the crowded highway and Pete's place, the rain decided to stop pouring, and the clouds chose to part, leaving a burst of bright-blue sky directly in the truck's path.

"Beautiful." Chaynie craned her neck to view the skies then pointed west. "And there's a rainbow!"

"Nice," Greg said.

He'd been right. It had only taken fortyish minutes from Morgan's Grove before he'd turned onto a nondescript empty road and driven toward an enormous steel-gray warehouse. "This is it... I think." He slowed the truck and checked his phone's GPS to make sure.

Chaynie read the sign coming into view. "'Pete's Movie Memories.' It's huge!"

Greg parked beside the only vehicle out front and clicked off the ignition. Chaynie pulled the leather tote from the floorboard then grabbed her purse and opened the truck door.

As they approached the warehouse, Chaynie noticed a door beneath an awning and figured they might as well try it.

She wouldn't tell Greg, but at that point, her hopes weren't very high that the inside would amount to anything special. Still, they were only there to confirm the projector and screen, so the interior didn't matter either way.

Greg pulled the door open for Chaynie, and she stepped inside.

"Whoa." She stopped short in the doorway, causing Greg to bump into her.

"Sorry," they said together.

She moved aside so he could see why she had paused.

"Whoa is right," he whispered.

They stood frozen together at the open door, gaping at what they saw—rows and rows of tables stacked with memorabilia, display cases stuffed with photographs and treasures, walls lined with movie posters, and bookcases stacked with books and DVDs.

"Incredible." Chaynie took a few steps inside as Greg shut the door behind them. "It's a time machine."

"Or a museum. Look at these." He pointed to a nearby glass case, which contained autographed scripts, movie ticket stubs, items of clothing labeled "Joan Crawford's scarf" and "Hedy Lamarr's broach."

They couldn't help themselves. Without another word, Greg and Chaynie drifted slowly down the center aisle of the enormous space—twenty thousand square feet, at least—and took it all in. Chaynie could spend an entire week there and never fully examine everything. Everywhere she looked, a new delight caught her attention: black-and-white photos of Gene Kelly and Fred Astaire, books devoted to TV and films, actual set props from *Lawrence of Arabia* and *The Sound of Music*. The entire warehouse was a treasure trove dedicated to classic films.

"My mom would love this place. I've got to bring her here," Chaynie mused, breaking the silence. Then she remembered her phone. Its camera wouldn't do the place justice, and the lighting wasn't great, but she could at least snap a few photos and show her mother tonight.

By the time they'd reached the midway point, Chaynie had returned her phone to her pocket while Greg had recalled their purpose for being there. "Pete! We haven't even tried to find him. He's been expecting us. I'll see if he's around." Greg stepped ahead of her and moved toward the back, calling out Pete's name. "Mr. Burrows? It's Greg Peterson. Mr. Burrows?"

Chaynie stopped to focus on a photo album filled with pictures taken behind the scenes on the set of *Funny Girl*. A candid shot showed Barbra Streisand, head tossed back, laughing at something another cast member had told her.

"Miss Mayfield?" A voice brought Chaynie out of her movie-induced trance. She shifted her attention from the album to see a mostly bald man with rosy cheeks approaching her. She assessed his age to be at least eighty-five. He extended a hand past his rather ample belly—his sweater was entirely too small for his stocky frame.

"Mr. Burrows. So nice to meet you." Chaynie shook his hand.

"Call me Pete."

"It's good to meet you, Pete. I'm in awe of what you've accumulated here." Chaynie slid her hands inside her jacket pockets, realizing when she shook Pete's hand how cold her own was. The chill from outside seemed to seep through the warehouse walls. "I've never heard of this place before. How do people find it?"

"Oh, the serious collectors know where we are. They pass the word along, and we've got an 'online presence.' Is that what they call it?"

"I believe so," Chaynie said.

Greg took a few steps to stand behind Chaynie, facing Pete. "He was just telling me that he opened this place twenty years ago with his wife."

Pete crossed his arms. "That's right. June. She and I got the idea for a collector's museum. Between the two of us, we already owned a couple hundred pieces of memorabilia—photographs, set props, costume jewelry worn by actresses, and so forth."

"Were you part of the movie business or only a fan?" Chaynie could easily pepper Pete all day with questions about this amazing venture of his.

"The wife and I met on the set of *The King and I*. She was a seamstress, and I was an extra. I've also worked as a stunt double. Between us, June and I worked on forty-four movie sets during the fifties and sixties."

"Wow," Chaynie and Greg mouthed together.

"But when the movie industry changed and musicals went by the wayside, well, we packed up and moved to Texas. June's family lived here. It was actually her idea to set up a space for all our memorabilia. At first, we were selling it out of our house, but then, as demand grew, we got serious—scouted out auctions, found some pieces through old Hollywood friends. Then we bought this place." He gestured around him then paused when his gaze landed on a photo nearby. "That's her. That's my June."

He lifted a black-and-white photo of a young woman with sleek blond hair who was hunched over a sewing table, her expression serious. Greg stepped in closer to Chaynie so he could get a glimpse as Pete passed her the photo. "She's been gone ten years."

"I'm sorry," Chaynie said. "How long were you married?"

"Fifty-one years."

"That's incredible," Greg noted, his deep voice resonating near Chaynie's ear.

She handed back the photo. "I would've loved to meet her. She sounds like a remarkable person."

"She was." Pete stared at the photo. "We lived a good life together. Oh, we had some rough patches, but nothing we couldn't handle." He looked up from the photo and addressed Greg and Chaynie together, moving his attention between them. "Young people nowadays have such a complicated view of love. They make it much harder than it needs to be, but it's simple, really. Appreciate the small things about that person every single day. Look at them with wonder, with fresh eyes. Like you're seeing them for the first time. That's the secret." He wagged his finger toward them.

"Oh." Chaynie understood Pete's assumption. She motioned between herself and Greg. "We're not..."

"No, we're not..." Greg added.

"We're just friends," Chaynie said.

Pete raised his eyebrows. "Are you sure about that?" He chuckled. "Sorry. That was overstepping. This is where my wife would've elbowed me in my enormous gut and scolded me. 'Pete! Leave these young people to their business. It's none of yours.'" He tucked the photo lovingly back in its place then clapped his hands together. "Well, you're both here to talk about a projector. Let's get to it!"

He plodded back down the aisle as Chaynie and Greg followed. He led them to a storeroom of the warehouse, a junky collection of odds and ends, and among them, a movie projector.

"It's old but in good condition," he assured them. "I keep it in tip-top shape, and you'd be surprised how often it's rented out. I've saved the date for your film viewing. February fourteenth?"

"Valentine's," Chaynie concurred. She looped her tote off her shoulder and searched for the flyer inside then drew it out. "This is the event. You can keep the flyer. It's a mock-up."

"Looks marvelous," Pete said. "A night under the stars. Nice idea." He folded the flyer and added, "I can deliver the projector to you that morning and stick around to run it. How does that sound?"

"Oh, yes. Please," Chaynie said. "I would feel much better if you were there during the film. I wouldn't have a clue how to run it."

"Then it's settled. As far as the screen goes..."

"You mentioned it was in another location?" Greg asked.

"I share it with another buddy of mine, and he's storing it at the moment. But I'll have it available on that date and will deliver it. He can help me load it."

"And I'll help unload it," Greg offered. "I've got a whole crew ready. You won't have to lift a finger."

Pete finished the deal by telling the rental amount—very reasonable and far below what Chaynie was expecting. She sifted through her purse to find the check Mary had given her from the library's account. "How much is the deposit?"

Pete waved his hand. "No need for that. I trust y'all."

"Oh, I insist. I'm all prepared to pay it."

"Well, in that case..." Pete pursed his lips in thought. "Ten bucks."

"Only ten?"

"I can go lower if you want."

Greg pulled out his wallet and swiftly handed Pete a ten-dollar bill.

"You two are impossible." Chaynie shook her head. "Tell your godmother to pay you back for that," she told Greg, slipping the check back into her purse. "Now." She looked at Pete. "The only thing missing is probably the most important element."

"What's that?"

"Which movie to show. I'm not sure what sort of selection would be available for an old projector."

"Right this way." Pete moved only a handful of steps toward the back wall. "Is this a wide enough selection for ya?"

Behind him stood a bookcase, floor to ceiling, filled with silver movie reel tins.

"My goodness." Chaynie approached the case. Pete, and presumably his wife, had carefully labeled each film below its tin, but they weren't in alphabetical order—or any sort of order at all: *Fiddler on the Roof, Top Hat, Psycho, Oklahoma, Citizen Kane, The Sound of Music.* The librarian in Chaynie was secretly dying to get her hands on it and create a better organizational system.

"What sort of movie did you want to show?" Pete asked.

"Light and happy, family-oriented, a musical."

"We have plenty of those. Browse as long as you want."

Pete and Greg stepped away, leaving Chaynie to contemplate her choice. She could hear the men chattering in the background.

Scouring the titles, overwhelmed by the selection and the pressure of being put on the spot to find *the perfect movie* everyone would enjoy, Chaynie went back in her mind to her favorite movie musicals growing up, the ones she'd watched with her family as a little girl. That, at least, would narrow it down. After several minutes of searching, her eyes landed on her top choice. She pulled it carefully from its slot.

"I found it!" she called out, holding the tin against her chest like the treasure it was.

"Well, that was fast." Pete approached with Greg then focused on the label. "Nice choice. June and I worked on this film together. I played Police Officer Number Two—uncredited—and Townsman Number Nine. June designed the costumes for the barbershop quartet."

Greg stepped closer to read the label. "*The Music Man.*" He confessed to Chaynie, "I've never actually seen it. Well, I've heard some of the songs but never sat down and watched the whole movie."

Chaynie gasped. "It's a total classic! How have you lived thirtysomething years on this planet and not seen *The Music Man*?"

"She's right." Pete grinned. "You should be ashamed of yourself."

"I have more good news," Greg said. "Pete and I discussed your library alcove, and I asked if he knew any special effects companies in Austin that might be able to help out or offer advice about that tree. After some deeper research last night, I realized that starting from scratch might be too expensive and time-consuming."

"We don't have to do a tree at all," Chaynie said. "If it's causing too much trouble, I mean."

"It's not, trust me. I'm committed to it," Greg assured her. "It's just a matter of finding the most practical way to get the job done right."

"I was telling Greg about UT's theater department," Pete added. "The dean there is a friend of mine. They put on top-rate productions each year with professional-looking set designs. I've seen 'em. They did *A Midsummer Night's Dream* a couple of years back. I could call the dean and see if they have any recyclable set pieces. Lots of greenery and trees were involved for the forest backdrop."

"What a great idea," Chaynie said. "We can pay for it."

"I have a feeling Nick would donate it. Specially when I tell him it's for a good cause."

Elated over so much good news packed into the past hour, Chaynie squeezed the tin closer to her chest. She had no idea their trip to Austin would bear such amazing fruit.

Greg interrupted her thoughts. "Well, I hate to say it, but I think we'd better get going. We don't want to fight the rush hour traffic in this weather."

"Good point," Chaynie agreed, handing the beloved film tin over to Pete. "It was such a pleasure meeting you, hearing your stories. I'm so glad we came."

"It was the highlight of my day, my week, my month. You two young folks give me hope that this world will end up in good hands long after I'm gone."

Chaynie smiled. "That's sweet of you to say. Oh, Greg texted you all our info, right?"

"Got it here," Pete assured her, patting his shirt pocket, where the rectangular outline of a phone showed through.

Greg and Chaynie walked the lengthy distance back through the warehouse, and she was tempted to linger. But Greg's wise comment about traffic pushed her toward the exit. They opened the door and left the warehouse time machine to see cloudy skies again, with a misty drizzle floating visibly in the air.

At the truck, Greg opened Chaynie's door. Settling in, she watched the drizzle transform suddenly into solid dollops of rain that pelted Greg's truck as he shut her door and sprinted to the driver's side.

Out of breath, he climbed in and flicked off the moisture beaded on his windbreaker. "Where did that come from?"

As he started the ignition, the dashboard lights only flickered, and the engine didn't respond.

"What's happening?"

"Nothing, unfortunately." He frowned and tried again. Still, nothing. Greg ran a hand through his damp hair, slicking it back.

"Is it the battery?" Chaynie wondered.

"Worse. It's the alternator."

"How can you tell?"

"I replaced the battery last week. Plus, the alternator light is on." Greg pointed at his dashboard with a sigh. "I'll see if Pete can give us a jump start." He dialed the number, and Pete answered immediately. Greg explained the situation, and through the phone, Chaynie could hear the cheery response. "Glad to help. Be right out!"

After ending the call, Greg made eye contact with Chaynie. "Even if we get a successful jump, driving with that alternator probably isn't safe enough for a return trip to Morgan's Grove. I'd feel better finding a garage nearby and getting the alternator replaced. It might take a while, and there's no reason for you to wait too. Can you call someone to come get you? Maybe your mom? Sorry there's not another option."

"Don't apologize. It's out of your control."

"What a day. First, I nearly kill us in traffic on the way here—"

"That was *not* your fault."

"And then my truck decides to break down."

Chaynie shrugged. "It doesn't change how great a day this was."

Greg offered a half smile. "True."

As she considered her options, Chaynie knew she wouldn't mind waiting around with Greg, but she did have some work to do, and there was no telling how long the repairs might take. She checked the time on her phone. Her mom would be finished teaching soon, but then she had another meeting that afternoon. Chaynie would have to try someone else. She dialed Savannah's number and explained the situation, including her location.

Savannah said she could be there "in a jiff."

Chaynie clicked off and told Greg, "Savannah to the rescue. No problem."

Through the rain-streaked windshield, Chaynie saw Pete open the door of his warehouse and wave. Greg scurried out of the truck to meet him under the awning before Pete could step out into the cold, wet weather. She watched them huddle together, using hand gestures. Greg patted Pete's shoulder twice then raced back to the cab.

Inside, he told Chaynie, "Pete knows a repair shop close by. He still needs to find his cables for the jump, though. My dad actually borrowed my cables last week, and we forgot to replace them in my truck. Glad Pete has some."

Several minutes later, in a stroke of good fortune, Savannah's car pulled up to the warehouse just as Pete successfully jump-started Greg's truck.

"What will you do if they have to order a part or keep the truck overnight?" Chaynie asked Greg after he'd darted beneath the awning to join her at the warehouse's entrance.

"My dad can pick me up." Greg returned Savannah's wave through her windshield. "Go on, I'll be fine. It's okay."

"I'll keep my phone on. Text if you need me."

"Will do."

Chaynie dodged the raindrops and raced to the passenger side of Savannah's car. "Thank you so much for doing this." She fiddled with the seat belt as Savannah pulled the car away.

"What are best friends for? Although I wouldn't mind being stuck with Greg. Did you have fun today on your excursion?"

Chaynie play-slapped Savannah's arm as her friend exited the property. "Yes. We did, actually."

Halfway to Morgan's Grove, after Chaynie had given a quick rundown about the incredible warehouse they'd explored, she remembered something. "I gave your number to Greg."

Savannah's eyes widened. "Did he ask for it?"

"No. Sorry. I need to explain." She told Savannah about Greg's parents needing a realtor. "And I thought of you. I hope it's okay. I didn't think to ask you first."

"Sure, I'm always grateful for new business."

"The thing is, Greg admitted his dad is stubborn. He wants to sell the ranch himself but admits to being clueless about how to find a home closer to town that will meet his needs. I think he'd be open to a realtor for that part, at least."

"I'm fine with that," Savannah said. "And maybe when he learns to trust my judgment, he'll let me take care of the ranch too."

"Good thinking."

The rain had lightened, and they were making good progress along the back roads that Greg had shown Chaynie earlier.

"So," Savannah said, turning down the car's heater. "Seriously. What is *up* with you and Greg? Every time I see you together, you're so... chummy."

"We are *not* chummy—not if chummy means what I think you want it to mean. We're friends."

It baffled Chaynie, why she had to keep explaining that to people. But even as she grew lightly frustrated with Savannah in the moment, her own words came back to bite her. Chaynie had gently accused her own mother and Mitch of being more than friends a couple of days before.

"Men and women can't be just friends," Savannah stated with a smirk. "It's a well-known fact."

"You sound so sure. Where do you get your proof?"

"*When Harry Met Sally*. I think you should rewatch that movie. You need a lesson in male-female friendships."

Chaynie suppressed a chuckle. "Well, that's a movie, and this is real life, so men and women *can* be just friends. It's more than possible. Besides, even if I were interested in Greg, it would be completely pointless. I'm trying to leave Morgan's Grove, remember?"

Savannah gasped. "Does that mean you've heard back on your applications?"

"Only a couple so far, both rejections, but there are still four more applications out there, and I'll send out a few more."

"Have you told your mom yet?"

Chaynie played with a loose thread on her glove. "Not yet. I tried to. Well, I meant to try. I haven't gotten up the courage yet. It's silly, but I feel like I'm abandoning her. I mean, I don't want her to be lonely. She's been through so much."

"She has, but she's a grown woman. You can't live your life for her. You have to do what *you* want to do, and your mom would tell you the same thing."

"You're right. I need to tell her soon. It's a matter of timing."

"So, back to Greg..."

Chaynie rolled her eyes. "The answer to your next question is *yes*. If you're interested in him, if you want to pursue him, then be my guest. He's a great guy. You have my blessing."

"That's exactly what I was hoping you'd say!" Savannah squeaked.

"I didn't know it would make you so happy. How long have you been waiting for my approval?"

"Honestly? Since the minute I saw Greg at the library. I didn't want to step on your toes... or create any weirdness between us. We've always done pretty well with not liking the same guy, or if one of us did, the other always backed off. I would *never* ruin our friendship over a guy. You know that."

"Neither would I. You can set your mind at ease. I'm not interested in Greg that way. Why would I want to start something serious with anyone when I'll probably be leaving? That's inviting heartbreak, and I've had plenty of that the last couple of years. So, I'm making the wise decision, the practical one. Greg's all yours."

Gazing out the car window, Chaynie envisioned all the various realities coming her way very soon—watching her best friend flirt openly with Greg and seeing him respond, eventually telling her mom about her career goals, then saying a permanent goodbye to Morgan's Grove.

That was what Chaynie wanted, what she'd been planning for months, but she felt unsettled thinking ahead, examining the details. Perhaps because she was leaving her comfort zone of Morgan's Grove, the library, the people most familiar to her. But there would be other cities and other people, too—a whole new reality in front of her. She just had to be bold enough to reach out and grab it.

Chapter Seven

Chaynie caught a generous whiff of the strong printer's ink as Angela handed over the finished flyer—glossy and colorful and perfect. Gazing closely at it only confirmed Chaynie's decision to order them from The Stationery Place. She could never have created a product so professional on her own, and she didn't have the time to try.

"Did I get the pink tones just the way you wanted?" Angela asked from behind the counter.

"Yes, and the hearts too." In the end, Chaynie had decided to embrace the symbols and traditional colors of Valentine's. *If you can't beat 'em...*

Chaynie paid for the flyers and clutched the paper bag, polishing up her pitch in her head. The stores in the square had a pretty strict policy about not cluttering the lampposts or windows with advertisements, but sometimes, they made exceptions. Surely, store owners would consider hanging up a flyer that would benefit their local library.

If they were amenable to the idea of flyers, Chaynie planned to tiptoe one step further and ask for donations for door prizes, such as coupons or gift cards or merchandise, to be given away during the movie night. And she hoped the restaurants might be interested in setting up food tables at the event. "It could be a unique advertisement for your place," she planned to tell them with great enthusiasm. But rehearsing pitches in her head only reminded her of the door-to-door panic that had ensued as a child whenever she sold Girl Scout cookies. That familiar fear of rejection returned, the awkwardness of trying to talk someone into buying something they didn't actually need. Salesmanship had never been in Chaynie's wheelhouse.

It's for the library, she reminded herself as she stepped onto the sidewalk.

She heard the *ching-ring* of a bell and saw Bob Turner—"Bicycle Bob," as the residents of Morgan's Grove called him—approaching swiftly.

"Good morning, Chaynie." He came to a full stop and tilted his bike to balance it. "How are things on this lovely Monday morning?"

Normally, Chaynie politely avoided long conversations with Bob as often as possible. He was nice enough but sometimes rambled on about town gossip or his grandchildren's detailed activities. But today, he was a welcome sight. He'd lived in Morgan's Grove his entire life, and since retiring, he seemed to know everyone's business. As the town's unofficial crier, Bob was the perfect person to tell about the event Under the Stars.

"Things are very well, thank you." She found an extra flyer and handed it over. "Have you heard about this yet? It's going to be the premiere event in Morgan's Grove for Valentine's Day."

Bob raised an eyebrow and scanned the flyer. "*Music Man*... families, dogs... all welcome. Sounds like a good time. I'll spread the word."

"Would you? I'd be so grateful. This is our first event, but if it's a success, we're hoping to make it an annual one, all for the good of the library."

"You can count on me!"

And she knew she could. After they exchanged good-byes, Chaynie made her way down the sidewalk to approach each store manager. By the time she'd reached the end of the block, Chaynie had garnered four hearty yeses.

She had planned on bypassing the bakery, since it was still weeks away from opening, but she caught a glimpse of someone closing the front door. Chaynie paused on the sidewalk and smiled at Jill Mc-Callister walking toward her, carrying paint swatches. Jill's curly hair spilled out from under the purple beanie she wore.

"I heard you're moving to Morgan's Grove permanently," Chaynie said when Jill came to a stop on the sidewalk. "I'm so happy you're staying, and Lucille is ecstatic."

"Thanks. I think Morgan's Grove was home from the minute I entered the square all those weeks ago. It just took me a little time to realize it." Jill's smile brightened.

"Now that you're here for good, does that mean you'll come and be a guest speaker at the library? We'd love to have you discuss your books. My friend Savannah teaches an honors creative writing class at the high school. Her students would enjoy hearing about your writing process. I would too."

"Sure. Send me some dates, and I'll check my schedule."

Jill's eyes drifted down toward the flyers Chaynie held.

"I was passing these out in the square for the businesses' windows." Chaynie tilted the flyers to show Jill.

"Under the Stars…"

Chaynie briefly explained the lawn-movie concept, using all the same pitch words she'd given the shop owners. "If the bakery were open, I'd offer a flyer to you, but—"

"We could still display one," Jill offered. "I'll check with the contractor first, make sure it won't mess with his renovations, but I don't see the harm in taping a flyer to a window. And, if it helps the library…"

"It would, thanks."

After she handed Jill a flyer, they parted, then Chaynie pivoted to make her way to Mrs. Haversham's bed-and-breakfast. It would be an easy pitch—Mrs. Haversham had brought her son and her nieces to the library every week when they were children. She was an advocate of the town and sat on many various committees. With her rosy cheeks and amiable nature, she was one of the most well-liked people in town.

Mrs. Haversham agreed to hang two library flyers in her window. On her way out, Chaynie saw the cardboard box planted near the door, a permanent fixture, usually stuffed with snacks and books and toiletries that the townspeople donated for Mrs. Haversham's son, stationed overseas. Chaynie made a mental note to add some books to the box next week.

A few stores down, The Pit wafted spicy barbecue scents throughout the block. The restaurant wouldn't open for another half hour, but Chaynie took a chance and knocked at the locked door. Tessa, one of the sisters who ran The Pit, opened the door.

"Oh, it's you. C'mon in, honey."

The smoky scent of barbecue only grew stronger as Chaynie stepped inside. "I'm sorry to bother you, but I'm making the rounds with these." She showed Tessa the flyer.

Before Chaynie could even begin her pitch, Tessa said, "I'll take two. One for the front window, and the other one at the counter."

"You're the best, thanks. Hey, would you also consider setting up a table at the event? Y'all could sell your barbecue sandwiches and chips, keep it simple?"

"And our Mississippi Mud?"

"Absolutely!"

"I'll run it by my sister, but I'm sure we can work it out. Count us in. Listen, how's your mom doing?"

"She's great. Busy with school. I feel like I never see her anymore."

"I know the holidays are still rough for you two... because of your dad. I'm glad she has you here. Give her my best." Tessa winked then opened the door for Chaynie.

As Chaynie continued her flyer mission, she felt a pinch of guilt. *I'm glad she has you here.* But not for much longer, perhaps. That morning, Chaynie had sent another three applications for head librarian positions in New Mexico, Georgia, and Vermont. She still hadn't told her mother.

By the time she made it to the other side of the square, Chaynie's sore feet were ready for a break, but she had given away nearly all her flyers and secured two more food tables from Juan's and the burger place.

She hadn't planned on stopping at Greg's work-in-progress office—she'd caught a quick glimpse of him earlier at the library, consulting with one of his guys on the roofing project, and assumed he would still be there—but as Chaynie passed by, she saw some movement behind the window and paused. Greg was dipping a paint brush into a bucket.

Chaynie tapped at the window, startling him. When he saw who it was, he set down the brush and came to unlock the door.

"I didn't expect you to be here." Chaynie stepped inside and immediately noticed the beginnings of a new paint job, half a wall completed. Greg had taken her advice on the neutral beige, and seeing the final unopened paint can, she knew he'd also trusted her about that forest-green accent wall she'd suggested.

"Yeah, trying to make some headway here whenever I can. It'll take some time to finish the job, but I'm not in a rush." He set down his brush and crossed his arms, peering at his own handiwork. "What do you think so far?"

"Very professional. The colors are soothing," Chaynie said then frowned. "But I forgot to do something last time I was here. It's very important." She set down her purse and the flyers on a nearby chair and drew out her phone, tapping out search words. "Do you have a pencil I can use?" she asked, absorbed in her search.

"I think so." Greg walked across the room to a box and sifted through some office supplies. He held up a yellow pencil then approached her with it. "You're being very mysterious."

"Just wait and see." Satisfied with the results of her online search, Chaynie took the pencil and tapped it lightly against her chin, wandering the room in search of the perfect spot. She stopped at the back corner. "Is this where your desk will go?"

"Probably."

She knelt down and found the right spot then consulted her phone again. She began to scribble on the unpainted wall.

"What's this?" Greg moved closer. "Some secret interior design trick?"

"Don't peek. Not yet."

He took a step back. "Okay, well, tell me when I can look."

It took a couple of minutes, but finally, Chaynie finished her task, double-checked her work, then moved aside, still squatting near the wall. She gave a ta-da motion with her hands. "Okay, you can look."

Greg knelt beside her and read the Frank Lloyd Wright quote aloud, his voice resonant, as Chaynie mouthed along. Then he touched the edge of the quote with his fingertips. "Wright is a huge inspiration. I took a couple of advanced classes about his style and philosophy."

Chaynie explained. "In college, I used to help my friends decorate their dorms and apartments, and I would always find the perfect quote for them—favorite song lyrics or quotes or mantras. And before we painted, I'd scribble it on an empty wall."

"Like the one we're about to paint over?" he asked with a semi-frown. "No one will see it."

"That's the point! Think of it as a sort of ceremonial christening, like the launch of a new ship, to mark the occasion. Your new office, a new chapter in your life."

Greg's frown curled into a smile. "I get it. You know how people place those mementos into the concrete that's being poured for a foundation? A sort of hidden blessing."

"Exactly. One that only you know about."

"And you, in this case." He tapped the quote.

"Right. And me."

Things suddenly became overcrowded for Chaynie, hunched in the tiny corner of the room, and she could feel herself getting flushed. She cleared her throat and gave him back the pencil. "I'm glad you like the quote."

When she tried to stand, she wobbled—her legs were jelly since she'd been squatting too long—and Greg put a strong hand under her elbow to right her.

After they stood together, Greg slipped his hands into his jeans pockets. "I talked to my folks about your friend Savannah being a re-altor. I gave them her contact info. They seemed interested, so they'll probably call her today. Thanks for the tip."

Chaynie knew how disappointed Savannah would be that Greg himself hadn't contacted her, even as a go-between for his parents. "I hope they find what they're looking for."

"I think they will, eventually."

Chaynie walked toward the chair to retrieve her items. "I deliv-ered most of the flyers this morning." She handed the finished prod-uct to Greg. "And I've been promised some door prize donations. It was easier than I thought."

"People love their library. I think it's the idea of community and heritage. Plus, most of them have used it over the years, brought their kids back, their grandkids. That building is in the center of the square for a reason."

"The heart of the town."

"Right." Greg examined the flyer. "These turned out great. How many can I have?"

"As many as you want."

"I'll take three."

Chaynie handed over two more flyers, and Greg found a roll of tape inside a box of office supplies then placed the flyers, inches apart, inside the front window.

"There. I've done my part for the library."

"Umm, I'd say you've done *more* than your part. How about renovating it? And driving all the way to Austin in the pouring rain, with a faulty alternator, to help with our big event?"

Greg had texted Chaynie an update that same night, letting her know that the repairs had been finished and he was on his way back to Morgan's Grove.

"Well, that wasn't any trouble. I enjoyed meeting Pete—and spending time with you." Greg paused then dipped his head. "I mean... I just... enjoyed having someone along with me, in the truck. Having company." It was the first time Chaynie had ever heard anything even close to a stutter from Greg.

Chaynie pushed the remaining flyers back inside their paper bag. "I'm glad I tagged along that day. Well, I'd better finish distributing these. Plus there's lots of work to catch up on at the library and also a meeting with Mary."

"And I should keep working on this wall. It's not gonna paint itself."

Greg opened the door for Chaynie. As she passed through, she could hear Savannah's proclamation rolling around in her head, *Men and women* can *be just friends*. Hopefully, it was true.

"MOM? ARE YOU HOME?" Chaynie laid her jacket across the sofa, patted Max's head as he slumbered there, and headed for the kitchen, where she noticed her mother's purse and keys splayed out on the table. That meant she was likely upstairs, resting. She often took naps after coming home from a long day spent with "energetic" students.

Flipping on the kitchen light, Chaynie saw all seven of her mother's gorgeous illustrations on display. She had pushed the breakfast table against the wall then flanked it with two easels to show the first and last illustrations. The others stood in between, in sequence, propped against the wall.

Chaynie hadn't seen them together, all laid out and finished. They told the story all by themselves. Chaynie moved closer, as though seeing them for the first time. She was in constant awe of her mother's artistic talents, the detail, the use of color, even the whimsy she somehow placed in the characters' eyes.

She should be a children's book illustrator, Chaynie thought. *As a profession. She's that good.*

Inspired, Chaynie darted upstairs for her pages—the ones she'd typed into her laptop and printed off several days ago, when the ending had finally come to her. Sorting through all those older children's books from the top shelf of her closet *had* helped, and she'd finished the story that same night.

Reentering the kitchen, Chaynie neatly fanned out her printed pages on the table, in front of the illustrations, with the title page showing: *The Library Mouse, by Chaynie Mayfield. Illustrated by Abby Mayfield.*

Chaynie decided she would make dinner for her mom, even though tonight wasn't officially her turn. They could celebrate the completion of their project. Those first ideas, all those months ago, had merely begun as the seeds of a brainstorm, some rough scribblings in a notebook to pass the time during her grief. She and her mother had never once talked about what to do once the story was complete. They simply kept scribbling and sketching away, week by week, when they had time. For the moment, it was enough knowing they had followed through to the end. That was an accomplishment all by itself.

Chaynie eyed the kitchen sink and saw the largest pan soaking. Her first order of business in making the meal would have to be cleaning the pan. Rolling up her sleeves, Chaynie turned on the faucet and dumped the old sudsy water into the sink. She didn't see the usual sponge lying around, so she kept the water running and opened the cabinet underneath in search of a new one. That was when she saw the puddle of water pooling at the bottom of the cabinet and beginning to drip down near her feet.

She gasped, sending Max flying into the room, curious about what was wrong. Heart pounding, Chaynie shut the faucet off, hoping that would at least contain the situation. *How long has the water been leaking?*

On her knees, Chaynie swiftly removed items from underneath the sink—cleaners and sponges and dishwashing tablets. All soaked.

"Ugh," she groaned. "Why now?"

Finishing her task, she found a roll of paper towels and carefully laid a thick stack on top of the standing water, which instantly soaked through the paper. After dabbing the water with more towels, Chaynie grabbed the flashlight that her mother kept nearby then assessed the situation. She couldn't tell the exact source of the leak, but water was dripping from a pipe.

Max stayed near her elbow, peering into the cabinet with her. Chaynie nudged him gently away as she clicked off the flashlight and searched the pantry for a bowl to hold the dripping water until the plumber could arrive. It was too late to phone him now—and in all the chaos of the last few minutes, she had entirely lost her motivation to cook an elaborate meal. After soaking up as much of the water as she could and placing a bowl beneath the drip, she found her phone with the intention of calling Juan's, a favorite Mexican food place beyond the square, for some take-out tacos. The phone rang in her hand before she could tap out the number. *Greg*, the screen told her.

Curious, Chaynie answered the call with the friendliest "Hi" she could muster.

"Hey. I just got off the phone with Pete. He says there's a larger screen available for the movie night. He told me the dimensions, and I think it's a better option. My guys have already measured to make sure, but I wanted to run it by you first. It'll cost more, though."

"Sure. Sounds good."

Greg paused. "You don't sound like your usual self."

Chaynie half-grinned at the phone. "Which self do I sound like?"

"Distracted... off. Is something wrong?"

"It's nothing. Not in the scheme of things. A minor household issue, a leaky kitchen sink. I've spent the last few minutes sopping up water. I can't find the source of the dripping."

"Want me to take a look?"

"Naw, it's fine. I'll call a plumber in the morning."

"I'm a block away. It's no trouble."

She remembered how Greg had fixed that broken chair last week with such ease, how comfortable he felt around tools. He was a handy guy, and he was offering. Maybe it was worth a try.

"Well, only if you're sure."

"I'm sure." Greg clicked off before Chaynie could change her mind.

Thankfully, she was still in her work clothes and not in the flannel pajamas she sometimes threw on the minute she came home from the library.

Greg arrived within five minutes. His knock came at the same time Chaynie's mother tapped downstairs with a deep yawn. She wore sweatpants and a sweater along with some fuzzy slippers.

"I'll get it." Chaynie twisted the doorknob.

"Greg?" Her mother reached the bottom of the stairs and paused, eyebrows raised, as Chaynie let him inside.

His jeans were stained with beige paint. Max circled Greg's shoes and gave out an approving "Meow!"

"He's here to fix the sink," Chaynie said before her mother could jump to any other conclusions.

"What's wrong with the sink?"

"It's leaking." Chaynie frowned. "Underneath the cabinet. It was soaked, but I cleaned most of it up. I was going to call a plumber, but then Greg called... about work, and—"

"And I insisted on taking a look." He raised his toolbox. "It's no trouble."

"A man of many talents," Chaynie's mother noted.

"I'm not sure about that," Greg confessed. "But I did work for a plumbing company while I was getting my degree a few years ago. Also worked construction and apprenticed as an electrician. I wanted to know the ins and outs of a house before I learned how to build them. Plus, those summers working for your husband..."

"At the hardware store. That probably gave you a good foundation, didn't it? Having to know all about the tools and products you were selling."

"Your husband taught me so much, and I soaked it up. In fact, it's probably partly what pushed me toward architecture—helping customers with ideas for their home renovations, watching them get excited about a new layout or addition to their house. It felt like they were getting a fresh start."

"I've never thought of architecture that way, but you know, one of the first things Chay and I did after Danny died was paint a couple of rooms upstairs. We just needed a new focus, I guess."

"Understandable." Greg nodded.

Before the natural sadness from mentioning her father's name permeated the room, Chaynie told Greg, "Let me show you to the kitchen."

"Sure, lead the way."

She guided Greg through the living room as Max and her mother followed.

"Oh! I forgot something upstairs," her mother claimed. "Back in a bit." Over Greg's shoulder, she gave Chaynie a knowing smile and left the room.

Very subtle, Mom.

Greg paused at the kitchen table and set down his toolbox. "What's all this?"

Chaynie had forgotten to clear away the illustrations before Greg arrived. Not that she minded anyone else seeing them, but up until then, it had been a private venture, a secret between only Chaynie and her mother.

"Well, it's sort of a children's story. It began with an idea I had last year—a mouse who runs away from home and takes up residence in a library. When I told my mom about it, she started making these gorgeous illustrations."

Greg stepped closer as Chaynie flicked on the overhead light.

"Mind if I...?" Greg pointed to the first illustration perched on the easel.

"Sure, go ahead."

He picked it up gingerly and scanned the details. "She's really good."

"I didn't get the artistic gene from her, unfortunately."

Greg set down the illustration as carefully as he'd retrieved it. "But this is yours?" He touched the fanned-out papers.

"Yeah, that's the story, finalized. Though I don't know exactly what finalized means."

"This isn't just a story." He tenderly slid the papers apart, careful not to put them out of order. "It's a book. You should submit it somewhere." He said it with absolute confidence, as though that were the only possible option for the pages he touched.

"Well, I haven't thought that far ahead. It's been a fun distraction. Plus, children's publishing is so competitive. I'd be crazy to try."

"Why crazy? I think you should. What do you have to lose?" Greg turned toward Chaynie, undaunted.

"Maybe I'm afraid my pride would be damaged."

"But that's if you're rejected. What if you succeed? What if someone says yes? There's a cliché about this. You'll never know..."

"Unless you try." Chaynie slowed down, considered Greg's advice, and gazed at her mother's illustrations through a new set of eyes—his. And when she did, Chaynie sensed the door of possibility crack open. She whispered, "Maybe it wouldn't hurt. To research a few publishers, take that first baby step."

"Why not?"

His confidence was beginning to rub off on her. "You're right. Why not?"

"So." Greg clapped his hands together then opened his toolbox. "The sink."

Chaynie pulled her focus from the illustrations and pointed. "It's all yours."

He removed his jacket then carried the toolbox over and kneeled down to have an initial peek, using his own light. He tugged on a pipe then peered deeper inside the cabinet.

"Max!" Chaynie whisper-yelled as the cat circled Greg, who was doing them a favor and didn't need any feline distractions. Greg didn't seem bothered by the cat, though, and after his inspection, he clicked off the flashlight and pushed away from the cabinet and into a sitting position.

"It's probably a retention nut that needs tightening."

"Let's hope it's that simple."

"Well, worst-case scenario, it's a pipe that needs some sealant. I'll rule out the retention nut first."

Chaynie offered him a bottled water while he finished the job, but he declined. The repair only took him a few strong twists of a wrench, then he tested out the faucet, and voilà.

"All fixed," he proclaimed, putting the wrench away and closing the toolbox. "You'll probably want to keep the cabinets open until they dry out—maybe use a fan. If the leak comes back, call me."

"I will."

Chaynie's mom reentered the kitchen in time to hear the end of their conversation. *How convenient.* "You fixed it! We have to thank you for this. Stay for dinner," she insisted.

Surprisingly, Chaynie didn't mind her mother's overt invitation. If she hadn't made the offer, Chaynie probably would have. It was the least they could do—Greg would surely refuse any payment for his time. Plus, their house hadn't seen any company in several weeks, aside from Mitch. It would be a nice change from the mundane.

"Thanks, but Mom's invited me for dinner at the ranch."

"Well, maybe another time, then. Are you staying with them? At the ranch?"

"No, ma'am. I've rented a small house outside the town square. Nearby, actually. But I'm searching for a more permanent place."

"Savannah could help with that!" Her mother pointed in Chaynie's direction. "Doesn't she still have her license?"

"Yep. I've already given Greg her info."

Greg found his jacket. "Well, I'd better get going."

"Promise me you'll return soon," Chaynie's mom said. "For dinner!"

"I promise." He glanced at Chaynie, almost seeking approval, probably wondering if it was all her mother's idea.

"Yes," Chaynie added. "And I might even make my special pasta—"

"Primavera!" her mother finished for her. "It's absolutely delicious."

"I look forward to it." Greg grasped his toolbox.

As he swiveled to leave the room, Max created a barrier, nearly causing Greg to trip over him.

"Max, come here! Silly cat." Chaynie bent over to scoop him up.

They followed Greg to the door, thanked him again, then shut out the cold.

"What should we do for dinner?" her mother asked.

"I'll cook your favorite dish," she decided on the spot. "It's a thank-you for all those gorgeous illustrations, a celebration of our book, finally finished." She wasn't planning to tell her mother about her publishing conversation with Greg. She refused to get her mother's hopes up for something that would probably never happen. *Why knowingly disappoint her?*

A couple of hours later, after the dishes were cleared and the coffee had been sipped beside the fire, Chaynie stole away, up to her bedroom, and eased open her laptop. Ever since Greg had left, she couldn't stop thinking about the children's book. He was right—it *was* a book, not just a mediocre story that had been cobbled together. After the countless hours spent creating it, the book was polished and waiting to be read. For the first time, she allowed herself to imagine some random little girl, wide-eyed, opening Chaynie's mouse book, diving into its pages, and falling in love with reading.

What if someone says yes? What do you have to lose?

Chaynie assumed that Greg's advice to her, and his absolute, unwavering tenacity that came along with it, had taken root in his childhood—a bullied little boy who never gave up, who worked hard to overcome his speech impediment then left for school and became an architect. It was nothing short of inspiring.

With no legitimate excuses remaining, Chaynie clicked on a jazz playlist from her phone, crossed her legs on the bed, and settled in for a couple of hours of research. She could easily contact Jill McCallister and pick her brain for some publishing advice and tips, but for now, Chaynie wished to keep the project to herself, her mother, and Greg. As she clicked to study publishers, guidelines, and websites for information, she recalled a children's writer visiting the library from Austin to give a talk last year at Mary's request. The author's lecture had included guest questions, and one of them had been about how to submit to publishers. "Give them whatever they ask for," the author had advised. "Follow their guidelines *to the letter* or risk a rejection." Chaynie followed that advice as she deepened her online search.

When she'd decided on three legitimate publishers, she read over their guidelines carefully. Then she crafted a query letter—thank goodness for the internet, which offered example letters posted online as guides—and polished it up.

At midnight, she heard Max scratching at her door to be let in, so she set aside her laptop. She hadn't moved from that bent-over position in hours, and the crick in her neck made her wince.

"Coming," she told Max then cracked the door open.

He rushed in, a dark-gray blur, and jumped onto her bed with acrobatic ease.

"Shoo." She waved him away from her laptop. The last thing she needed was for his paws to dance across the keyboard and accidentally send a nonsense letter to a potential publisher. "I'm almost finished."

As though understanding, he perched obediently at the corner of her bed, closed his eyes, and licked his paw.

Several clicks later, Chaynie had done it. She'd submitted three professional letters to three small publishers—and included the entire manuscript of her children's book along with scans of her mother's illustrations, which she'd hastily snapped with her phone while her mother was preoccupied with stoking the fire after dinner.

Chaynie heard the *ding* of new email, and she held her breath. Surely, they wouldn't respond *that* quickly. But what she saw instead was a rejection of another kind from the university library in Vermont. *We regret to inform you... position has already been filled...*

Chaynie closed her laptop, making more room for Max.

The full, busy day had suddenly caught up with her, and nothing sounded better than a warm blanket and soft pillow, with visions of publisher acceptances dancing in her head.

Chapter Eight

A*lcove party tonight??*

Chaynie paused, clicked send, then focused again on the ladies' discussion of a character's insecurity.

"Julie's making too much of their ages," Ginger noted. "Why does she care what her children think of the romance, anyway?"

Chaynie's phone vibrated in her palm, and she peered down discreetly. She sat in the corner of the conference room as usual, hidden from view as the Sassy Ladies were gathered around the table. Even so, Chaynie felt guilty reading Greg's response. She was breaking her *own* cardinal rule—no cell phones during meetings.

Party? I'm there. When? And why?

Chaynie started to type out her explanation when she heard an obvious and lengthy pause in the ladies' conversation, then a throat being cleared. She looked up sheepishly to see Doris staring at her, far across the room at the head of the elongated table. Chaynie felt like a second grader writing notes to a friend, caught by the stern teacher.

"Sorry. Library business." Which was a half-truth—the alcove *was* located inside the library.

Doris softened. "Of course, dear. It's just that Lucille wanted your thoughts on the Shakespeare play. We're hoping to compare this subplot with *Romeo and Juliet's*."

"Oh, sure, I can help with that." She turned to Lucille. "Would you repeat your question?" Chaynie abandoned her phone entirely and shifted her full focus to the ladies, knowing she was leaving Greg hanging. He would have to wait.

After the meeting, Greg was easy to find, standing right outside the conference door in anticipation. "You never finished your text," he teased, holding up his phone.

Chaynie studied him as she exited the room. Something was different from when Greg had left her house the night before. He'd gotten a haircut. Only a trim, but enough for Chaynie to notice.

She smiled up at him. "Have you been standing here, waiting, all this time?"

"Nope. I was already working on the second floor and knew I could catch you after the book club. So, what's all this about a party?"

Chaynie walked with him a few yards toward the alcove, where a pair of twin boys and their mother sat on the floor, flipping through a book. Nothing had changed inside the alcove since the day they'd talked about renovations, but Greg had texted her that morning with mysterious photos of what looked like tree props. He said he would explain in person.

Chaynie kept her voice at a whisper. "First, you. Tell me about those tree photos you sent."

"Dad and I went to visit Nick at UT early this morning. He showed us the storage room where they keep props from past productions. Pete was right—the set designs for *A Midsummer Night's Dream* were really professional and well-preserved. They had a tree trunk prop that's the right size for the alcove. It needs branches and leaves, but that won't be a problem. Nick said if we make arrangements to pick up the trunk, it's ours free of charge."

"I can't believe our luck."

"Neither can I. As much as I wanted to start the project from scratch, it didn't make sense for the timeline I promised. I can hire some guys to help transport it. It's probably best to have the trunk delivered to the alcove on a weekend, after hours. Okay, your turn. Alcove party?"

"Right, so this morning, I had this idea. My mom's already on board to paint the mural, and you're underway with the tree, so why not combine all our efforts? Mom could begin sketching out the mural on that back wall, and maybe I could pitch in, too, paint the chairs?"

"Sure. Dad's nearly finished making the base. We'll mount the tree on top of it, which should give the project a more polished look. Dad's idea. We can bring the base tonight, get to work securing it."

"Perfect. We can order pizza, play some music, make a party out of it. We're not going to finish in one night—and I'm not trying to rush the job—but at least it could be a fun start?"

They discussed possible colors for the new chairs, and Chaynie insisted on purchasing the paint. "It's the least I can do," she told Greg. "Let this be my contribution."

She would buy it from her dad's old hardware store. It had been purchased last year and completely overhauled by some big corporation from Austin with all the departments either spruced up beyond recognition or completely moved around—which, though heartbreaking for Chaynie, was also a relief. On the rare occasion when she visited the store to purchase a necessary item, she wasn't quite so eerily reminded that her dad should still be there, running it.

"Seven, then?" Greg confirmed.

"Yeah. I'll run this by Mary out of courtesy, but I'm sure she'll be fine with it."

They parted with a wave, and Chaynie walked to her office to sort through her morning messages and return some calls that couldn't wait.

CHAYNIE LEANED INTO the passenger seat of her six-year-old Camry and removed two plastic bags. Savannah had requested tacos, so Chaynie had picked them up from Juan's.

Occasionally, Chaynie would drive to the high school a couple of miles outside the square and bring food to Savannah, especially on those challenging days when all the teachers and students were stressed over their required standardized testing. Savannah never felt she could do enough to prepare the students. She often fretted over their test scores which ended up being, rightly or wrongly, a reflection on her teaching skills.

Chaynie received her security guest badge from Marge at the high school's front desk—"Mmm, you're making me hungry," Marge told her after getting a whiff of the tacos Chaynie carried—and then made her way down the long, familiar corridor toward Savannah's classroom.

The halls contained countless memories of friendships, heartbreaks, laughter, and tears. She could still visualize her teenage self gossiping with a teenage Savannah in between class periods at their side-by-side lockers. They'd first met in third grade, soon after Chaynie's family had moved to Morgan's Grove, but their friendship had strengthened the most in high school. While other friendships had waxed and waned, Savannah and Chaynie had hung on to each other through the tumultuous teenage years, becoming each other's port in the storm.

Chaynie plodded on toward Savannah's classroom and mused that the building hadn't changed one iota. The floors were still depressingly gray, the walls still displayed announcements, and the sickly fluorescent lighting still glowed above. In spite of the spicy taco scent wafting from the bag she carried, Chaynie could still smell that distinctive high school odor that never changed—an odd mixture of sweat, cafeteria food, and cleaning products. Maybe the walls had been infused with those odors over the many years.

As Chaynie turned the corner of another hallway, the bell rang. Out spilled hundreds of noisy, chatty, immature teenagers nearly bumping into her as they moved carelessly to their next class, cell phones in every palm. Chaynie had to hold tightly to her treasured food, and finally, she made it to Savannah's classroom in one piece. She waited for the last student to exit then swiftly entered the room and closed the door, shutting out the hallway chaos.

"Special delivery!" Chaynie announced in a singsong voice, but when she approached Savannah at her desk, she saw that their current moods did not match.

Savannah seemed particularly harried and frazzled as she scribbled something down then looked up with a frown.

"Hard morning?" Chaynie winced.

"You wouldn't believe." Savannah blew out an audible sigh then threw down her pen. "Jimmy has the flu but came to school anyway, so I had to send him home—praying I didn't catch it myself. I caught Avery and Britney cheating and had to take them to the principal. Then Thomas's mother phoned me for a conference this afternoon. That woman is impossible."

"Sounds like you need a break."

"I do!" Savannah watched Chaynie open the bag from Juan's. "Thank you for doing this. It smells amazing. I'll try to shift out of grump mode."

"It's okay. I'd be grumpy, too, in your position. So, how long do we have?"

Savannah checked the wall clock. "Thirty-three minutes of freedom left."

"That's plenty." Chaynie removed her coat then pulled up a chair to Savannah's desk. The room was neatly kept with desks in order, bookshelves tidy, and walls decorated with posters dedicated to Savannah's favorite writers—Steinbeck, Poe, Shakespeare, Angelou, and Milton.

Chaynie distributed napkins while Savannah uncapped two bottled waters. They spent the first five minutes in silence, eating the flavorful tacos. That was partly what Chaynie valued about their long-time friendship. They didn't have to talk all the time. They read each other well and knew exactly when to give each other space and when to offer support.

Savannah and Chaynie had been through every possible situation together over the years—boyfriend breakups, elation over new loves, failing grades, passing grades, then other, more serious life events, such as Savannah's parents divorcing or Chaynie's father passing away. After high school, they'd gone their separate ways for college, but they'd still managed to sustain their friendship over the miles with phone calls and frequent campus visits. Chaynie suspected that, someday, when one or both of them got married and started families, their friendship might necessarily be pushed aside due to new and daunting responsibilities. But for the moment, she would treasure what they had.

Finishing her taco, Chaynie peered out the classroom window toward the sports field. In the distance, she could see the athletes stretching on the oval track that bordered the field.

"Oh, there's Mitch," she mused, unwrapping a second taco. She watched him cross his arms and survey the athletes. "He's been over to the house a couple of times recently."

"Has he?" Savannah raised her eyebrows. "What does that mean?"

"Mom says they're on some committee together and that's why she's spending more time with him. But they text each other a lot, too, and she's... different around him now. She laughs at his corny jokes. She never used to do that."

"Do you think something's happening with them?"

"I asked her, and she denied it, using the 'only friends' line. But I think there's more. She just won't admit it yet."

"Is it weird for you? Seeing your mom with someone else?"

Chaynie reached for her bottled water. "Sure. I mean, I pictured my parents together forever. They were each other's first love. But he's gone, and I know my dad wouldn't want her to be lonely. Mitch is a good guy. He's been a rock for my mom since Daddy passed, not just one of those people who brings a meal or two at first then stops calling. He's been checking on us, genuinely concerned, all these months. I think he really cares about my mom."

Savannah thoughtfully snapped off a piece of her taco shell. "Yeah, I like Mitch. We don't cross paths much, but all the teachers are buzzing lately about how he helped that student last month."

Chaynie tilted her head. "What student?"

"Some freshman kid on the football team had been bullied, and apparently, Mitch took him under his wing. He talked the kid out of suicide and got him some help. He saved his life."

Chaynie glanced outside again at Mitch, who was gesturing toward his athletes as he instructed them. "I had no idea." She gave it some thought. "He's got this semi-tough exterior sometimes, probably from being a coach, but he's always been sweet with my mom and me. He's got this soft spot."

"Yeah, he's a good guy."

"I wonder if my mom knows," Chaynie mused. "About the kid he helped."

Before Savannah could respond, her classroom door creaked open, drawing Chaynie and Savannah's attention. A man in his late twenties with longish brown hair and wearing a long-sleeved shirt and tie stepped hesitantly inside.

"Sorry to bother you, Savannah. You were going to give me a copy of that text? I need it before my next class."

Savannah wiped her mouth with a napkin. "Oh, sure. I set it aside but then forgot to bring it to you. This morning has been crazy."

The man stepped closer then stretched out his hand for the book Savannah was holding—a text on mythological terminology. "Thanks. I'll have this back to you next week," he assured her.

Savannah waved a hand. "Just keep it. I have another copy at home."

He attempted a grateful smile, but it was wasted on Savannah, who'd already shifted her attention back to the tacos.

When the man shut the door behind him, Chaynie widened her eyes toward Savannah. "Is *that* the teacher-crush? Lucas?"

Savannah wadded up her napkin. "Yeah, that's him. Gorgeous, eh? But completely unattainable."

"Still? You're not invisible if he's coming to your room, asking for textbooks."

Savannah shrugged. "It's only because the department head paired us up last week. I'm acting as his mentor, answering questions, giving guidance. This is his first year of teaching. So every single one of our interactions has been strictly professional."

"Well, who's to say it won't lead to something strictly personal? That's how these things start, you know."

"Don't get my hopes up." Savannah clucked. "I've been proud of myself, keeping Lucas at arm's length, not anticipating anything beyond work. I'm tired of being disappointed. Besides, I've seen Amy Curtis salivating in his direction. She's got her sights on him, and I don't need the hassle of competition. It's not worth the trouble."

"Well, okay. But I'd say you should always keep an open mind."

"Listen to us! I think we've switched roles. How am I suddenly the realistic one and you're the Pollyanna? This feels too weird. Let's switch back."

Before they knew it, the bell had rung again, proclaiming lunchtime was over. Chaynie and Savannah gathered the trash and discarded it hastily, then Savannah leaned forward for a tight hug. As usual, Chaynie had to bend down to reach her petite friend.

"Thanks for bringing lunch—and for putting up with my sour mood. I needed some girl time."

"Me too."

"Oh, I completely forgot to tell you that Greg's parents phoned this morning. They've agreed to let me try to sell their ranch! No more 'by owner.'"

"That's fantastic news! I didn't think Mr. Peterson would ever cave, and the commission on a property that size…"

"Oh my gosh, amazing. I'm trying not to get my hopes too high. It's not exactly a seller's market, but at least Mr. Peterson has decided to trust me with it."

As Chaynie pushed her arm through her coat sleeve, Savannah added, "Hey, why don't we do something tonight? That suspense movie just premiered. I've been dying to see it."

"I'd love to, but I've sorta got plans. Recently made. We're working on the alcove tonight after the library closes."

"We?"

"Yeah. Me, Greg, his dad, my mom, and maybe Sam. We're all helping out with the alcove renovation together. You should come! We could use an extra set of hands."

"Okay, I might. Sounds like fun. Text me when y'all get there. Can I bring anything?"

"Just yourself."

By then, students were streaming into the classroom, bringing their raucous volume with them.

"Back to the grind," Savannah mouthed.

Chaynie attempted to wade through the students in the crowded hall toward the freedom of the parking lot. Years ago, Chaynie had actually taught classes after receiving her bachelor's in literature, but after two years at an Austin high school, she wasn't cut out for it—the paperwork, the standardization, the faculty meetings, the griping parents, the indifferent students. No, she much preferred her job at the library, teaching students how to love books early on.

Chapter Nine

"Want some help with that?" Chaynie's mother offered, but she already had a full load of her own and couldn't possibly lighten her daughter's.

"Nope, I've got it," Chaynie assured her, securing the three large pizza boxes inside the crook of her arm and inserting the key into the library door with her other hand.

They had taken the risk of a ticket—no parking in the square—in order to pull the car up to the library's curb and unload. Pizzas and art supplies first, then the paint cans that Chaynie had bought that afternoon.

As they made their way upstairs, they could hear male voices growing stronger.

"Greg and his dad," Chaynie assumed. "They beat us here!"

When Chaynie and her mom reached the alcove on the second floor, her suspicions were confirmed. Greg and his father, along with Sam, had begun the process. They had moved Chaynie's reading chair aside and stood with arms crossed, studying the circular wooden disc set before them and discussing the best approach for securing it.

Sam was the first to notice the new arrivals and extended a hand to Chaynie's mother. "It's been a long while. How are you these days?"

She set down her bag of supplies and her sketch pad then took Sam's hand. "So nice seeing you. We're doing well, keeping busy. How about yourself?"

"Staying busy too." Sam shook her hand heartily.

Greg and his father stepped closer to Chaynie, who made the introductions between her mother and Greg's dad. They exchanged greetings while Greg raised his eyebrows toward Chaynie, who still held the pizzas.

"You got pepperoni, right?"

"Just like you asked."

Greg moved toward her and offered to take the pizza boxes, placing them on a kiddie-sized table nearby. Their parents and Sam chatted as Greg's dad explained the renovation vision to her mother.

"Were you able to get the paint?" Greg asked.

"It's in the car. I'm illegally parked." Chaynie grimaced.

"Yeah, that's how we got all this up here." He waved toward the tools and the stacks of kid-sized chairs his father had built. "We had to park my dad's truck out front and hope we wouldn't get ticketed or towed."

"Oh, look at these!" Chaynie gave a tiny squeal and squatted near one of the new chairs, touching its smooth surface, smelling the strong scent of fresh wood. "They turned out perfect! So sturdy! How did your dad finish these so quickly?"

"He had help. A couple of shop students at the high school needed an apprenticeship for a class project, and Dad was assigned a couple of them last month. They've been working with him every day after school."

"That's fantastic." She paused then frowned. "Oh no. The paint for the chairs, I think I made a stupid mistake."

"What do you mean?"

Chaynie rose to face Greg. "Well, I got all the dust cloths to protect the carpet—we can paint the chairs right here." She gestured. "But they'll still be wet tomorrow, and the library's open. We can't use them in the alcove, so what do we do? Close off the area till they dry?"

Sam had overheard and joined them with a suggestion. "I think we have a couple of pieces of plywood, so let's set the chairs on top of them. When you finish painting, I can roll a good-sized platform cart in here, and we'll lift the plywood onto the cart and steer the wet chairs into the storage room to dry for a couple of days."

"We can use the old chairs until everything in the alcove is finished, all ready at once for the big reveal." Chaynie clapped her hands together. "Good, that's settled. Hey, the pizza's getting cold. Sam, you want a slice?"

"Sure." He drifted toward the box and opened it.

"Greg and I are going to get the paint. Right?"

"Right, boss."

"Pizza, everyone! Please dive in while it's hot!" Chaynie announced as she and Greg headed downstairs.

The night air was unseasonably warm for mid-January, even in Texas. Chaynie barely felt the need for the light jacket she wore as she led Greg toward her car. "Oh, I wanted to thank you for something." She opened the back door. "I mean, besides your fixing the sink last night... you gave me the publisher idea, for the book."

Greg smiled. "So, we're officially calling it a book?"

"Yes, we are. I spent a few hours last night researching publishers, in fact. And I sent the manuscript, with Mom's illustrations, to three of them." She took in a breath. "It makes me nervous thinking about it!"

"Why? It deserves to be seen. It deserves to be *published*. Kids would love that kind of book."

"Thanks. But it's still a new idea for me, stepping out on this particular limb, trying to get a book published. It all happened so fast. I've never seen myself as an author."

"It makes perfect sense, though, doesn't it? You know all about books. You're around them all day, grew up with them. Besides, maybe this is the best way to handle things—no time to think about submitting to publishers, no time to lose your courage. Just do it, like you did. I'm proud of you." Under the glow of the streetlamp, Chaynie noticed his gaze linger a split second longer than she expected, and she found herself looking away.

"Well, anyway, thanks for the support," she whispered. "I'm sorta proud of me too."

Greg lifted a bag of paint supplies from the backseat and handed it to Chaynie, then leaned deep inside to retrieve the paint cans on the car floor.

"Hey, guys!" someone shouted in a high-pitched voice nearby.

Chaynie craned her neck to see a familiar figure walking toward them. "You made it!"

Savannah approached the car. "Yeah, I needed a break from essay grading. If I have to mark one more comma splice, I'll probably lose the will to live."

"So, you'd prefer to paint chairs instead?" Chaynie teased. "It's not very glamorous."

"*Any*thing is better than grading. Trust me. It's the bane of my existence." Savannah paused as she watched Greg reemerge with two paint cans. "Hi, Greg."

"Hey, Savannah."

"I have an idea. Why don't I take this from you?" Savannah grabbed the bag from Chaynie's grasp. "You should go park the car before you get into trouble. I saw Officer Charlie around the corner."

"Oh, yikes. Good idea." Thankfully, Chaynie's keys were inside her jacket pocket. "I'll meet you both inside. Savannah, there's pizza upstairs!"

"Sausage?"

"Of course."

Savannah shut the car door for Greg, who somehow managed to balance three paint cans, then led him toward the library's entrance and opened the door.

By the time Chaynie had parked nearby, walked the half block to the library, and returned to the alcove, the party was in full swing. The only missing element was music. While everyone finished their pizza and found their posts—Greg, his dad, and Sam working on the tree's base at one end, Chaynie's mom working on the wall mural at the other end, and Savannah preparing to paint the chairs in the center—Chaynie clicked a playlist on her phone and cued up the first song.

"Does anyone object to Sinatra?" she asked, as his familiar silky voice crooned the first few notes of "The Way You Look Tonight."

"No objection!" was the immediate consensus, so Sinatra sang them through the first half hour of work.

Chaynie soon realized she had to teach Savannah how to paint the chairs. "Have you never done this before?" she teased, watching Savannah barely dip her brush into the dark-green paint then push the bristles hesitantly against the wood, creating a few splotches.

Savannah elbowed her with a giggle. "Actually, no."

Chaynie showed her by example, using her own chair. "Be generous. Don't be afraid to use a thick coat. You're not going to mess this up."

"Now, you know me better than that. I'll probably find *some* way to mess this up."

Savannah got the hang of it and became quite good at her technique. They went to work, and after her second chair was completed, Chaynie glanced over to see how her mother was coming along. She hadn't meant for her job to be such a solitary one, stuck in the corner while everyone else was paired off, but her mother's focus seemed intense, with her face near the wall as she sketched out toads and streams and tall grass waving in the wind.

Chaynie stood to stretch her back then changed the playlist to an upbeat mix of seventies and eighties pop. She noticed that Sam had left. He'd mentioned earlier that he had some other pressing duties in the library but would return to check on everyone's progress.

"Hey, that's really coming along," she told Greg and his dad. "It's easier to envision the proportions of the trunk now."

They were almost finished securing the tree trunk's base.

Greg had paused his drill and was kneeling at the far end. "It doesn't look like much yet, but this is the first step."

"It's a big one," Savannah noted, standing to stretch too.

"I need a volunteer," Greg said to no one in particular. "Can someone hand me a half-inch drill bit? I picked up the wrong one."

"I can help!" Savannah stepped forward. "Describe it to me."

"Um, it's a metal piece with grooves. It should be in that yellow toolbox, in one of the compartments." He pointed to the corner of the alcove while Savannah moved toward it.

Delicately picking up and putting down various pieces of hardware, she asked, "Is this it?" and brought it closer to Greg, who squinted at it from across the base.

"Nope, it's the one next to it, I think. The measurement should be inscribed in the metal." He started to put down his drill. "Here, I can just—"

"Hang on. I'll try again."

Amused, Chaynie couldn't take her eyes off the scene as Savannah sifted through the toolbox once more.

"Got it," she said with great confidence. She cupped her hand and placed the bit inside it then returned to Greg, careful to stretch across the base and not touch it with her shoes.

Greg leaned forward and lifted the bit from her palm then replaced it with the other one.

"Did I get it right?" she asked.

"Yep, that's the one. Thanks."

"No problem at all."

Savannah didn't return to Chaynie and the chairs right away. Instead, she stepped back a couple of feet and watched Greg secure the bit and resume drilling. Savannah inserted her hands into her back jeans pockets and swayed a little. Chaynie instantly recognized it as Savannah's flirting stance, but Greg was too busy working to notice.

"So, what will the end result be?" Savannah asked. "I mean, what's the trunk going to be made of?"

Greg paused the drill again. "It's actually chicken wire and foam, but it looks like a real tree trunk with divots and painted moss. Dad and I need to attach fake branches and leaves up top, that sort of thing."

"Wow, it's a huge project."

"Well, it could be, if we'd started from scratch. But we found the trunk from another source. Lucky break."

"Chaynie?" Her mother was suddenly at her side, holding her phone. "It's Mitch. He wanted to meet me for coffee and bring some paperwork for tomorrow's meeting, but I told him I was here at the library."

"Mom, the mural can wait. You should join him."

"I'd rather stay here. I'm enjoying myself, making some real progress. I thought maybe Mitch could come here to meet me instead?"

"Sure. But we might just put him to work." Chaynie winked.

"He could handle that." Abby squeezed her daughter's elbow. "I'll go downstairs and let him in."

By then, Savannah had returned to her post and taken up her paintbrush. "This is fun!" She dipped the brush into the paint. "*So* much better than grading."

Chaynie eyed Greg in his hunched-over position and grinned. "I'll bet."

Soon, Mitch and Abby rejoined the group, and Chaynie made the necessary introductions. When Mitch followed Chaynie's mom over to the alcove's back corner, Chaynie could hear him audibly gasp, impressed with her mother's sketch. She wondered if her mom had ever shown him her art before.

An hour later, Chaynie could overhear her mother chuckling with Mitch. She caught snippets of their conversation. "Right here!... overnight... worried sick," then they said Chaynie's name.

"Okay, you two, I've *got* to know what you're talking about." Chaynie abandoned her paintbrush. "It sounds too entertaining to keep to yourselves. Share!"

"Your mom was telling me about the time you ran away here, to the library."

"I hope you don't mind, honey." Her mother winced. "Being in the Children's Corner reminded me of it."

"Oh, I remember that story!" Savannah said, getting everyone's full attention.

Greg had finished with the base and was taking a break. "What story?" He grabbed a bottled water and took a swig.

"You don't mind me telling it, do you, honey?" Chaynie's mom asked.

"Well, it's pretty much public knowledge, so—"

"In fact, didn't the story make the newspaper the next day?" Savannah teased her friend. "You have to tell it, Mrs. Mayfield. Every detail."

And tell it she did, beginning with the grounding of little Chaynie to her room that evening for misbehavior then, two hours later, peeking in and realizing her daughter was missing, followed by the frantic search that ensued—including a call to the police station—and the great relief at seeing Sam at her door, his arm around Chaynie's shoulder, bringing her home safe and sound.

Hearing it told through her mother's eyes, Chaynie felt the sting of guilt from the panic she had put her parents through. But her mother wore a wistful expression as she retold the story, and Chaynie knew that those moments of panic and fear had melted away long ago, replaced by a charming story to tell.

"Where did you hide out?" Greg asked. "Do you remember?"

Chaynie pointed to the corner behind Greg. "Right there. It was dark and quiet, and I burrowed myself where nobody could find me, or so I thought…"

"That's right." Sam stood at the alcove's opening, his arms crossed. "You weren't stealthy enough for me." He added his own nostalgic details to the story. "I remember seeing an unusual light in that corner as I collected the trash on this floor. I came in to see Chaynie, sound asleep in a bean bag chair, a book splayed across her lap."

Chaynie confirmed his version. "He woke me up and talked me into going back home. It wasn't a hard sell. I wanted my warm bed." She looked over at her mom. "And I missed my folks."

"We were just glad you were safe."

"So that's why this alcove is so special for you?" Mitch asked. "And why we're renovating it?"

"Yeah, I guess so. It's still my safe place. Speaking of renovations, I've said it a dozen times already, but thanks to everyone for your hard work tonight. Look at how much progress we've made!"

Chaynie glanced at her mother's wall mural sketch, one-third completed, then at their painted chairs—only two to go—and the sturdy base that Greg and his dad had finished.

"In fact, why don't we put a pause on things?" Chaynie suggested. "As my mom would say, 'It's a school night,' and we're all probably tired. Maybe we can hold another party next week? Food's on me."

Everyone agreed then began the cleanup process. Greg returned Chaynie's reading chair to its usual spot while his father draped a black cloth over the new base to hide the project from the children, then they gathered their tools while Chaynie and Savannah finished painting the final chairs.

"This was fun." Chaynie's mom squeezed her daughter's shoulder. "I think we'll get going. Mitch still wants to have coffee so we can discuss the meeting."

Mitch came to stand beside her. "Thanks for letting me join y'all."

"Come for the next party, too, if you want," Chaynie offered.

"See you later," her mother said. "Mitch can drive me home after coffee."

It sounds like a date, Chaynie couldn't help thinking as Savannah confirmed that interpretation with wide eyes. Mitch and her mother turned the corner to leave together.

After the final strokes of paint, Savannah and Chaynie closed the paint-can lids and backed away so Sam and Greg and his father could lift the plywood slat carefully onto the lengthy cart Sam had wheeled in. It would clearly take more than one trip to get all the chairs, supplies, and paint cans to the storage room.

"We can help out," Chaynie said, folding up the dust cloth with Savannah. They collected the paint cans then followed the men, and the chairs, to the storage room.

"Painting is more fun than I thought it would be," Savannah mused. "Am I invited to the next party too?"

"Of course. I enjoyed you being here. And I could never have made that much progress on my own."

It only took a few minutes with all hands on deck for the freshly painted chairs and equipment to be transferred to the storage room and the alcove to be cleaned up, shipshape again.

After grabbing coats and purses and leftover toolboxes, the group left the library and paused while Chaynie locked the door. Sam waved good night and walked away, then Chaynie asked Savannah where she'd parked.

"I'm behind The Pit."

"We're parked behind Greg's office. Come with us, and I'll drive you to your car. It's safer that way, this time of night."

Savannah clucked. "Nothing bad ever happens in Morgan's Grove."

"Thankfully true, but indulge me. I'd feel better this way."

"You sound like an overprotective big sister."

"I'm okay with that role." Chaynie elbowed her friend as they walked alongside Greg and his father.

Bright stars studded a navy sky above, and a cool breeze lifted Chaynie's hair away from her face. Though every part of her body was exhausted and sore after a full workday followed by physical labor, the rest of her felt blissful. They'd gotten so much done, everyone working in harmony toward the same cause, everyone in a good mood. It almost reminded her of her college days—late nights spent on a group project, with music and food, her best friends by her side. *How many times in someone's adult life does that ever happen?*

"Mr. Peterson, I meant to tell you," Savannah said, "I've already gotten some interest on your ranch. A couple from Austin wants to view it next week. A property in town that fits your needs is also opening up this weekend. I'll let you know the details, and maybe we can visit the open house?"

Mr. Peterson nodded his reply as he walked.

"You should come too." Savannah gestured toward Greg. "To give some input, I mean."

"Maybe. If I have time."

As they approached their vehicles, Greg's father waved good night and entered the driver's side of his truck while Chaynie clicked her remote to unlock the passenger side for Savannah, which left Greg and Chaynie sandwiched between their two vehicles. Savannah had already opened the door to crawl into the passenger side, but Chaynie decided to linger with Greg.

"You and your dad did amazing work tonight."

Greg stood a few inches away from her, hand on the truck's door handle, a shadow cast over half his face in the moonlight.

"The party was a good idea. It made the work seem... less like work."

Chaynie was about to open her door when Greg continued, his voice softening to a lower volume than usual. "That story. The one your mom told about you running away."

Chaynie shook her head, embarrassed.

"That's where the idea came from. Your mouse story."

"Yeah. I guess I'm the runaway mouse."

"I learn more about you every day, Chaynie Mayfield." She could hear the grin in his voice.

Chaynie whispered goodbye then crawled into the driver's seat and started the engine.

"What was all that?" Savannah asked.

"Oh, sorry. I was just thanking Greg for their hard work tonight."

It was the perfect chance to tell Savannah—her best friend—about the mouse story, the illustrations, the publishers. But for whatever reason, she couldn't form the words. She wanted to believe it was because she didn't want to jinx the submissions she'd sent to the publishers, but deep down, maybe she wanted to keep it a secret between herself and Greg a bit longer.

Chapter Ten

The next morning, Chaynie awakened from a vivid dream involving her mouse-library book, as she followed the characters and their escapades, watching them wriggle out of situations and resolve them. At the end of the dream, before bubbling up toward consciousness, Chaynie's brain crafted the clear seeds of an idea for a sequel—another library mouse story that involved a missing ancient manuscript, a high-speed chase along the library's hallways, and a heart-stopping ending.

Bleary-eyed, pulse racing, Chaynie clicked on the bedside lamp, not having a clue what time it was, and reached for her notepad. In the light of the day, her ideas would likely end up seeming ridiculous and nonsensical, as dreams often did. But she had to obey her muse.

In the process of finding her notepad, she accidentally brushed her childhood charm bracelet onto the carpet, where Max snatched it then batted and played with it as he might a coveted piece of string.

Chaynie threw back the covers, forgetting the notepad. "Max! That is not a toy!"

It took her several seconds to wrench the bracelet carefully away from Max's claws and teeth without damaging the jewelry, but finally she did, chiding herself for not putting the bracelet in a less precarious area.

"Silly cat." She opened the nightstand drawer and dropped the bracelet deep inside the corner, safe and sound.

Returning to her notepad, she jotted down the details of her dream. As she finished the final phrase, she heard her phone *ping*, notifying her of a new email. Setting aside her brainstorming, she clicked onto the message and gasped. "From Mr. Baines, Publisher."

When she tapped open the email, she immediately knew it was a rejection. One of those over-the-top, politely worded form letters meant to cushion the blow. *Dear Miss Mayfield: Thank you for your submission. Although it is obvious that you've spent energy and dedication on this project, unfortunately, it does not suit our needs at this time. All the best.*

Best of what? Chaynie deleted the email with a quiet grunt.

She had at least hoped for some insight, some small reason for the rejection—the illustrations weren't detailed enough, the story was stupid and implausible, the writing was too simple or too complex for the targeted age group, the plot had been done and redone a million other times. She would never know.

That was why Chaynie had been so nervous, so apprehensive about submitting. The self-doubt immediately crept in after letting someone read, then coldly reject, her work. It was humiliating, a punch to the gut.

But even in the midst of the self-doubt, Chaynie could hear that annoyingly earnest tone of Greg's rah-rah enthusiasm in her head, countering her negative thoughts. *It's only one rejection. They weren't the right fit for you. It takes time. Don't give up.*

Brushing off the desire to lie back in bed and sulk for a while, Chaynie decided to face the workday.

Downstairs, her mother had made coffee, which instantly lifted Chaynie's mood. She poured a cup as Max perched at her feet.

"You look tired," her mother noted from her seat at the breakfast table.

"Is that code for awful?" Chaynie smirked and took her first sip. She'd already noticed the bags under her eyes when she'd applied her makeup a few minutes ago. "I didn't sleep well."

"It must be contagious. I didn't either." Her mother was nursing her own mug, shoulders hunched.

"Is anything wrong?" Chaynie pulled up a chair and sat.

"Not wrong. Just... bothersome."

Chaynie waited through the pause, watching her mother focus on her mug. Then she prompted, "Is it Mitch? You got home pretty late last night."

She made eye contact with Chaynie and bit her lip gently. "I think I sort of lied to you. Unintentionally. Back when you asked me if I had feelings for Mitch, I told you I only thought of him as a friend, but..."

"It's more?" Chaynie softened her voice, not wanting to push too hard. It wasn't easy for her mother to be brutally honest with her own emotions sometimes. Vulnerability could mean weakness.

"I think so, but I didn't realize it until last night. Truly. We were sitting at the café, sharing donuts and coffee, and talking about school, or maybe music. I don't even remember. I looked across at him when he wasn't looking at me, and out of nowhere, I felt this... slight pang in my chest." She motioned toward that area. "Like a teenager gets when she sees her crush entering the room, an extra heartbeat, a flutter."

"Well, you've spent a lot of time with him lately. Maybe that's part of it."

"Maybe, but it confuses me, having these feelings." She peered down then whispered, "I still love your father. I think about him dozens of times every single day. I still miss him." Her gaze returned to Chaynie, eyes glossy with tears. "So, what does this mean? This interest in another man? And not just any man—it's your father's best friend. I don't know if I can handle this. It's all too soon."

"Oh, Mom." Chaynie leaned in and placed a hand on top of her mother's. "It's okay to be confused. There's no timeline you have to follow, no right or wrong way of doing things or feeling things. I think it's fine for you to be attracted to Mitch, to enjoy his company. He's a good man. In fact, Savannah told me something about him yesterday. He helped talk a student out of suicide. Did you know about that?"

"Yes, I'd heard. He was too humble to tell me himself, but it's the talk of the school. You're right. He is a good man."

"And I think it's okay for you to spend time with a good man. What's wrong with that? Mom, you're still young. You have time ahead of you for romance if that's what you want. And—prepare yourself for the cliché—Dad would want you to be happy. Wouldn't he?"

Her mother sniffed back tears. "You're right, but this is too weird for me, too fresh and unexpected. I wasn't looking for this."

"I know you weren't. What does Mitch think? I mean, has he pressured you to be more than friends?"

"Not at all. He's very respectful. In fact, I don't know *how* he feels about me. And here I am, making mountains out of molehills that don't even exist." She wiped a tear from the corner of her eye before it could fall. "Maybe I'm having a lonely moment. Valentine's is coming, after all."

"Don't remind me." Chaynie rolled her eyes. "It's impossible to ignore as we get closer—romantic songs, red-and-pink decorations everywhere, cheesy commercials and movies. Mom, why don't you take it slow with Mitch, see what happens? Open yourself up to the possibility, at least. There's nothing wrong with that."

"It's great advice. Maybe you should listen to it too."

Chaynie frowned. "What do you mean?"

"Greg Peterson."

Chaynie removed her hand from her mother's and sat back in her chair. "Mom, that's not fair."

"Why isn't it fair? You and Greg spend all sorts of time together, every single day, practically. He's handsome and kind. You can't tell me it hasn't crossed your mind at least once... being more than friends."

Chaynie let out a long, thoughtful sigh. "Okay, yes, he's handsome. Yes, he's amazing and kind and sensitive, and yes, I do enjoy hanging out with him. There, I said it."

"Then why can't you open yourself up to the possibility, at least?"

There's a very good reason, actually. Chaynie wasn't planning to have the new-job conversation with her mother in the few minutes before work, but she felt cornered into it. She leaned forward and focused on the placemat, unable to make eye contact. "Mom, there's something I haven't told you about my future plans. I've been thinking about my career goals lately, long-term." She raised her gaze to her mother. "You know how much I love Morgan's Grove, and I love this library. But it's Mary's library. As long as she's around, I'll only be the technician, an assistant, and I want more than that. Honestly, it's time for me to make the big decisions, set the tone for an entire library, and be responsible for its success. Right now, I'm only treading water."

"I can see where this is going."

"After New Year's, I applied to several libraries for the head position. I've gotten some rejections, but I'm still hopeful."

"Well, that's good. I'm sure it will all work out."

"The catch is none of the libraries is located in Texas, which is why I can't start anything with Greg or anybody else."

"I see. Well, if you're moving far away, it's a sensible way to look at things."

"Mom, I've been nervous about telling you. I've considered a move for a few months now. I'm happy in Morgan's Grove, but I want more."

Her mother pushed aside her coffee and placed her palms faceup on the table. Chaynie placed her hands in them. They used to do that when Chaynie was a little girl and her mother needed to grab her full attention.

"Honey, I want the best for you. Okay, so I'm not crazy about your moving to another state—you know how much I hate flying—but if that's where you're meant to be, then let it happen. I support you. And don't worry about me. If I thought you were staying behind in Morgan's Grove just for me, it would make me feel old and sad and rather pathetic." She shrugged. "Actually, after your father died, I fully expected you to leave, maybe back to Austin or somewhere to pursue your dreams. But you stayed, and it's been a gift for me, having you here this long." She squeezed Chaynie's hands. "The time has come for you to fly. I'll be fine, more than fine. I have friendships here, my job, this wonderful house. I have a life here. You don't need to stay because of me."

"Thanks, Mom. I didn't know how to tell you."

"You can tell me anything. Always."

She leaned forward for a hug, which Chaynie reciprocated. She could smell her mother's strawberry shampoo as she breathed in, relieved.

A LAZY SATURDAY—AN actual stay-home, sleep-late, no-make-up, watch-cheesy-movies-by-the-fire Saturday—was exactly what Chaynie had been craving ever since the holidays had ended. She'd been so busy with the library's Valentine's project plus the book club readings as well as her usual library duties that she'd been spending at least part of each weekend working. Today would be different.

Downstairs, still in her pj's, Chaynie had a late breakfast of buttered toast and microwaved bacon, then turned on the gas fireplace and settled onto the sofa. She sipped a second cup of coffee while she tucked a velour blanket around her legs and clicked on the television.

Max startled her by jumping onto the sofa and nestling himself near her feet, kneading the blanket before settling into a gray ball of fur. From the nearby coffee table, a *ping!* caught Chaynie's attention. She'd intended to have a cell-free Saturday, too, but couldn't stop from checking the message. Muting the television, she picked up her phone and clicked through to her email. Surely it was spam or some political ad she would end up deleting.

But a familiar name caught her eye. It was another publisher's response. Before her heart could lift with hope, Chaynie forced it back down, remembering that in the past week, she'd received two out of three rejections. This was surely the final one, the nail in the rejection coffin of dead publishing dreams.

Bracing herself for Mr. Bullard, a small publisher located in North Carolina, to offer all the usual clichés—"not for us," "good luck on your literary journey," "publishing is a subjective business"—Chaynie clicked the email open with a wince.

Dear Ms. Mayfield:

We are happy to inform you that...

Happy? Chaynie gasped, clinging to her phone, shifting her feet from underneath the blanket and moving to a sitting position, disturbing Max in the process.

... we enjoyed your children's story, The Library Mouse, *and are very interested in publishing it. We have attached a boilerplate contract for you to review. We're eager to set up a phone conference with you on Monday, if possible, at your convenience.*

All the best...

Chaynie surprised Max with a loud shriek, causing him to jump off the sofa and scamper away. She read the email again, this time out loud in between puffs of shallow breaths. When she was absolutely *sure* she wasn't dreaming, Chaynie clutched the phone to her chest and let out another squeak of delight.

This is happening. This is really, really happening. They want to publish our book!

She'd read from her research online about the rare possibility of a fast response, a quick yes from a publisher, a swift contract offered. Sometimes it happened that way, but never in a thousand years had Chaynie believed it would happen for her.

Still breathless, mind racing, Chaynie threw off the blanket and wondered what to do next. She hadn't seen her mother yet that morning, probably because she was sleeping late, too, but she was the first person Chaynie wanted to tell, *had* to tell.

Rushing up the staircase, taking two steps at a time, phone still in hand, Chaynie paused at her mother's bedroom door and tapped. "Mom?"

"Come in."

Chaynie pushed open the door to find her mother stepping out of the bathroom and flicking off the light.

"What's wrong?" Her mother's eyes grew wide, and she halted midstep.

"Nothing's wrong. It's the opposite." She slowed down and remembered that her mother knew nothing about the publishers. Chaynie had to handle this the right way, set it up, not just blurt out the good news. It would take some finesse.

"Can we sit? I have some news."

"Sure, honey." Her mother led her to the two chairs that sat at her window alcove with morning sunlight beaming through.

Chaynie took in a long breath. "I did something last week. Well, Greg urged me to, and I decided he was right."

Her mother grinned and frowned at the same time. "Chaynie, you're not making much sense so far. Have you had your coffee yet?"

"Yes. Two cups already. Forget the coffee. I have some news. So, Greg saw your illustrations last week sitting out on the table, and I told him all about our book. He said I should try to get it published.

That night, on a whim, I took his advice and researched some publishers and sent the book to three of them."

"Why didn't you tell me any of this?"

"I didn't want you to be disappointed if we got rejections—and we did, two, right off the bat. But this morning..." Chaynie raised up her phone between them, turning the screen to face her mother. "Read this."

Her mother squinted and took the phone from Chaynie. She mumbled the words, "Happy to inform... interested in publishing... boilerplate contract..." She lowered the phone, and looked across at Chaynie without blinking. "Are you pulling my leg?"

"No! This is happening. Your book—our book—is getting published."

Her mother shook her head. "I don't know what to say, how to feel."

"I know it's a shock, but it's a good shock, right?"

She noticed her mother's face begin to change, to lighten, as she processed the news, and then it dawned. "We have a book that's *actually* going to be published. In print. For other people to read."

"Yes, Mom! It's surreal, isn't it? Of course, I still have to study the contract, and we need to speak with the publisher, iron out the details. I don't know how any of this works." Chaynie chewed her lip as she thought it over. "I've been thinking of contacting Jill McCallister. You know, she wrote all those cozy mysteries, sold tons of books. She would know what advice to give."

"Our book is going to be published!" Her mother's expression transformed into a full, open-mouthed smile of sheer joy. She leaned forward and clasped her daughter's shoulders. "I can't believe this!" They stood together as she closed the gap between them and squeezed Chaynie in a tight hug.

Her mother backed away with a small jolt. "I have so many questions! There's a lot to process."

"Yes, but we're in this together. We'll make all the decisions together. And we won't rush into anything. We'll do this right—have the contract analyzed then develop some questions for the publisher before our conference call."

"So, what's next? Did you respond to his email?"

"Not yet. I had to come tell you first! But we need to reply soon. Short and professional?" Chaynie tapped out her response then read it aloud. "What about this? 'Dear Mr. Bullard, we are thrilled about your acceptance of our manuscript and are eager to speak with you on Monday afternoon. Thank you for your interest in the book!' And then I'll sign both our names?"

"Sounds good enough to me."

Chaynie read the email once more for any errors then clicked send.

Her mother stamped her feet lightly on the floor and let out the same squeal Chaynie had, minutes ago, downstairs. "Can you imagine *our* book—your words, my illustrations—in a bound copy, available in bookstores or libraries? In the hands of children and parents? Can you?"

"I haven't even gone there yet. It's still very surreal."

"But it's happening!"

"Yes! It's happening."

By then, Max had gathered enough courage to slink into the bedroom to see what all the ruckus was about. He sat at the end of the bed and watched Chaynie and her mother at the window, then decided all was well and began grooming his front paw.

Chaynie noticed him sitting there. "Hey, Max, guess what. We're going to be published!"

Max paused at the sound of her voice then closed his eyes to groom his other paw.

THE NEXT LOGICAL PERSON to tell about the good news was the one who had encouraged her in the first place—Greg. Chaynie had considered phoning him, but it needed to be done in person. She needed to *see* his face light up. So, she abandoned all her lazy-Saturday plans, got dressed in a sweater and jeans, then headed outside.

Earlier, she had texted Greg to see where she could find him on a Saturday morning, but she'd gotten no response. So she tried the closest venue first, his office in the square.

With the surreal news in the forefront of her thoughts, everything looked brighter and more in focus. The sky was a vacant blue, the air crisp and cold. Chaynie breathed it in, still letting the thrill of the news wash over her. The publisher had responded immediately to Chaynie's email, "delighted" with her answer, and had suggested a five-o'clock conference call on Monday, which would be perfect—Chaynie and her mother could work a full day then both be present for the call at their house. They would have a couple of days to breathe, to process the news, to jot down some questions, and even do some online research about how to handle the situation.

Chaynie waved to Bicycle Bob as he passed by then to Lucille as she walked the corgis toward her soon-to-be-finished bakery. She approached Greg's office and heard music pulsating through the cracked door. He was inside finishing the final wall. He stood high on a ladder, carefully painting the crown molding with a petite brush.

Chaynie entered the office and cleared her throat loudly.

Greg heard and swiveled around. "Hey!" He placed the brush in the tray on the ladder's shelf.

"You're nearly finished! It looks fantastic."

Greg climbed down then clicked the music on his phone to pause it. "Thanks." He was slightly out of breath. "I worked hard last night and thought I might as well finish today, get it over with."

Chaynie couldn't wait any longer. "So, I have news!" She clasped her hands together as her giddiness returned. "I heard from a publisher this morning. He emailed me, and it wasn't a rejection."

Greg's eyes widened. "You mean..."

"They want to publish our book! He emailed a contract and everything!"

"That's incredible!"

In an instant, Greg took two steps closer and swept Chaynie into his arms. She reciprocated, wrapping her hands around his broad shoulders.

"This is the best news," he told her, squeezing tight. "You deserve it!" He released her then studied her face. "You must be..."

"Ecstatic. In shock. Over the moon. All of the above."

"I can imagine." He crossed his arms. "Did you tell your mom?"

"About an hour ago. She's in heaven, can't believe it's happening. I hadn't told her anything about the publishers, so she had no idea! She's still in shock."

"You said you have a contract?"

"Yeah, a boilerplate. I know nothing about these things, so I'll be researching tonight, reading it over. We have a conference call with the publisher on Monday to finalize things."

Greg looked away, deep in thought, his eyes searching the newly painted walls. "You know, I have a friend in Austin who could give advice on the contract, if you want. He's a lawyer. He'd do it as a favor to me."

"Are you sure?"

"Totally sure. I'll give him a call this afternoon."

"That would be so helpful. I mean, I want to be smart about this and not dive in eyes closed. I researched this publisher before I submitted, and he's legitimate, but I want to follow all the right steps, not get too swept up in the emotion of it."

"Smart thinking. I'll help in any way I can."

"You already have! If it hadn't been for you encouraging me to submit in the first place, this book would've been collecting dust in some drawer for years. I never would've sent it out to publishers without you having such faith in it."

"I didn't do anything. Just gave you my honest opinion. You and your mom did all the work."

"You're too humble for your own good." She soft-pinched his arm.

Greg made sudden eye contact with her, as though an idea had struck. "We should celebrate, maybe this week. Dinner or something?"

Chaynie hadn't expected a dinner invitation. She wasn't sure how to respond.

Possibly because of her lengthy hesitation, Greg quickly added, "And your mom too. I mean, to mark the occasion. This is a big deal."

"Sure. Maybe. I mean, we're inching closer to the big Valentine's night, so I'll be swamped with that. It's hard to commit to anything these days."

"I understand. We can wait and see."

"Okay. Well, I'd better scoot. I still need to see Mary and let her know. She'll be shocked!"

"Yeah, and I need to finish this." He pointed behind him to the wall in progress. "Thanks for telling me about the book."

She turned to leave Greg to his painting job and shrugged off the notion that "celebrate" had possibly been a substitute word for date. But maybe he'd gotten caught up in the moment.

"I'M DYING, HERE. WHAT'S the big secret news?" Savannah sat across from Chaynie at one of the picnic benches inside The Pit. Chaynie had texted her friend right after leaving Mary's office to see if she had time for lunch. She couldn't resist teasing Savannah with *I have news. BIG news.*

They'd met at The Pit, placed their order at the counter, then found a table near the old-fashioned jukebox that only ever played country music. Brad Paisley's "Whiskey Lullaby" strummed in the background.

"Okay, brace yourself," Chaynie told Savannah, who was wide-eyed at that point, her foot tapping in anticipation. As with her mother, Chaynie first had to rewind and give her friend some background information about the book. "Remember that story idea I had a while back about a mouse who runs away to the library?" She had mentioned it to Savannah vaguely, months ago.

Savannah frowned and searched the air. "That sounds familiar, I guess, but I thought nothing came of it. You haven't said anything since."

Chaynie lowered her voice to an excited half whisper. "That idea flourished into a full-blown story, and my mom even got involved—she's made these gorgeous illustrations to go along with it. We've been working on it for months."

"Why haven't I heard about this? You never told me how much progress you'd made."

"I guess because I thought nothing would ever come of it. I mean, it was this side hobby we did at home in our spare time. Nothing to tell."

"So, your good news has to do with this book?"

Chaynie leaned forward. "Last week, I decided to take a chance and submit it to publishers."

Savannah clamped a hand over her mouth.

"I got two rejections really fast, but this morning..." Chaynie fished out her phone and tapped the email already waiting to be displayed. She flipped the screen around so Savannah could read the words for herself.

Savannah's eyes darted across the screen then widened and focused on Chaynie. She removed her hand from her mouth. "It's getting *published*? As in, glossy hardcover, sold in stores, read in libraries? Published?"

"I don't have all the details—this is a small publisher, so I don't know about distribution or covers. But, yes. It will be an actual book with my mother's illustrations and my words to be read by actual children."

Savannah grasped Chaynie's hands across the table, causing the phone to plunk against the surface, and squeezed tightly. "This is the best news ever! I can't believe it. My best friend, a published author! You're going to be famous!"

Chaynie chuckled. "Well, I don't know about that."

"I do! It can happen. Chay, I'm so proud of you and your mom. How did she take the news?"

"She was ecstatic."

Savannah let go of Chaynie's hands, stood, and scurried over to her friend's side of the table for a tight hug. "I am so happy for you!" She released Chaynie when Tessa interrupted to bring their baskets of ribs and fries to the table.

"She's going to be published!" Savannah shouted to the entire restaurant. "Chaynie Mayfield is going to become a famous author!"

Someone in the corner gave a hesitant smattering of applause, and Tessa set down the baskets as Savannah took her seat again.

"Honey, that's amazing," Tessa offered. "Congratulations. The food's on us today."

"Oh, Tessa, you don't have to—"

"It's not every day we get a published author in the restaurant. I'll even throw in some Mississippi Mud."

"We'll take it!" Savannah insisted. "Thanks, Tessa!"

Finally, when the commotion died down and the other patrons returned to their meals, Savannah whispered across the table, "Sorry

if I embarrassed you. I couldn't help myself. This deserves to be cele-
brated! And you have to promise I get a signed copy."

"Absolutely!"

As they focused on their food, Chaynie couldn't erase her smile,
even as she brought the first french fry to her lips. She had to be living in some wonderful dream. But even in the midst of her joy, a
miniscule prick of pain emerged. The one thing missing from it all
was her father. She wished so badly he'd been there to see their success. He would've been the proudest one of all.

Chapter Eleven

Chaynie reached the end of her checklist and marked a penciled line through her final question—*Clause 6.b??*—with a satisfied nod. "Thank you, Mr. Bullard. That makes more sense now."

Chaynie's mother squeezed her daughter's elbow, surely in an effort to suppress her elation. They had to remain entirely professional until the call ended.

They sat at the kitchen table, where, exactly one hour ago, Mr. Bullard had phoned Chaynie's cell for their conference call, which had gone better than expected. He had been cordial, and Chaynie and her mother had managed to sound like they knew what they were doing. By the call's end, Chaynie couldn't think of anything else to ask Mr. Bullard. He had answered all her questions—the book would be published in both e-book and hard cover, distribution would be online and in libraries with a goal of putting the book into limited bookstores next year, and edits would begin shortly after the contract was signed, a process that could take up to three months.

"Oh, there was one other point." Mr. Bullard's voice echoed through the phone's speaker. "I wanted to ask about your future goals. Is there another book in mind?"

Chaynie leaned forward with confidence. "Yes, we're actually brainstorming a sequel." She could feel her mother lightly pinch at her elbow but ignored it. "We don't have all the details finalized yet, but I can send you a draft of it in the coming weeks."

"Fine, fine. Yes, I'd like to get a move on this to consider your mouse book as a series. I think it would work very well for this age of readers."

They all said their polite goodbyes. When Chaynie clicked to end the call, her mother turned to her, mouth agape. "A sequel? Did you just lie to our new publisher?"

"No, no. In all the bluster over the weekend, I forgot to tell you—I was thinking up story ideas for a sequel, even before we heard from Mr. Bullard. I had a dream one morning and jotted down all the details. The plot is about a lost manuscript, and Martin and his family get involved to solve the case inside the library."

"You've really thought about this. Why didn't you tell me?"

"Well, I wasn't sure if it was worth pursuing. Plus..."

"You might not be here by then, in Morgan's Grove, to work on it."

"But you know we can work long-distance if we have to—Skype, email, all the rest."

"Of course."

Chaynie knew her mother was being brave, trying not to dampen the exciting moment. If Chaynie was being honest, she was having trouble picturing *not* being in Morgan's Grove, working on the new project right alongside her mother.

"Well, anyway, I'm so glad Greg had his friend look over the contract and give it a thumbs-up," her mother said. "We were more confident talking about clauses and legalese."

"Yes. And I called Jill yesterday too. She helped me know which specific questions to ask the publisher. I felt very prepared. Speaking of Greg..." Chaynie leaned back in her seat and fiddled with the pencil, twirling it between her fingers. "He mentioned wanting to celebrate the book getting published this week. With me. And with you."

"That's nice."

Chaynie shrugged. "At first, it didn't sound like the three of us together. He added you on at the end. It sounded more like a..."

"What?"

"A date."

"That's not so surprising, is it? You're spending all this extra time together." Her mother waited for Chaynie's eye contact. "Honey. Does he even know you're planning on leaving Morgan's Grove?"

"I told him, actually, weeks ago, but we barely knew each other then. It didn't seem to matter whether I left or stayed."

"Is it starting to matter now?"

"I haven't lost the desire to become a head librarian, but honestly, I don't think I've allowed myself to picture leaving Morgan's Grove permanently. I mean, it's something I'll have to face if I'm offered a position."

"I understand. It's complicated. Well, as for the dinner, I have an idea. Let's remove all the awkwardness and have it here at the house—a cozy, relaxed supper, the three of us. Remember our rain check offer to Greg when he fixed the sink? I had invited him back for supper, anyway, so it's the perfect excuse. No pressure, no weirdness, just a nice meal together, a casual celebration."

"Perfect idea! I'll let him know."

"PUBLISHED? A CHILDREN'S book?" Doris gasped from her place at the head of the conference table. The Sassy Ladies had gotten seated with their snacks, and Doris had asked the group if they wanted to share any news or ask questions before they got down to business. Chaynie had raised a shy hand from her spot in the corner and told them about the publisher.

"Can you believe it?" Chaynie was still brimming with excitement.

All heads had swiveled toward her, and the layers of congratulations and gasps had multiplied. The ladies launched into all the usual questions. "When will it be published?" "Can I get a signed copy?"

"Will you become a famous author, make lots of money, be able to quit your job?" Chaynie answered them patiently with "I'm not sure yet," "Definitely yes," and "Definitely not."

When the excitement died down and the ladies returned to their meeting, Chaynie flipped open her book—they'd already moved on to the sequel, *Julie and Romeo Get Lucky*—and followed along as Doris began the book discussion.

Truthfully, Chaynie had only skimmed the assigned chapters the night before. She'd spent most of the evening cross-legged on her bed with Max, coming up with more ideas for the library-mouse sequel. It was important to have a firm grasp on the main plot before her mother could begin sketching the illustrations.

Thankfully, the ladies didn't have any book questions for her, and she even had time to jot down stronger story details in her notepad without them noticing.

After the group broke up and Chaynie locked the conference room door, she made her way to the Children's Corner to take a peek. Greg had mentioned that he and his dad might be able to work on the tree after hours during the week. She was anxious to see the final result, but it would be at least two or three more weeks, nearer to Valentine's, before the renovations would all be complete.

She hadn't seen Greg around the library that morning, so she texted to see if he could take a quick break and meet her there.

Within a couple of minutes, she heard a "Hey" behind her and pivoted to see Greg.

"I wasn't sure where you'd be this morning," Chaynie told him.

He was clean-shaven and wore an uncharacteristically colorful teal sweater, which made his eyes change colors. "Yeah, we're finishing up the HVAC repairs. They're coming along."

"That's good."

He pointed toward the alcove. "It looks like the trunk delivery from UT will happen sometime this weekend. When the trunk is secured, we can start attaching the greenery and branches."

"Is it anything I can help with? I mean, I *am* good with a staple gun," Chaynie bragged.

"Normally, I would say yes, but I want the end result to be a surprise for you."

"But I've already seen those photos of the trunk, remember?"

"Yeah, but the whole thing, put together with the details and the leaves draping down... that's worth waiting for. Indulge me?"

"Patience is not my strong suit, but okay. It'll be worth the wait. Maybe we could have another alcove party soon? I'm sure Savannah and my mom would be up for it, maybe even Mitch and Sam."

"Sounds good."

"Oh, the reason I texted," Chaynie remembered. "Mom wanted to invite you to the house for dinner this week as a rain check for helping us with the sink, plus we could celebrate the book getting published. Does tomorrow night sound good?"

Greg searched the air. "I think that'll work. Yeah. I'll make it work."

"Great. I'll let her know."

"What can I bring?"

"Just yourself. How does Italian sound?"

"My favorite."

They decided on a time then said hasty goodbyes as they both received work-related texts at nearly the same time.

IT DIDN'T *seem* like an overly ambitious meal on the surface—bow tie pasta with two kinds of sauces and garlic bread on the side—but with two cooks in the kitchen, both tired after a full day's work, and a curious cat in the mix, Chaynie and her mom found themselves bumping into each other as they shut off beeping timers, reached over each other for utensils, and tried not to let the sauces boil over on the stove, all while Max sauntered underneath their feet, wanting to be part of the action or hoping food would fall from the sky for him to catch.

Chaynie nearly stepped on his tail twice before finally having the good sense to abandon her post and banish him to his carrier in the next room. "Just until dinner is over," she promised as she gently shut the door.

The front bell rang as Max meowed his protest, and Chaynie shouted, "I'll get it!" over another timer going off in the kitchen. She smoothed out her maroon-colored blouse, a favorite, then opened the door to see Greg standing on the porch with a box in his hands.

"You weren't supposed to bring anything," she chided, hand on hip, as she let him pass through.

"Mama raised me right, so I had to bring something. I've heard cheesecake goes well with Italian."

"It certainly does." She took the white box from him and saw the label. "Mm, my favorite." It was from Christine's.

Greg shut the door and paused, then pointed downward. "Cute reindeer."

Chaynie had forgotten all about her fuzzy Christmas slippers—the only footwear she ever wore around the house. "Oops. I think my flats are in the living room."

"Well, don't change out of those for me. I like reindeer."

Chaynie's grin widened as she let her reindeer slippers lead him toward the kitchen.

Greg removed his coat, revealing a black blazer and an eggplant-colored shirt underneath. He always seemed put-together, as though he hadn't primped or spent any time with the mirror at all. Chaynie almost assumed he rolled out of bed that way, effortless.

"Just sling your coat over the chair," she suggested, setting down his cheesecake.

"Hi, Greg!" her mom called out over a steaming bowl of pasta as she strained it into the sink. "Dinner's almost ready."

He rubbed his palms together. "The garlic smells amazing. Can I help?"

"Nope, we've got everything covered. Oh! The bread!" Chaynie remembered then swiped a potholder from the counter and crossed swiftly to the oven. The bread was light brown and crusty on the edges and hopefully tender and buttery in the middle. She brought the pan to rest on the counter.

"Honey, grab that bowl for me, will you?" her mother asked.

Chaynie brought the huge white bowl within her mother's reach so she could pour the bow tie pasta into it.

Chaynie stirred the marinara once more on the stove then set it to simmer.

"Y'all are good at this," Greg noted.

"We're not usually *this* coordinated." Chaynie smirked. "We normally cook alone, taking turns, but tonight, we decided to work together."

It only took a few minutes for the sauces to be poured into bowls, the bread basket to be assembled, and the drinks to be set at the table.

Greg helped with those, pouring sweet tea into glasses. "You gave me the easy job."

"You're our guest," Chaynie reminded him. "Guests in this house never work. Mom's motto."

"That's exactly right," her mother confirmed. "Guests of mine never lift a finger in this house. It's the Southern way."

"My mama's philosophy, too," Greg agreed.

They sat together at the dining table, where Chaynie and her mother had rarely shared a meal since her father passed away. Her mother settled in at the head of the table then led them in a brief prayer to bless the food.

"Amen," they whispered together at the end.

"Before we start"—Greg raised his tea glass—"a toast. To publication success, and more where that came from."

"I'll toast to that!" Chaynie raised her glass along with her mother, and they all clinked together in the center.

Chaynie hadn't realized how hungry she was until she saw everything set before her at once, steam rising, the garlicky scent permeating the atmosphere. They passed the bowls politely around, pouring out sauces, grabbing hunks of bread from the basket. Chaynie could hear Max in the other room clawing inside his carrier.

"I'll get you in a minute, boy," she told him. "Max is a pest during mealtimes. He's a little beggar."

Greg nodded. "Yeah, my folks have cats at the ranch, but they're outdoors. It's our chocolate lab, Buddy, who's the beggar in the family."

They ate in silence at first, enjoying every bite of garlicky goodness, but soon, Chaynie's mother peppered Greg with gentle questions about when he'd first become interested in architecture—questions Chaynie had been wanting to ask, too, but had never gotten around to.

Greg wiped his mouth with the cloth napkin before responding. "Well, I've always built things. With Lincoln Logs as a little boy, then erector sets and model airplanes later on. I guess it's the precision I enjoy, creating something that takes patience and strategy. It's fulfilling to spend all that time and energy on a project, then step back and see a finished result."

"But your specialty is historic buildings," Chaynie prodded. "What made you go in that direction?"

"That's an easy answer. It was a trip to Italy before college. I back-packed around for a couple of weeks, soaking up the architecture, and was fascinated. The history of those buildings and their intricate construction—they tell a story just by existing. They deserve to be carefully preserved."

Chaynie's mother chimed in. "Yes! Danny and I got to see some marvelous cathedrals in person. We went to Italy for our honeymoon then went back again for our twentieth anniversary—Sorrento, Rome, Florence."

Her faraway gaze told Chaynie that her mother was flicking through specific memories in her mind, like snapshots in her hand.

Abby blinked away her thoughts. "Anyway. Italy is a special place."

"I want go back someday," Greg agreed.

After a brief gap in conversation, Chaynie sipped her tea then sat back in her chair. "I have a confession to make. It's an irrational fear I've been having lately about the Valentine's movie night."

Her mother speared two bow ties with her fork and looked up. "Fear? About what? You've been so careful with the planning."

"But... what if nobody shows up? I mean, we've never done any-thing this ambitious before at the library, and most people have their Valentine's Day plans set. They've made reservations weeks ago, months ago. Probably half the town goes to Austin for a fancy din-ner. What if we go to all this trouble and only a smattering of people come?"

Greg tore off a corner of his bread. "I think you'll have a good turnout. But even if you don't, remember why you're doing it. Aside from bringing people to the library, you're giving them another op-tion for Valentine's, and I think they'll take it. You'll be surprised."

"He's right, honey. Plus, this is a brand-new event! You need to give it time to grow, for word to spread, which it will in this town."

Chaynie sighed. "True. I guess it's nerve-racking, being the one in charge. If it doesn't go well, it's on me. And let's hope the weather cooperates."

"Now, that's one thing you *really* can't control," her mother admitted. "Especially in Texas."

At the end of the meal, Chaynie's mother rose to clear the table.

"No, Mom. Let me. You needed to check your email, anyway, remember? That new rubric the principal sent you for the committee?"

"Oh, that's right. I need to call Mitch first. He was hoping for my feedback right after school, but I forgot." She winced toward Greg. "Please excuse me. This shouldn't take long."

"Of course. No problem at all."

As she left the room, her mother called out, "Do you want me to let Max out?"

"Sure!" Chaynie shouted back as she stacked her empty plate on top of her mother's.

Greg rose and gathered his plate, the bread basket, and the sweet tea pitcher.

"You're not supposed to do that!" Chaynie whispered across the table.

"Too late. It's already done. Your mom will never know."

As they carried plates and bowls to the kitchen, Max darted into the room and ran toward his water bowl for a drink. Chaynie and Greg cleared the whole table in two trips, then Chaynie began rinsing the dishes. Greg stepped in beside her and took a plate.

"You're not supposed to be doing that either!" Chaynie flicked a dry dish towel in his direction.

"I'll take full responsibility for it if your mom catches us. All my fault."

They stood nearly shoulder to shoulder working in sync and finished the job in mere minutes. After she'd stacked the last dish, Chaynie noticed the box on the kitchen table. "We forgot the cheesecake!"

She found three clean saucers and forks then stepped toward the table. The fresh smell of collective ingredients—the sugar, butter, cream cheese, vanilla, and graham cracker crust—hit her senses as she opened the box. *Congratulations!* was spelled out in special blue icing on top.

"Greg, that's so nice. Thank you."

She sliced two pieces, carefully leaving most of the writing intact so her mother could see it later, then saved her mother a fork and saucer and closed the lid again.

"She won't mind us diving in without her. And maybe I can whip us up some hot chocolate," Chaynie suggested. "You wanna take these into the den and start the fire? It's gas. The knob is on the right." She handed him her cheesecake.

It only took a few minutes for Chaynie to scoop out the home-made cocoa mix and add it to water, microwave the mugs, plop in some mini-marshmallows, and join Greg on the sofa. Max had already nestled himself right up against Greg, hoping for a bite.

"Scoot!" Chaynie ordered the cat as she gave Greg his mug. She noticed he'd removed his blazer and tossed it over a nearby chair.

Max jumped off the couch obediently then sat at Greg's foot, tail twitching. Chaynie joined Greg at a comfortable distance on the sofa—not too far away, not too close. She took a quick sip of her cocoa, set down the mug, tucked her reindeer slippers underneath her legs, then adjusted the velvety blanket around her hips as Greg handed her the plate of dessert.

"How is it?" she asked.

"I was waiting for you."

Chaynie took her first luxurious bite. "Delicious. It's so creamy."

Greg followed suit and agreed. "Melts in your mouth."

The fire flickered behind the glass doors in a mesmerizing dance. The carbs from the pasta, along with the cocoa, fire, and blanket, were making Chaynie drowsy.

"I love this colder weather we've been having." She leaned her head against the sofa cushion and lowered the plate to her lap. "It's nice to have an *actual* winter in Texas."

"It's supposed to snow over the weekend."

Chaynie popped up. "Is it? I didn't think we'd get any more this season." She took another bite of cheesecake as Greg sank his fork into his dessert.

"Well, that's what the forecaster said this morning, but you know how wrong they can be."

"I won't get my hopes too high."

She watched the fire, but Greg was still in her eyeline. She looked at his profile, watched him savor the last bite, then set down his plate. Rarely was Chaynie *this* relaxed in a male's presence—except for her dad or brother. Normally, in adulthood, being around a guy, especially a still-new-in-her-life guy, made her... nervous wasn't the right word. On guard, self-aware, conscious of basic things like her hair, her makeup, her gestures, her tone of voice. But not with Greg. He always put her at ease, as though he would accept her in whatever state, mood, or appearance she was in. Always.

"Why weren't we friends in high school?" Chaynie heard herself ask. She had actually intended it as a question to ponder internally, but it came out as a question to Greg.

He shifted on the sofa and tilted his head toward her.

"I just mean," she explained, "things are easy with you. Relaxed. I think we would've made great friends back then. Don't take this the wrong way, but I can't even remember specifically which classes we took together. We weren't in each other's... orbits."

"From what I remember, we first had Mrs. Cranford together then a couple of classes in junior high and—"

"Chemistry in tenth grade!" Chaynie added, her memory jogged. "Mr. Miller's class. I remember where you sat. Back of the room, right corner, by the window."

"Yep. I always chose the back of the room if we weren't alphabetized. There was less of a chance to be called on to answer questions." Greg shifted and retrieved his mug. "I had a speech impediment back in those days, especially grade school, a pretty bad stutter, actually." He stared at his mug, at the reflection of flames dancing on its surface. "So, I had a pretty strong shy streak. I sort of disappeared into the background, made myself invisible."

Chaynie wondered if Greg had ever confessed that to anyone or talked about it at all. She remained still, hoping he would feel comfortable enough to continue.

He took a sip, put his mug down again, then settled back in and gave her a side glance. "My mom was overprotective about the stuttering early on. She even wanted to try homeschooling to avoid all the teasing from other kids, but Dad thought it was a cop-out, the easy way out. So they compromised and paid for a speech therapist while I kept going to school. I saw the therapist every day after classes and worked on these weird vocal exercises. It was hard—I had to retrain my brain. By junior high, I'd gotten the stutter mostly under control except for when I got stressed out about something, but..." He removed a piece of lint from his jeans. "I guess all those years of being self-conscious stayed with me. So I kept to myself through high school. Easier that way."

"I'm sorry." Chaynie had meant it in an empathetic way but realized it could be interpreted as patronizing. "That we weren't friends back then, I mean," she clarified. "And that you endured any cruelty."

Chaynie felt ashamed that she'd never reached out to Greg in those days. At the least, she could've been nicer to the shy boy in the back who'd kept to himself, maybe tried to draw him into her group of friends, make the effort. But she had probably been self-centered, as kids generally were.

"It's all a distant memory," Greg reassured her. "But there were some nice kids too. Like you."

"Me?"

"I'll never forget one day in fourth grade, how the teacher told us to pick partners for peer review on a paragraph we wrote. Immediately, everyone paired up, snagged their best friend as a partner, but I didn't have a best friend. The teacher pointed straight at me and announced, 'Greg's the odd man out.' She meant 'odd,' as in an odd number of students, not odd 'weird,' but as a kid, I took it as 'weird' and slunk down in my chair. Then she turned to the whole class and asked for a volunteer to be my partner. Suddenly, the spotlight was on me. It was probably only a couple of seconds, but it seemed like hours as everyone in the room stared. Out of the corner of the room, you raised your hand high. 'I'll do it,' you said. And after that, everyone got back to work, no big deal. You took the spotlight away. The teacher walked your paper over to mine and swapped them for us, and when she gave back the papers, I saw that you'd drawn this friendly smiley face at the bottom of it. A small gesture, but it meant everything that day."

Chaynie actually *didn't* remember the gesture but was so proud of her fourth-grade self. She could only imagine what might've been the outcome that day if a random student, especially a potential bully, had been called upon to swap papers instead.

"I had no idea," Chaynie confessed. "I'm glad it helped."

"It did." He shook his head. "I'm not sure how we got on such a serious topic. I didn't mean to weigh the conversation down."

Instinctively, for reassurance, Chaynie moved her hand to his shoulder, placing her fingers there for a couple of seconds then lifting back up. "You didn't. I'm glad you shared it with me."

"Well, anyway, I'm glad we're friends now. I enjoy spending time with you."

"It's mutual."

HOURS LATER, AFTER Greg had departed and the fire had been extinguished, Chaynie and her mother walked upstairs. As they paused at her mother's bedroom door, Chaynie said, "Mom, he told me about the stuttering. Greg did, I mean. When you were upstairs checking your email."

"Oh?" Her mother paused, too, hand on her bedroom door handle. "How detailed did he get?"

"Surprisingly detailed. He opened up about some of the bullying, the self-consciousness, and he said that I actually helped him one day in school. That I was kind to him."

"Well, that's not surprising at all. You're just like your father, always lending a hand, trying to make people feel as comfortable as possible."

"I didn't expect Greg to do that," Chaynie said softly, her mind still on their fireside conversation. "To open up that way."

"He must trust you. That's a big step."

"Toward what?"

"Toward whatever you want it to be."

Her mother smiled as she opened her bedroom door, leaving a question mark hovering in the air as Chaynie headed for bed in her reindeer slippers.

Chapter Twelve

Chaynie pinched off the corner of her blueberry scone, watching the crumbs fall onto the plate.

"I texted you last night, but you never answered. You must've had your phone off." Savannah tucked her silky black hair behind one ear.

"Sorry. By the time I saw your texts, it was pretty late. I didn't wanna wake you up since it was a school night." Chaynie ate the bite of scone, feeling the guilt return. She *had* seen Savannah's first text last night, right before Greg had arrived at the house, but had decided to shut down her phone rather than respond. She hadn't been sure how to explain the dinner.

An hour ago, Savannah had texted again while Chaynie had been leaving an impromptu meeting with Mary at the library. *Join me for coffee?*

Since Savannah's teacher workshop had let out early and Chaynie had no pressing issues or duties for the next hour, they'd both dropped everything to grab a table at the coffee shop in the square.

"Were you busy working on the new book last night, with your mom?" Savannah asked.

"Not exactly." Chaynie stirred her black coffee and tapped the spoon on the mug's edge. "We had company for dinner."

Savannah raised her eyebrows over her latte and set down the cup. "Mitch?"

"No, actually. It was Greg." Before Savannah could jump to all sorts of conclusions, Chaynie quickly added, "It was *all* my mom's idea, very last minute. Remember I told you that Greg fixed the kitchen sink last week? Well, Mom insisted on a dinner to thank him. You know what she always says. 'There's no better thank-you—"

"'Than food.'" Savannah finished the sentence with a grin and a nod. "That's your mom, Southern hospitality at its finest."

"You know how she hates being indebted to people. So, we kept it simple, made some pasta and garlic bread, had a quick meal. Debt repaid."

Savannah cut into her muffin with a fork. "Does he ever... does Greg, I mean...?"

"What?"

"Does he ever ask about me or mention me?"

Chaynie felt a second wave of guilt. *How am I supposed to answer this question without lying or hurting her feelings?* "I don't think so, but we mostly only talk about work stuff. You know, the library renovations or the movie night."

Which was partly true—they had, indeed, talked about the movie night at the dinner table last evening.

"I'm having trouble reading him," Savannah said. "I mean, the handful of times we've come in contact, he's polite and sweet. He has the best smile, doesn't he?"

It's true, Chaynie admitted privately. *He does.*

"But I can't figure out," Savannah continued, "whether he's disinterested and just being nice or he's interested but too shy to express it? I mean, I've dropped as many hints as I can, flirting a little, asking him to tag along to see properties for his folks, working on the library alcove near him. Maybe he's distracted? Busy with other things?"

"Greg is *definitely* a busy guy, always working at the library or at his office, and I know he's helping his dad pack up part of the ranch."

"Okay. So maybe that's it. He's busy, and when things settle down, he'll have more time for new interests." Savannah took a sip of her latte.

Chaynie hoped the Greg portion of the conversation was finally over. She didn't know how much more metaphorical tap dancing she could do. Just as she'd come up with a different topic to offer, a man approached their table and halted.

"Hey," Savannah said.

Chaynie swiveled her head to see Lucas.

"I guess we had the same idea," he told Savannah. "For coffee, I mean. We need some caffeine after those meetings, eh? How many of those things have you had to attend? I can barely stand them." He finally noticed Chaynie and gave a cursory nod. "Hi again."

She nodded back then watched Savannah's body language—not flirty and open, like she was with Greg at the alcove party, but reserved and subtle. Cautious.

"Yeah," Savannah agreed. "They can be torturous, but it's part of the job, so I usually take them in stride. I let my mind wander when someone drones on, or I even get some grading done."

"Lucas?" the barista called from the counter.

"That's me," he said cheerily then turned to retrieve his coffee.

Chaynie ate the last bite of her scone then twisted around to grab her coat, hanging on the seat back.

"Leaving already?" Savannah pouted. "We barely sat down."

"Sorry. I remembered some work I have to do—lots of calls to return, and we're expecting a shipment of books this afternoon."

Before Savannah had a chance to rush her snack and join her in leaving, Lucas approached again with his coffee, as Chaynie had secretly hoped he would.

"Here. Take my seat," she insisted. "I'm leaving, and I don't think Savannah's finished yet."

She grinned toward her friend, who shot her a friendly glare behind Lucas's back.

"Thanks," he said. "I will."

Chaynie cleared her side of the table to give him room then told Savannah, "I'll text you later. We can do something this afternoon, maybe?"

"Okay."

As Chaynie knew it would, politeness trumped frustration for Savannah, whose face relaxed as Lucas took his seat.

When Chaynie opened the door to leave, she could hear Lucas chattering away about the meeting and wondered if Savannah was right—that Lucas only saw her through the lens of work, as a helpful mentor. But the gleam in his eye when he'd first seen Savannah had told Chaynie otherwise. *Time will tell.*

"HEY, BOSS!" BRITNEY tapped at Chaynie's office door.

"Perfect timing." Chaynie waved her inside. "I just received another three donations from shops around the square."

"For Under the Stars?"

"Yep, and it brings our grand total to nine so far! I guess the word is spreading. We'll have more than enough door prizes."

"And tons of library card sign-ups!"

"Here's hoping!" Chaynie sifted through the gift cards and coupons, then pushed them into an envelope and slid it across the desk. Last week, she'd given Britney the task of coordinating all the incoming door prizes—sorting them, cataloging them, and writing up thank-you notes to the various vendors.

Chaynie heard another knock and looked up to see Greg leaning against the doorframe.

"Hey! Come in," she told him.

"I'll take care of these," Britney reassured Chaynie, patting the envelope then passing Greg to leave.

"Thanks again for last night." Greg stood across the desk from her. "The food was great. Tell your mom too."

"I will."

"So, I was thinking, how about having another alcove party this weekend? My dad's available, and I think we could make some real progress. Maybe even enough to finish by Valentine's."

Chaynie thought about her plans for the weekend. "Sure. I think Saturday night is doable. I'll talk to my mom, and I can text Savannah. She's probably free too."

Chaynie gauged Greg's expression for any reaction at the mention of Savannah's name but saw only the tiniest nod of acknowledgement, which could've meant approval for *any*thing Chaynie had just said—Saturday night, her mom's involvement, Savannah's help.

Greg's cell buzzed in his hand. "Gotta go," he said after seeing the screen. "Text me about Saturday, and I'll let my dad know."

"Will do."

As Greg left the room, Chaynie considered what Savannah had said earlier, that Greg was hard to read. Generally, it wasn't true for Chaynie. Most of the time, she found Greg quite easy to read because he'd chosen to let her in over the past few weeks. Remembering what he'd told her last night on the couch about his childhood experiences, Chaynie knew that building trust wasn't an easy task for Greg. But it seemed she'd already earned that trust with him, unknowingly, way back in fourth grade. Chaynie doodled a smiley face on a nearby notepad and smiled back at it.

Chapter Thirteen

When Chaynie and her mother arrived at the library, armed with barbecue sandwiches from The Pit, they discovered a tree trunk—in two enormous pieces—sitting outside the alcove upstairs. Chaynie set down the food at a table outside the alcove and marveled at the craftsmanship. She removed her gloves to touch the deep brown crevices in the foam.

"It looks so real, doesn't it?"

"My goodness, it does." Her mother set down the satchel of painting supplies and joined Chaynie in the middle of the room.

From there, Chaynie could see Greg, his father, and Sam securing the first piece of the trunk, on top of the base, inside the alcove.

"I hate to disturb them. Look at that concentration," Chaynie whispered to her mother. The men hadn't noticed them yet and were hard at work with loud drills and instructions to each other. "Lower on your side." "I've got it." "That'll work."

When they'd secured the first piece, Greg stepped back and exhaled. Chaynie took advantage of the pause and moved into the alcove to view their handiwork.

"Look at this!" she marveled. "Lots of progress already, and the trunk pieces look completely authentic."

Greg saw her and flashed a smile. "Glad you like it. I was hoping you would."

"It's coming along well," Greg's dad agreed, out of breath, drill in hand.

Her mother had already read Chaynie's mind and popped over to retrieve the food, the ultimate thank-you. "Anyone hungry?" She laid out the sandwiches and chips on the two kid-sized tables inside the alcove.

Chaynie helped out as Greg walked over.

"Here." She raised a foil-covered disc between them. As he accepted the sandwich, she added, "It's just us tonight. Savannah's got a UIL competition in Austin with her seniors. Mitch might be able to come for a few minutes and lend a hand."

"I'll get the chairs from storage," Sam offered, leaving the room before Chaynie could protest, offer a sandwich, and tell him, "It can wait."

After munching on barbecue and sharing snippets of their work-week, everyone was back to business—her mother perched at the mural, intensely focused, squinting, leaning back to see the overall result, then leaning in again; all the guys working on the trunk, one piece at a time, making sure the job was done right.

Chaynie's primary duty was to add foresty details to the chairs she and Savannah had painted last time. Thankfully, the details weren't original creations. Her mom had bought stencils, which became cheat sheets for branches and woodland creatures Chaynie could paint onto the chairs with incredible ease. Minimal effort, little room for mistakes, a beautiful outcome, and all she needed to do was choose the right colors and tape on the stencil, straight and steady, then paint.

When she was half-finished with the job, Chaynie remembered to snap several photos of the alcove for Savannah: the chairs she'd completed, the men working on the trunk, her mother's mural. She sifted through the photos to decide which ones to send, and one caught her eye—Greg helping lift one of the trunk pieces, holding it high with Sam for his father to attach. Chaynie zoomed in. Greg wore a short-sleeved shirt, something she'd rarely seen him in during the winter weeks, revealing strong forearms Chaynie hadn't been aware of. Greg was tall with a lean frame, so the muscle definition was unexpected.

Shaking off the thought, Chaynie selected the photos—*not* including the Greg-forearm one—and texted Savannah. *Wish you were here.*

The moment she clicked send, her mother received a text of her own and stood up. "Mitch is here. I'll go let him in."

Everyone greeted Mitch when he arrived, and Chaynie heard her mother whisper to him, "I saved you a sandwich with extra sauce and some chips." Her mother loved taking care of people, and Mitch was no exception.

Chaynie missed Savannah's presence. Stencil painting wasn't a difficult job, but it was a lonely occupation. Everyone else seemed to have partners and helpers, but Chaynie was on her own, and the stenciling became quite backbreaking if she didn't occasionally stand and stretch.

Nearly three hours later, when she finally finished the stencil on the last chair, Chaynie rocked back on her heels and took account. Not only of the chairs, but of everything else in sight—the trunk that finally looked like a tree, the mural that stretched across the back wall, the freshly stenciled chairs. Chaynie fast-forwarded time, envisioning the completed space, the children perched in sturdy new chairs while reading stories, the incredible sensory impact of the tree and finished branches, and the lasting work of art on the wall that kids and adults alike would enjoy and marvel over for decades to come. She only wished the space had been so creative and elaborate when she was a child. Although, if it had been, she probably would never have wanted to leave. She certainly would have run away from home more than once.

Watching everyone hard at work, Chaynie was filled with gratitude. She felt a specific warmth, a unique appreciation that came from the knowledge that these people, each important to her in various ways, had spent their own time and money to make the alcove dream a reality for her, for the children, for the library. Those types of selfless group efforts always reaffirmed her confidence in humanity. The world did contain great good. In fact, it was filled with compassionate and giving spirits, and it all began on a small scale—paint on a mural, foam for a tree.

"You're finished!"

During Chaynie's introspective daze, she hadn't noticed that her mother had taken a few steps toward her. She stood, hands on hips, peering down to assess Chaynie's handiwork.

"You did a marvelous job with these. The kids will be so pleased."

"Thanks. Once we get these sealed, they'll be all finished. The mural is coming along too." Chaynie stood to meet her mother and gestured toward the back wall.

"I'm almost finished. I want you to see something."

Chaynie followed her to the wall, where Mitch stood carefully filling in a white cloud at the edge of the mural. No doubt, her mother had given him the easy tasks and guided him every step of the way, including which color to use, how to fill in the carefully sketched lines. She could've easily completed the entire wall without anyone's help, and probably would have preferred it that way, but she obviously wanted Mitch to feel involved and included.

Mitch paused his painting. "Hey, congrats on the book. Your mother told me all about it."

"It's hard to believe it's really happening. We're very excited."

"I want your opinion on this." Her mother pointed toward a corner of the mural.

Chaynie leaned in, searching, unsure of what exactly her mother wanted her opinion on. Then she recognized Martin the Mouse, peeking out through a hole in the ground.

"Oh, Mom, that makes it perfect." She leaned in for a squeeze. "Thank you for making it so special. This space wouldn't be the same without your art in it."

They pulled out of the hug, and Chaynie studied the rest of the half-finished mural—all sorts of woodland creatures at play, including rabbits and deer and birds; a beautiful pastoral setting of brooks and streams and valleys; a carpet of thick, lush grass as the mural's base; towering trees hanging with vibrant-green leaves.

"You've outdone yourself, Mom." Chaynie pulled her cell from her pocket. "Can I snap some photos for Savannah?"

"Of course! I'm sorry she couldn't be here."

Chaynie took close-ups of the mural, sent them to Savannah, and returned to the center of the room to see that Greg and his crew had finished the job. Chaynie snapped another photo of the completed trunk and sent the image to Savannah, who'd been responding with smileys and wow emojis.

Sam joined Chaynie to assess their work after the last piece of trunk was secured.

"Not too shabby, eh?"

Chaynie nudged his arm. "Yeah, I'd say it's pretty darned amazing. Way above my expectations." She made eye contact. "You've stayed after hours more than once for this project. You should be long gone, resting at home."

Sam, ever the humble worker, shrugged. "I did it for the library, for Mary, and for you. And for all the kids who will end up discovering books because of this place. It's special to me, too, you know."

"I know."

"Well, that's the trunk, done," Greg announced, wiping his hands and stepping back toward Chaynie.

"It's incredible, Greg. Bigger and better than I even imagined. I can't wait to see the branches and leaves when it all comes together."

"Honey, I think I'll get going," Chaynie's mother said as Mitch helped her into her coat. "I'm addicted to these sugared donuts the diner started serving, and Mitch has agreed to go sit with me. It'll be a post-work treat for both of us. Want to join?"

"No thanks. I'm still full from the barbecue. Have fun," Chaynie insisted, glad that her mother had taken her advice—not to bolt and run from Mitch but to gently, slowly see where things might lead.

Chaynie noticed Sam loading up the chairs, preparing to take a trip to the storage room to let them dry. Greg and his dad were busy draping the ample sheet across the trunk, tucking down the sides to secure it from nosy children who might be tempted to take a peek on Monday.

Chaynie discarded the trash from The Pit then began folding the paint-spattered dust cloth, a work of art in its own right.

"Here, let me help." Greg gathered the cloth's other end and walked it toward her.

They met in the middle, arms raised, nearly chest-to-chest, and Chaynie grasped the ends of the cloth from him before the corners could fall to the floor. She backed away and folded the rest of the cloth on her own as Greg and his father lugged the ladder and equipment off to the storage room.

When they entered the alcove again, Greg's dad asked him, "Ready, son?"

"Yeah." Greg took the folded cloth from Chaynie and threw it onto an empty space on Sam's cart—by then, he had returned for the final load of chairs. They all gathered their coats as Chaynie said good night to Sam then headed downstairs with Greg and his father.

When Chaynie opened the library's front door, she gave a little gasp. The town square had been utterly transformed from when she'd walked inside the library hours ago. The entire city was blanketed with a bright-white layer of snow, and flakes were still falling from a dark sky.

She opened the door wider and walked through, making room for Greg and his father to see what she saw. They'd only been inside the library four or five hours, but it had been long enough for the snow to cover every streetlamp, bench, hedge, and shop sign in sight. The pathway to the library only contained the faint footprints of her mother and Mitch leaving for the coffee shop.

Long ago, Chaynie had gotten used to being in a bubble inside the library. The stained glass windows never revealed the weather going on outside, but it was an easy compromise to make since the stained glass was so beautiful. It felt like being in an art museum or an English cathedral, and it made the surprise of weather that much more striking when she opened the door to leave. Especially tonight.

"The weather guy finally got it right!" Greg extended a gloved hand to let the snowflakes fall into his palm.

Greg's dad seemed unimpressed and shrank down into his jacket, pulling the collar up higher. "Glad I put the horses in the barn before we came. We're in for a long, cold night."

Greg asked Chaynie, who had just locked the library's door, "Did you park near my office again?"

"Not this time. Mom and I walked since we didn't have so many loads to carry. We didn't think it would actually snow!"

"We'll give you a ride." His dad took his first step onto the snowy path.

"Oh, that's okay," Chaynie reassured him. "I'm only a block or so away. Besides, I'd like to walk home in the snow, enjoy it for a while. Thanks anyway."

Greg's father nodded, thrust his bare hands into his coat pockets, and began walking briskly toward Greg's office. "You coming, son?" he asked, not slowing his pace.

"You go on. I'll walk Chaynie home," Greg called out. "See you tomorrow!"

"Suit yourself." His father's voice faded in the distance as he trekked across the freshly powdered library lawn.

"You don't have to come," Chaynie told Greg. "Your jacket is too light."

"I'll be fine. A good walk will clear my head."

Chaynie stepped onto the library's pathway and took it all in. "Texas snow. An oxymoron?"

"I think that would qualify." His words puffed out in cold vapors. "It's really beautiful, isn't it?"

"It's another world. And listen." Chaynie paused on the walkway, snowflakes dusting her shoulders. "There's a silence that always comes with the snow. Why is that?"

"I guess because people go inside and hunker down in their homes. Which means we get the square all to ourselves."

"I think it's something else too." Chaynie raised her face to the sky, let the snowflakes melt on her cheeks, then turned to Greg. "It's almost like the snow hushes everything else on purpose. It forces us to pay attention."

"Your explanation is better than mine. Leave it to the writer..."

They shuffled through the snow in silence, side by side. Chaynie breathed in the cold air, letting it fill her lungs, fill her senses. Snowy evenings *were* rare, especially in Texas. Since she'd moved to Morgan's Grove as a little girl, Chaynie had only experienced maybe a dozen days of snow. So when they happened, they were magical.

Hearing the squeak of Greg's boots in the snow beside her, keeping her pace, she was grateful for his company, glad that he'd offered to walk her home and happy she hadn't waved him away out of politeness. It might've been lonely, trekking through the beautiful scene all on her own. Snow sometimes held a melancholy quality—a bleakness, a starkness—but Greg's presence was like a warm, comforting blanket. On that snowy night, with no one else around and no signs of human life, they were the only two people on the planet.

When they reached her mom's house, Chaynie approached the porch and noticed the pillowed snow lying on the three broad steps. The warm glow of the overhead light enhanced the snow's crystalline elements, which resembled tiny sparkling diamonds.

Chaynie had a sudden playful idea. She inserted her gloved hand straight into the middle of the porch step and pushed the snow toward her other hand, creating a generous block of snow between her palms. She stood and packed the snow together, creating a large ball, and saw Greg in her peripheral vision.

He had stopped short behind her and raised his hands in surrender.

She frowned, confused. "What are you doing?"

"Aren't you about to chuck that thing at me?" He grinned, raising his hands higher in preparation.

"A snowball fight? What do you think we are—a couple of six-year-olds? How juvenile. No, this project requires *at least* a seven-year-old's mentality."

She fashioned the snow into the size and shape of a volleyball then stooped to set it gently in the fresh snow on the top porch step.

"I see where this is going." Greg lowered his hands and scooped up some snow of his own, shaping the ball while gauging the size of the base Chaynie had just set down. "I'll handle the middle section."

"And I'll create the head." Chaynie stooped to gather more snow.

"Isn't he, um... kinda small?" Greg asked, still packing down his snowball. "For a snowman, I mean."

"Well, it's late, and I don't have the energy for a life-sized one. Maybe tomorrow, if the snow sticks, but this can be our practice run."

Greg had finished with his, perfectly round, as she would expect from an architect. But before placing it down, he paused to shave off a bit of snow from the top and bottom of the ball.

"What's this technique?" she asked.

"It gives the ball a flatter surface, less chance of it rolling off the base." He leaned forward to brush a bit of snow from Chaynie's largest snowball before setting his on top of it. "Flat surface to flat surface."

"Clever trick. You're pretty good at this."

"I've built a few snowmen in my day." He stepped away, dusting snow from his gloves with confidence. "Your turn."

Learning from Greg's example, she flattened the bottom of her final snowball then placed it gingerly on top of his. It wobbled at first, so she steadied it, pushing more firmly until it felt secure. "There." She backed away and assessed their final product with a frown.

"What is it?" Greg wondered.

"He doesn't have any eyes." She had a brainstorm. "Oh, wait."

She removed a glove and shoved her bare hand deep inside her pocket, producing a small plastic pouch containing two extra buttons. She handed one button to Greg, which he delicately placed into a socket of snow he dug with his fingertip. He did it so well that she handed over the other button, which he placed symmetrically beside it.

"Now we need a nose." Chaynie glanced around and saw a branch peeking out of the snow. She broke the branch to make it the right size and slipped it into the snowman's face below the eyes.

"No mouth?" Greg asked.

"Yeah, no mouth. I guess he's a mute snowman. No hat either."

"A mute, balding snowman."

"Exactly." She snickered and replaced her glove, then crossed her arms and took a step backward. "I like him. He's quirky." With that last observation, Chaynie realized how cold she was getting. "You should come inside for a bit. Hot cocoa? A warm fire? An obnoxious cat who begs for belly rubs?"

Greg shook his head. "I wish I could, but I've got an early start tomorrow."

"On a Sunday morning?"

"Yeah, Mom's planning on packing up the guest room at the ranch, and if I'm not there to help—"

"She'll do it all herself, right? Sounds exactly like my mom, stubborn to a fault."

"Yep. I told her I'd swing by before church and help her out. Plus, I need to get a heating pad on this back tonight." Greg stretched and winced.

"No wonder, with all the labor you've done at the alcove. I can drive you home. You've earned it. I mean, snowman building *is* taxing work."

"That's okay. My rental house is less than a block from here. Rain check on the cocoa?"

"You mean snow check?"

"Right. Snow check." He thrust out his palm to catch more flakes, which hadn't slowed down since the walk home from the library. Moving his gaze toward Chaynie, he took a step forward and tugged gently at the snow-covered hair spilling out from under her knit cap. A few flakes fell from her shoulder. "Looks like you're turning into a snowman yourself." He stepped back again and crinkled his eyebrows. "Snowwoman? Snowperson?"

Chaynie snickered. "I think you need some sleep."

"Agreed." He pivoted to leave as he told Chaynie, "Stay warm."

"You too."

Chaynie lingered on the porch for a bit, taking in the serene scene—the lamplight on the street corner outlining the drifting flakes, the pattern of steps she and Greg had recently created in the thick snow, and the thin black tree branches coated with white frosting. And Greg trudging home for a well-deserved slumber.

Chapter Fourteen

"Thank you for saying yes. This will be the highlight of our event!" Chaynie said, her voice laced with excitement.

"It's our pleasure," Stan Edwards replied. "And all for a good cause. My daughter learned how to read in that library. It means a lot to my family."

"I'm sorry again for the late notice. I know it's only two weeks before the event."

Stan tsked. "That's no problem. We'll already be out and about that day, singing Valen-tunes to various couples. We can add one more venue to the list."

Chaynie finalized the details with Mr. Edwards before ending the call then sat back in her chair. It was all coming together. That morning, on her way to the library, she'd gotten another idea for Valentine's Under the Stars—to call up the lead singer of Morgan's Grove's local barbershop quartet, Then and Now, and ask if they might be willing to sing a couple of songs before the movie began. In fact, weeks ago, the quartet had given a concert in Morgan's Grove and had included the *Music Man* medley of "Goodnight, Ladies" and "Lida Rose." What a perfect way to kick off the Valentine's event.

Chaynie frowned, remembering something. "The flyers," she muttered. They would need to be updated. Having the quartet at the event was sure to draw even more interest from the townspeople, but they wouldn't hear about it unless the quartet was advertised. The new flyers would surely be well worth the time and expense of reprinting and redistributing to the stores. In the end, it was a smart business move.

As Chaynie opened her laptop and tapped out the necessary tweaks on the old flyer, her cell phone buzzed. She tapped the screen to see a text response from Greg. *RIP, Snowman.*

An hour ago, walking down the wet steps of her mother's house on the way to work, Chaynie had noticed the sad-looking remnants of their porch snowman—mostly melted, only one eye button left, the twig nose sinking toward his navel. Chaynie had snapped a photo and texted it to Greg with a sad-face emoji.

She grinned at his answer and texted Greg back. *He had a good life. Brief, but good.*

The snow had continued to fall the night they'd created the snowman, but by Sunday evening, the bright sun and increased temperatures had melted much of it until all that remained were scattered white pillows around town and the remnants of a pitiful snowman.

BY WEDNESDAY AFTERNOON, all the old flyers in the square had been replaced with new ones, heralding the quartet's involvement on the big night. Every shop owner had been more than happy to make the change—"We love the quartet!" "Aren't they a town treasure?" "What a great idea, having them open for *The Music Man*!"—and Chaynie only hoped their enthusiasm would spill over to the townspeople, translating into increased numbers on the lawn.

Before returning to the library, Chaynie stopped at the coffee shop for a hot chocolate and a couple of heart-shaped iced sugar cookies to get her through the remainder of the day. She usually found her work interesting, but the rest of the afternoon would only hold mundane tasks such as cataloguing books, returning phone calls, and tutoring a senior group at the downstairs bank of computers.

Chaynie entered the library with her sugary treats but halted when she saw Greg consulting with a man in a hard hat near the elevator. They pointed toward it, saying something about gears.

"Hey," she said when Greg had finished his conversation.

"Oh. Hey." He turned to greet her.

"Problems with the elevator?"

"Yeah, enough to replace the whole system, unfortunately. It's not safe."

"I could've told you that. It's the grinding noise it makes when it rises, then there's that unsettling jump that happens when it reaches the second floor. I always take the stairs."

"Well then, it sounds like we're here just in time."

"To save the day," Chaynie added. "Here. You need a cookie for your efforts." She handed over the paper bag with an iced cookie peeking out.

Greg slipped the cookie out of its sleeve then took a bite. "Mm. Good."

"Oh, and I have this for you too." She sifted through the new flyers and gave him three. "Would you mind replacing the other ones in your office window with these?"

"Sure. Why the change?" Greg took another bite of cookie then examined the flyer.

"I got that local barbershop quartet booked! I forgot to tell you. They'll sing a couple of actual songs from *The Music Man* right before the movie starts."

"Genius idea," Greg admitted. "Why didn't I think of that?"

Before she could conjure up a witty response, Chaynie felt her phone buzz in her hand. "Sorry, let me check this."

As she tilted the screen, a crewman pulled Greg away with another elevator question.

The text was from Savannah. Somewhere in the deluge of all the exclamation points and smiley faces, Chaynie managed to determine the good news. *I sold it!!! Greg's parents' ranch!!! So happy!!!*

Chaynie started to tap out her response but paused when Greg returned to her side. "This is Savannah," she explained, waving her phone.

"Oh. That's probably about the ranch," Greg acknowledged. "Yeah, Mom called me a minute ago."

Chaynie attempted to read his expression. "It's good news, isn't it? The ranch being sold?"

"Yep. It is."

"But that's also your childhood home."

"Yep. It is."

Chaynie understood Greg's flat response, the opposite of Savannah's. Chaynie would be quietly heartbroken if her mother sold her childhood home. So many memories still lingered in those walls, inside those rooms—especially of her dad. She imagined that selling a beloved home might feel like a piece of one's childhood being handed over to total strangers.

Greg popped the last piece of the cookie into his mouth and tried to wave away any doubts. "It's all good. It's what my folks want. Now they can downsize, find something affordable."

"That's the logical way of seeing it," Chaynie mused.

Greg shrugged. "It's the only way to see it. It's just a house, land, property."

No matter how sincere his tone, Chaynie knew better. She suspected that, for an architect especially, a house was never just a house—a hollow, meaningless structure of plaster and brick. A house had a soul, a personality all its own, carefully crafted, lovingly built.

Savannah texted again, and Chaynie assumed her friend was anxiously awaiting a phone chat.

"Well, have a good rest of the day," she told Greg. "I'll see you around?"

"Sure. I'll be working on the alcove this week. No peeking."

"I promise."

Upstairs in her office, Chaynie made the call Savannah was expecting and heard a shrill shriek in response. "Isn't this exciting? It only took the second potential buyer! I got the phone call this morning. It's the biggest property I've ever sold, Chay. I won't even have to take a summer job this year, and maybe it'll get me some more clients. I love teaching—well, most of the time—but this will give me options. I won't feel so stuck!"

"That's incredible, Savannah. I'm proud of you." And she *was* proud. Her friend had worked hard, taken risks, and it had all paid off in a huge way.

"Let's celebrate! How about this Saturday, in Austin? We could try that Italian place everyone's raving about. My treat."

"Sure, I'm up for that, but why your treat? We're celebrating *you*, remember? It should be my treat."

"Well, okay, Dutch treat, then. We'll celebrate my house sale and your book sale, but I'm buying dessert."

Savannah paused for a moment, and Chaynie thought she'd lost the connection. "Are you still there? Savannah?"

"I'm here. I was just thinking... remember when we were kids, and we would look ahead, dream of what our lives would be as adults? I was going to be either a veterinarian or a newscaster—"

"And I was going to be a famous singer or a scientist." Chaynie chuckled. "What were we thinking?"

"Hey, we were only ten or eleven. We were dreaming big, but I'd say our ten-year-old selves would be pretty proud of us. You, a soon-to-be-famous children's author, and me, having two successful careers. It's happening, Chay. We're coming into our own."

They said their goodbyes, and Chaynie hung up, imagining those two little girls they used to be—hearts full of potential, eyes toward the stars, and ready for whatever the future might hold.

But remembering the sixth rejection she'd received that morning from a university library, she only hoped Savannah was right about coming into *her* own someday.

Chapter Fifteen

The soft rush of water from the faucet and the gentle clanking of dishes were the only sounds that morning as Chaynie finished washing up. She and her mother had decided on a Saturday brunch at home of French toast and bacon, a working meal as they brainstormed together on the Martin Mouse sequel. Her mother had scribbled notes down as Chaynie had told her about the opening she'd already written out last week.

"Yep. That will work," her mother had agreed, scanning the notes. "Martin can be in his cubbyhole for that scene, surrounded by his little bookshelves and tiny lamp, etcetera."

It was almost a shorthand between them by then—her mother knew the characters as well as Chaynie did. Leaving her mother to sketch at the table, Chaynie had collected the dishes and started washing them, still answering occasional story questions as her mother posed them.

"Your phone," her mother said, eyes remaining on her sketch.

"Oh. I thought I'd shut it off." Chaynie heard the quiet buzz then dried her hands on a dish towel and approached the table.

The text was from Greg. *Plans this afternoon?*

She cocked her head and studied the text. It was nearly noon, which still gave her several empty hours, especially since her celebration dinner with Savannah had been pushed to seven o'clock. She tapped out her reply. *I'm free. Why?*

Want to show you something at the ranch.

I can be there in twenty minutes. Directions?

Two miles north of the main square on Old Oak Road. Wear boots.

"What's that look about?" her mother asked as Chaynie clicked off her phone.

"Curiosity. Greg wants to see me at the ranch. He said to wear boots, but I don't even own a pair."

"Yes, you do." Her mother paused her pencil. "In your bedroom closet. I think they're still there. Remember those red boots you had to buy in college for that party?"

"I remember! My sorority was throwing a rodeo-themed benefit. You still have them?"

"I think so. You only wore them once, and I thought it would be a shame to throw out a perfectly good pair of boots."

"But... they're red."

"They were all the rage when you were in college, I guess. Surely Greg won't care about the color. What does he want to show you?"

"He was cryptic. Maybe it's about the sale. He probably just wants my opinion on something and didn't want me to get my good shoes dirty."

"If it's about the sale, why didn't he call Savannah?" her mother mused.

"Who knows? But I'm committed now. I told him I'd be there soon. Do you still need me for this?" She pointed toward the pad.

"Nope. I've got everything I need. I can finish this one in the next few hours, at least the sketch of it. In fact, it'll be best for me to have an empty house. No offense, of course."

"None taken." She understood her mother's desire for silence, to let the creative process take over while she worked. Chaynie headed upstairs to seek out her old college boots, hoping they still fit.

THE RANCH WAS EASY to find, and Chaynie made good time, arriving earlier than expected. She rolled her Toyota through the broad, opened gates and approached the ranch house—a two-story rustic structure made of part brick and part stone. Chaynie wondered if its architectural style had influenced Greg, growing up.

The day was overcast and gloomy, but the temperatures were mild enough for only a light jacket. A warm front had abruptly followed the cold front from the week before, which was completely normal for Texas.

Exiting the car and shutting the door, Chaynie noticed Greg in the distance crouched between two saddled-up horses. She understood the boot requirement. As she stepped hesitantly closer, she could see that Greg was tightening the girth on one of the saddles.

"You made it," he said, remaining focused on his chore. He managed to steal a glance at Chaynie's footwear. "Colorful boots."

"They were the only ones I had."

"They'll do fine," he assured her.

One of the horses snorted and dipped its head toward Chaynie, forcing her to take a step back. She loved the *idea* of horses—beautiful, regal creatures featured in some of her favorite children's books, like *Black Beauty*—but wasn't comfortable actually being in their presence. In fact, she hadn't been so near a horse in over two decades. Her father had once taken her to a county fair and paid five dollars to walk alongside her as she rode in a broad circle behind other child riders. Even in that structured environment, she remembered the enormous animal trying to nip at her hair while her father's back was turned so he could pay the man.

"Jeb's playing his game with me," Greg explained, still hunched over, pausing with his hands on the belt. "He waits until I cinch up the girth then inhales a deep breath to give himself more room, hoping I'll make the saddle looser. But I'm onto him. I just have to be patient."

Chaynie watched the horse finally blow out a long gust of air, and the moment he did, Greg tightened the buckle.

"Gotcha," he told Jeb then patted his neck.

Chaynie marveled at the confidence and knowledge Greg displayed. His movements and demeanor held no hesitation like she'd observed on other occasions. He seemed in his element on the ranch, among the horses. He knew what he was doing.

"Have you ridden?" Greg asked, breaking her thoughts.

Chaynie shuddered at the vivid horse-nipping memory and shook her head. "Not really."

Jeb snorted again, this time toward Chaynie.

"He's harmless, I promise," Greg assured her. "I thought we could go for a ride. These two have to be ridden together, and my parents are busy inside, so..."

"You need a partner."

"Exactly." He reached for the reins of the other horse, who seemed to have fallen asleep standing up, and rubbed its long nose. "Dad actually sold these two yesterday. They'll be picked up by a neighboring ranch tomorrow."

"So this will be their last ride?"

"Yep."

How can I possibly say no? Chaynie gathered up all her courage and shoved down her horse fears, remembering she was in safe, confident hands with Greg. "Well then, let's give them a ride to remember."

Greg's face said it all as he beamed. "All right, then! You take Cinder. She's a gentle old mare, totally trustworthy."

"I'll take your word for it." Chaynie stepped forward and approached the horse's nose with an extended hand, which Cinder sniffed.

"She likes you."

Chaynie's cell phone jingled unexpectedly inside her jacket pocket, spooking Jeb. He reared back and whinnied.

"Gosh, sorry." She took a few steps out of the way to glance at a text from Mary, confirming a Monday meeting. "I'll put it on silent."

"That's probably best." Greg grabbed the reins. "Jeb hates ringtones. I should've warned you."

Chaynie clicked off her phone then stared again at Cinder and tried to recall how to get *onto* a horse.

"Want some help?" Greg flicked the reins over Jeb's mane then walked to Chaynie's side.

"Sure." Chaynie was tall, but she wasn't tall enough to mount the enormous equine without toppling over. She placed her left boot awkwardly into the stirrup then felt Greg's strong hand at her waist, guiding her upward as she plunked into the saddle.

Proud of herself, and of Cinder for not moving a single muscle, Chaynie leaned forward to hold onto the saddle horn with one hand and pat the mare's neck with the other. "Her fur is so thick."

"Yeah, it gets that way in the winter, but during the summer, her coat will be thin and sleek to accommodate the hot days."

Greg mounted Jeb with incredible ease and maneuvered the horse toward an open pasture. "I can show you the ranch. Well, not the *whole* ranch—it's forty acres—but we can walk some of it."

Chaynie observed the way Greg kicked Jeb's ribs and followed suit, giving Cinder's sides a polite nudge. "C'mon, girl," she urged, and Cinder obeyed, starting off at a leisurely stroll.

It took a few minutes for Chaynie to push past her initial nerves, but soon, she discovered exactly why riding was so popular with some people. When she was certain Cinder wouldn't spook and throw her off, Chaynie relaxed her grip on the saddle horn and took everything in.

Perched high in the saddle, she could see the world from a totally different angle. Her view from up there was broader, more complete. She was also forced into channeling all her energy and all her focus onto one thing, her animal—how to guide her, how to avoid losing her own balance, how to stay in rhythm with her gait—and consequently, all other cares on Chaynie's mind magically melted away. Nothing else mattered but that horse and that moment, as she sauntered along with Cinder, enjoying the hypnotic pace of her walk.

As she grew even more comfortable, Chaynie was able to gaze out and determine how beautiful the Petersons' land was, with its peaks and valleys, thick groves of trees, and a small stream. She imagined it in the springtime, when everything would be green and lush again.

"You must've loved growing up here," she noted, riding by Greg's side.

He'd been there all along, keeping a slow, steady pace with Jeb.

When she looked over to hear his response, she saw that Greg's focus was on the land, too, as he scanned the hills. He was a natural in the saddle. With a relaxed hand holding the reins and him wearing his old boots and jeans and brown leather jacket, Greg could've been a cowboy straight out of a western. All he needed was a hat to complete the image. Chaynie assumed he had one stashed away in a closet somewhere.

"What were you saying?" He turned his attention to her. "Sorry, I get kinda preoccupied when I ride."

"Just that it's beautiful here."

"Yeah, there's nothing like it. I don't think it hit me until today—that the ranch will be someone else's. I can't come here whenever I want and slow down, escape things for a while."

Chaynie wondered if he'd done that all his life, if he had often "escaped" the bullies in grade school by jumping on a horse and riding far, far away.

Greg leaned forward to pat Jeb's coat. "I'll miss these guys, too, but it's time for them to retire." He pointed over to Chaynie's mare. "Cinder is nearly thirty years old. My dad bought her a couple of years after I was born."

"I didn't know a horse could live that long."

"They're hearty animals if they're well cared for."

They continued in silence except for a rushing stream and some birds calling out, answering each other in the distance.

An hour into the ride, Greg gave Chaynie a side glance and asked, "Wanna speed things up a bit?"

By then, Chaynie trusted Cinder completely. "Sure. A gentle trot? If there is such a thing."

"There is. It won't be full speed. I don't think Cinder's capable of more than a light gallop. Just give her a small kick in the sides. Let her know you want to increase the speed."

Chaynie puffed out her nerves then kicked twice. Almost immediately, Cinder obeyed and burst into a brisk walk, then a trot, leaving Chaynie to grasp the saddle horn with a squeal. She bounced in the saddle, but she wasn't afraid. She was exhilarated.

"Faster!" she yelled over to Greg. If she could handle a trot, she could surely handle something close to a gallop.

"You sure?" he called back.

"I'm sure."

"Give her another kick."

And so, she did. As Cinder shifted into a stronger run, Chaynie couldn't stop smiling. She was flying. Greg galloped alongside her, and Chaynie could sense his protective stare.

"You okay?" he shouted.

"This is amazing!" she shouted back, hearing the swoosh of wind in her ears, hanging on for dear life. She hadn't experienced that kind of rush in a very long time.

Out of breath, even though Cinder had been the one running, Chaynie finally pulled on the reins to slow her down to a trot then to a relaxed walk. Taking her cue, Greg slowed Jeb beside her.

"I galloped!" she told Greg with a proud smile.

"I'm a witness."

"When I first saw you standing with the horses... I didn't admit this, but... I was sort of petrified," she confessed through still-ragged breaths.

"Yeah, I could tell." Greg grinned.

"But I can see why people love this. It feels like freedom, doesn't it? I never knew."

"It's an escape from everything. Hard to describe. I try to ride every day. Well, tried. Past tense. It's going to be hard to let these two go."

"Can you visit them at their new ranch? Surely the owners would let you ride now and then."

"Probably, but it wouldn't be the same. It would be someone else's land, someone else's horses." Greg clucked and shifted his reins to turn Jeb around. "We'd better head back."

They turned the horses toward the ranch house, but that part of the ride became noticeably different in tone than the first half—sadder, more final. Maybe the horses could sense it too. The last ride.

When they approached the house, Chaynie saw a woman on the porch. When she noticed the horses, the woman waved. "Come inside, you two!" she called out then disappeared inside the house.

"Your mom?" Chaynie asked.

"You should go meet her," Greg suggested. "I can put the horses up."

When they slowed to a stop, Greg dismounted and steadied Jeb then came straight to Chaynie's side. She had already made an awkward effort to dismount, but when she'd swung her leg around the saddle, both her thighs felt like they were made of jelly instead of muscle. She barely had any control over them.

She attempted to slide carefully down the saddle, realizing how ungraceful she probably looked. When her other foot got caught in the stirrup, Chaynie wobbled and reached instinctively for Greg, who placed his hands around her waist, catching her before she could fall.

"I've gotcha," he whispered.

Leaning on Greg gave Chaynie the chance to loosen her boot from the stirrup and right herself. When she stood tall, she swiveled in his arms and met him eye to eye. "Thanks," she said, out of breath again.

The sky held the beginnings of an intense sunset, and Greg's eyes caught the sunbeams' reflection as he responded. "No problem." He dropped his hands from her waist then took a step back.

"You knew I'd need your help getting down," she mused.

"First-timers usually do. They forget how weak their muscles are after the first ride, especially if it's a long one. You'll be sore tomorrow—have a heating pad ready."

"What do you mean 'tomorrow'? I'm sore right now!"

Greg took Cinder's reins then Jeb's. "I'll only be a few minutes. Mom has some sweet tea waiting for you."

"How do you know?"

"She always has it waiting after a ride."

Something else Greg would miss, no doubt. It was a bittersweet day for him all around.

As he headed toward the barn, Chaynie moved in the direction of the ranch house and padded up the porch stairs in slow motion, one weak leg at a time, then knocked on the screen door. Hearing a "Come in!" she entered and immediately heard a clicking sound on the wood floors. A chocolate lab ambled toward her, tongue wagging.

"You must be Buddy!" Chaynie stooped to pet his head. Buddy panted and rubbed his back against her leg in response. He gazed up at her with soulful brown eyes.

Even through the sudden burst of canine activity, Chaynie could smell a heavenly scent wafting from the kitchen a few feet away.

Chaynie looked up to see Mrs. Peterson standing at a respectful distance. She approached Buddy with a "Shoo. She's our guest. You've given her enough hellos."

Buddy obeyed, tail wagging, and jogged to the corner of the room, then circled twice and settled into his soft pillow bed.

As predicted, Mrs. Peterson held a glass of amber-colored liquid clinking with ice cubes and handed it over. "You must be parched after your ride."

"I am. Thank you, Mrs. Peterson." Chaynie accepted the glass.

"Call me Margie. We're informal around here."

Margie had salt-and-pepper hair, pulled back into a ponytail at the nape of her neck, and wore casual jeans and a peach blouse. Her dark eyes were kind and sincere, putting Chaynie at ease. Margie looked familiar to Chaynie. In a town the size of Morgan's Grove, they had likely seen each other a handful of times over the years but hadn't officially met.

"And you're Chaynie, Danny's daughter." Margie gave a single nod. "He was a good man. I was sorry to hear he passed. He was kind to my Greg."

"Yes" was all Chaynie could utter. The mention of her father's name always seemed to startle her, reminding her that he was really gone.

Greg's father entered the room and headed straight for the refrigerator.

"Buck. Leave that and come greet our guest," his wife chided.

"Oh. Hello, Chaynie. I didn't know you were here." He closed the fridge door and came to stand next to his wife. "Nice to see you."

Behind Chaynie, the patio door banged shut as Greg entered the ranch house, wiping his dusty hands on his jeans. Buddy bolted from his spot in the corner and raced to Greg's side, whimpering with excitement.

"Hey, boy." Greg knelt to meet him, rubbing the dog's back vigorously.

"You two had better wash up." Margie made her way toward the kitchen to quiet a dinging timer on the oven. "Dinner's almost ready."

"Oh. I don't think I can—" Chaynie started to protest as politely as possible.

"I won't take no for an answer," Margie insisted. "You're our guest. Didn't Greg invite you?"

"I was going to," Greg admitted. "I hadn't had a chance yet."

"Well, you're officially invited, Chaynie. We'd love to have you stay," Margie assured her.

"I don't think you have a choice," Greg whispered out of his mom's earshot. "Might as well take off your coat."

Chaynie peeked at the rooster clock on the wall and saw that she had plenty of time before she was supposed to meet Savannah. Surely, she could do both—accept the Peterson's impromptu invitation and still make Savannah's dinner without missing a beat. She could eat light at the Petersons', treat the meal as a sort of appetizer, and save room for the Italian main course with Savannah.

"Of course I'll stay. Thank you." Chaynie removed her jacket and handed it to Greg. "Can I do anything to help?"

Margie shook her head. "It's all under control." She stepped to the range and stirred something in a pot. "Oven-fried chicken, mashed potatoes, biscuits, salad, and cobbler for dessert. It's almost ready, but you two have time to wash up first."

"I'll show you where." Greg paused to let Chaynie walk ahead of him toward a hallway.

As she passed by the ample living room, she noticed how homey and rustic the house's interior was with antiques and quilts and collections of cookie jars decorating the space. Even so, the overall architecture was still quite upscale with detailed crown moldings and dark hardwood floors. She could see why Savannah had no trouble selling the property so quickly.

Greg led her to the half bath beneath the staircase, and Chaynie washed her hands then combed out her windblown hair with her fingers. Her makeup needed some touching up, but her purse with a spare makeup bag was in the car. It didn't matter anyway. Nobody in this household would care if she didn't have on enough blush or lip gloss. Chaynie used a tissue to remove a couple of dark eyeliner smudges from beneath her eyes then examined the results in the mirror. *Good enough.*

She exited the bathroom, expecting Greg to be waiting on her, next in line, but he ambled down the nearby staircase. He'd apparently washed up in his room upstairs, removed his jacket, and changed his jeans as well.

"Greg, honey? Would you come take out the biscuits?" Margie called from the kitchen.

"Sure." Greg let Chaynie walk down the hallway first then picked up his pace and grabbed a potholder on the way to the oven. He removed a pan of biscuits, baked to perfection. They were obviously made from scratch, as were the potatoes, Chaynie noted, seeing the remnants of peelings left in the sink.

"This looks so delicious," Chaynie said. "I didn't know I was this hungry."

Greg set the biscuits on the counter. "It's the riding. It'll make you famished every time."

"Like swimming. Every time I went swimming as a kid, I got out of the pool totally ravenous." Chaynie's eyes skimmed the kitchen and paused on the stacked-up silverware and napkins. "May I set the table, at least?"

Before his mother could protest, Greg said, "I'll help."

He took charge of the napkins and let Chaynie take the silverware. They made their way around the dining table together side by side, as though they'd done that very task a million times before.

Within minutes, the meal was ready, piping hot, the entire spread laid out in bowls and on huge plates in the middle of the table, family style.

"You two sit over there," Margie instructed, pointing across the table, "and we'll sit here."

Greg pulled out Chaynie's chair—she saw that Greg's father did the same for his mother—then they sat and placed napkins in their laps. Margie offered her hands out, palms up. "Who wants to give the blessing?"

"I will." Greg opened his palm to Chaynie. She laid her hand on top of his, and he enclosed it in a warm grip. "Lord, we thank you for your many blessings, including this wonderful food. We thank you for the fellowship here tonight, for family, and for the special guest at our table. Amen."

"Amen," everyone echoed then politely clanked dishes as they served themselves.

Presented with such a feast, Chaynie couldn't commit to her previous plan of eating light. The mashed potatoes looked too buttery and creamy, the chicken too crisp and golden, and the biscuits too flakey and light. She piled on generous helpings, realizing everyone else was doing the same. *I'm merely being a good guest*, she told herself as she globbed a second spoonful of mashed potatoes onto her plate.

Chaynie was grateful there wasn't much conversation during dinner beyond some general chatter about each other's workweek because she was too busy being hungry to pause her fork over her food for long periods of time and answer a lot of in-depth questions. Still, rather than shovel the food into her mouth, she watched her pacing and tried to match the others. By the time she finished her food, they had all nearly cleared their plates, and Greg had started on seconds.

"Save room for cobbler," Margie told him. "You know it's your favorite."

Greg wiped his mouth with a paper napkin. "It's award-winning. Mom's too humble to say, but it won five years in a row at the state fair."

"*Second* prize, one year," Margie corrected.

"I can't wait to try it," Chaynie said.

"Why don't you two make a fire in the pit while we clear the table?" Margie told Greg and Chaynie. "I'll bring out dessert."

Drowsy from all the carbs she'd eaten as well as the earlier ride, Chaynie dutifully obeyed, pushing back her chair as Greg pulled it out farther for her.

"I'll get your jacket." He walked ahead to retrieve it from the coat rack then balanced the jacket on Chaynie's shoulders as she slipped her arms through the sleeves. "It's probably overkill, but we have blankets, too," he offered as he led her down the hallway and toward the back door. A few thick quilts were stacked inside a large basket nearby. He selected two and handed one to Chaynie then opened the door.

"Dad and I built this a few years back." Greg nodded toward the firepit that sat several yards away from the house. It was constructed with large beige stones, surrounded by six wooden lawn chairs.

"And these too?" Chaynie touched one of the chairs.

"Yeah, those too."

"I'm learning something new about you every day." Seeing the empty firepit, she asked, "Can I help out? Gather wood?"

"Naw, just pick a seat and get warm. I'll do the rest. We've got lots of wood stacked against the house. This won't take long."

He was right. In a matter of minutes, Greg had created and stoked a blazing fire, and Chaynie, bundled up in her quilt to protect her from the chilly night air, sat before it, mesmerized. With her happily full belly, she could easily fall asleep there, under the growing twilight, watching the flames flicker upward.

"Here we are!" Chaynie heard someone approaching from behind. Before she knew it, a steaming plate of peach cobbler had been placed in front of her.

She wriggled her hands out from under the blanket and told her hostess, "Thank you. This smells incredible!"

Margie handed Greg his portion—he had settled into the seat next to Chaynie—then began to leave.

"Aren't you joining us?" Chaynie asked.

"I have some household things to attend to, and Bill has some packing to do. We'll leave you young people to enjoy the evening." She squeezed Chaynie's arm then went back inside.

"I like your folks." Chaynie pierced her first bite of cobbler with her fork. The dessert was too hot to eat, but she didn't care. She blew twice on the surface then tried a bite, which dissolved in her mouth. The fruit was fresh and syrupy, the crust flaky and buttery. "Oh my gosh," she said, still chewing. "This *is* incredible." Her eyes grew wide as she looked over at Greg, who'd just cut into his first bite.

They sat in silence except for the crackling, popping fire and a bird calling in the distance. It was Chaynie's favorite time of day, those few moments right after sunset, when the sky turned a special kind of velvety technicolor blue that soon evaporated into dark night. She rarely got to experience it this way, on an open range with clear skies, near a blazing fire, and holding an award-winning cobbler. Usually, she was in her mom's house or walking home from the library, where shop buildings and tall trees got in the way of the view. But here, she could take in the gradient of colors at the skyline, the occasional twinkling star, the hint of the sun's glow as it continued to set.

Finishing her cobbler—so much for her efforts to restrain her appetite—Chaynie set the plate on the ground then snuggled back underneath the quilt. "This is heaven," she said, letting the drowsiness have its way.

Greg finished his cobbler and abandoned his plate then pulled his blanket up to his waist. "Yeah, I like this time of the day. The busy stuff is behind you. The new day hasn't come yet. It's this in-between part where you can relax, ponder things."

Curious, she rolled her neck to see him. "You're philosophical tonight. What things are you pondering?"

Greg shrugged. "You said you're learning things about me. I guess I'm learning new things about you too."

"Such as?"

Greg met her gaze, the firelight reflecting off his stubbled cheek. "Well, I discovered tonight that you're a cat lover who also appreciates dogs."

"True, but how can anyone not love Buddy?"

"Also, you push past your fears, even if it's out of politeness, to try new things."

"Like riding horses."

"Yep, and you have this knack for..." Greg pondered his words. "For turning a bad thing into a good thing."

"How so?"

"Well, tonight you could tell I was having a hard time letting go of the ranch, and the horses, this place. And you had all the right words. You weren't patronizing, and you didn't throw platitudes at me. You just... listened a lot. You helped turn something bad into something good or, at least, something better."

"I didn't know I was doing that."

"You do it a lot. In fact, back when we met—or met again as adults is more accurate—you hated Valentine's Day because of that jerk boyfriend. But when you were forced to head the Valentine's event, you didn't go through the motions or tell Mary no. You accepted it, pushed down your personal feelings about it, and now you're making the holiday positive for everyone else. Not everybody can do that."

Chaynie was glad he couldn't see her blushing in the fireside's glow. "Well, I don't know about that. I mean, I did have some help. If I remember correctly, *you* were the one who encouraged me to make the Valentine's event accessible to everyone. So maybe you have that unique talent too? Turning good into bad. I've seen it more than once in you."

Greg dipped his head. "Fair enough."

"So, speaking of Blake—"

"Who?"

"The 'jerk boyfriend.'" Chaynie grinned at the accurate description. "It got me thinking. I've told you about my humiliating breakup, but what about you? Did someone ever break your heart, or vice versa?"

Greg stared into the fire and nodded. "Both, I guess. Senior year of college was Jane. We were study partners, and it turned into more. She wanted to go faster in the relationship than I did, and I got cold feet. But honestly, I wasn't in love with her. I thought it was cruel to stay with her when I already knew that. I didn't want to lead her on."

"You did the right thing. Trust me." Chaynie remembered a college romance where she had felt the guy pulling away. She'd wanted to believe he was busy or distracted, but deep inside, she'd known he wasn't "in" the relationship and hadn't been for a long time.

"As for *my* heart getting broken," Greg continued, "that honor goes to Emily Maines, a colleague at the last firm where I worked. We dated for a couple of years—even talked about marriage—but she connected with an old boyfriend on social media, and the rest is history. I couldn't compete with a first love."

"That's rough. I'm sorry."

Chaynie heard the porch door slam and twisted her neck to see Buddy bounding down the steps, toward the firepit.

"Hey, Buddy!" Greg called.

The lab bypassed Chaynie and rushed straight to Greg, who leaned forward to cup the dog's head in his hands.

"Did you wanna come see us? You needed to go out, didn't you? Wanna sit by the fire?"

Buddy whined his response and gazed sweetly into Greg's face. It was clear whose dog Buddy really was. Greg stooped to offer Buddy the crumbs off his plate.

"Good boy," he whispered, stroking Buddy's fur.

Carpenter's hands, Chaynie realized, even in the faint light of the fire. Greg's hands were masculine, strong, and well-defined, accustomed to working on furniture and renovation projects.

In that moment, watching Greg's attentiveness to Buddy while completely unaware that he was being watched, Chaynie felt something unexpected rising in her. It started in the depths of her stomach and lifted toward her chest and shoulders, a wave of emotion she couldn't quite identify—a gentle nervousness, a quicker heartbeat, a flutter. Just like her mother had described about Mitch. *A pang*.

And just like her mother's, the pang was happening while Greg was doing an incredibly mundane and unimportant activity. He wasn't lifting equipment high over his head or helping her build a snowman or being chivalrous and pulling out chairs or helping her down from the saddle. Chaynie hadn't experienced a single flutter during those acts.

But it appeared inside a moment when Greg was oblivious to her stare, when he was petting a dog, simply navigating his natural environment, being himself. Being the person she'd grown incredibly fond of over the last several weeks. The person she was comfortable being her true self with. The person she'd recently begun talking to first, above anyone else, whenever she received news, good or bad, throughout the day. She hadn't noticed it until then, but Greg had, somewhere along the way, become her first text or first call—even above Savannah and her mother.

Savannah.

Chaynie sat straight up in her chair, dropping the quilt to the dusty ground. "What time is it?"

Greg paused his petting and looked across at her. "Not sure. I don't have my phone out here."

Chaynie stood and reached deep inside her jacket pocket to feel for hers, then turned the device on, her knee bobbling anxiously. When the screen finally came to life, it told her how late she was—7:02. She was supposed to meet Savannah at her mom's house at six thirty so they could drive to Austin together for their seven-o'clock dinner reservation.

Chaynie saw the bubbles of texts Savannah had already left her—*Where are you? Did I get the time wrong? Waiting at your house*—and hastily texted her back.

SO sorry. I'm on my way. Will explain later.

Chaynie lowered her phone and noticed Greg's confusion. He stood up with a frown while Buddy happily moved on to lick Chaynie's discarded plate.

"I didn't know it was so late," she said. "I need to be somewhere. I needed to be somewhere thirty minutes ago, actually. Plans with Savannah." She picked up the quilt and placed it on the chair.

"Don't worry about that. I'll get it," Greg said.

He walked her back into the house, where his parents were placing carefully wrapped items into boxes in the living room.

"I need to rush out," Chaynie explained. "I'm late for something. The time got away from me. Thank you for the meal, the cobbler, for everything. This has been such a lovely day."

Margie's warmth put her at ease. "You're very welcome. We were glad to have you join us. We'll do it again. Soon."

Chaynie waved a final goodbye then headed out the front door with Greg.

"Drive safe, okay?" he urged from the porch as she tapped down the stairs. "You seem a little… stressed out."

She turned to face him. "Sorry. I hate leaving in such a rush."

"You don't have to be sorry." Greg smiled through the shadows cast by the porch light. "I had a good time."

"So did I."

She walked briskly to her car and got in, clicking her seat belt then starting the engine. She could see Greg lingering, hands in his jeans pockets, watching her leave. As she pulled away from the ranch house, an uncomfortable thought presented itself. She wondered whether her hasty departure was really about the embarrassment over being late to meet Savannah, or whether it was more about escaping a certain unexpected pang.

Chapter Sixteen

"You're doing that thing you do," Savannah noted.

Chaynie peered across the restaurant table at her friend. "What thing?"

"That thing when you're distracted. You zone out of the conversation, and your eyes go sort of glassy. Your mind is in another place."

Chaynie winced. "Sorry."

"And stop apologizing. That's, like, the fourteenth sorry I've gotten since you rushed over to your mom's house. You just lost track of time and had your phone off. You explained it already, so quit feeling bad. And, hey, we still made it to Portofino's, and they had a table ready for us."

"I can't help it. You know how I hate to be late for anything, especially when I've committed to it. Plus, this is your big celebration."

"*Our* big celebration," Savannah corrected. "Of both our accomplishments. But I have to say, your appetite doesn't seem very celebratory. You've hardly touched your manicotti. I thought it was your favorite."

Chaynie looked down at her plate, at the bite that had been sitting on her fork for too long. She couldn't tell Savannah she was still bulging from the hearty meal Mrs. Peterson had made—it would be too awkward to explain what she was doing at the ranch in the first place. Because she wasn't actually sure.

At first, Greg had innocently wanted to show her the horses, but then the day had shifted into something else, all on its own. No matter how she framed it, Chaynie knew Savannah would only interpret the day at the ranch as a date. *Horseback riding, a family meal, dessert by the fire outside, how else could it seem?* Still, nothing *had* actually happened between Chaynie and Greg. She shouldn't have a guilty conscience.

"No, the manicotti's delicious. You're right. I'm just distracted. Work stuff."

"Your Under the Stars night. Don't worry. You've put so much work into it already, all the planning and details. If you build it..."

"They will come?" Chaynie snickered. "Let's hope so. This could be either a roaring success or a raging failure."

"Well, I predict success." Savannah waved her empty fork to punctuate the air then speared a tortellini.

Chaynie tried to relax and remember why she was there, at that lovely Italian restaurant in Austin, with its crisp white linens, fancy silverware, and exquisite décor. She was celebrating with her best friend. Chaynie needed to be there, in the moment. Her mind *had* been elsewhere, but she had the power to change it, to nudge her thoughts back to the present. The here and now was what mattered most.

Chaynie raised her wine glass and waited for Savannah to join her. "To both our future successes."

"Now *that's* more like it!" Savannah clinked her glass against Chaynie's.

BY THE TIME SHE CRAWLED into bed at midnight, exhausted, Chaynie was entirely convinced that the flutter over Greg wasn't a flutter at all. She had mistaken it for something else, probably related to her digestion. Maybe it was the fried chicken, or maybe it was the euphoria of a horse ride, followed by a relaxing dinner, followed by a crackling fireside. *That* was the feeling she'd actually had—an emotional warmth, an easy comfort. Not a romantic pang of any sort.

Her eyes had happened to focus on Greg when that warm sensation hit, which explained why she'd mistakenly associated it with him.

Satisfied, she burrowed deep inside her sheets and pulled the flannel blanket up to her chin, hoping to let sleep carry her away.

CHAYNIE AND HER MOTHER walked out of Morgan's Grove's oldest, most-attended church and into a crisp, cold day. The sky was a turquoise blue, and birds chirped overhead in the bare trees.

Pastor Dan, a gregarious Sam Elliott lookalike, always greeted the parting churchgoers outside the exit with handshakes and well wishes for the week ahead. Chaynie released his hand with a smile, reminded that the whole church experience always gave her a sense of renewal, of hope and refreshment, no matter what was going on in her life. The reverent music and encouraging scriptures seemed to plant her feet more firmly, to shape her days with more order and perspective. She'd needed it today in particular, knowing she would face her most hectic week since she'd moved back to Morgan's Grove. Only a few more days remained until the big Valentine's event, and it all fell solidly upon her shoulders.

"There you are!" Doris huffed out as she leaned on her cane, touching Chaynie's arm with her free hand. "I was hoping to catch you. Can we talk?"

"Of course."

Doris pulled Chaynie aside, letting the stream of worshippers continue their exit behind them.

"Is anything wrong?" Chaynie asked as they settled on a bench nearby. The strong ache in her thighs from the horse ride was still present as she sat down.

"No, no. The opposite." Doris shifted her cane to her other hand. She hunched toward Chaynie with a whisper. "Did you realize it's Mary's birthday this coming week? Her *seventieth*?"

Chaynie's eyes widened. "I had no idea!"

"She let it slip this morning during Bible study. She thought nobody else heard, but I did." She stared into Chaynie's face with a mischievous grin that extended up to the crinkles around her eyes. "I think we should celebrate, throw a surprise party."

"Do you know the date?"

"Tuesday."

"Day after tomorrow?" Chaynie pondered for a moment. *A lovely idea on the surface, but how much extra work will that mean?* Her plate was already so full.

"The date falls on our final book club meeting, the anniversary party! We have cake and decorations ready to go. We'll turn it into a double celebration—add an extra birthday cake, some birthday balloons, voilà! Mary's already invited, so we won't have to concoct a lie to coax her there. We could quietly spread the word and add a few more folks to the list, have them bring cards or presents for her. It shouldn't require much planning."

Music to my ears.

"I've already spoken to Lucille and a couple of the other ladies I've seen at church, but I wanted to get your opinion."

Chaynie clutched Doris's hand. "I think it's a sweet idea. Mary will love it. Count me in."

"Wonderful!"

"The only hiccup could be the timing. Knowing Mary, she'll arrive at your anniversary party early, trying to help out. No chance for people to pop up and tell her 'Surprise!' at the right moment."

"Mm. Good point. Would you be willing to distract her, keep her away until on-the-dot meeting time? I can get everyone ready and shushed before then."

"That shouldn't be a problem."

And just like that, the party was set.

Chaynie's phone vibrated in her coat pocket, so she and Doris said their goodbyes and parted ways. She checked the screen to see a new email from the University of Virginia. When she clicked it open, the email appeared to be the typical form letter, a polite "thanks, but no thanks" that she had become very familiar with in recent weeks. She almost swiped the email to the trash, but a phrase in the second sentence caught her attention. ... *and your application has moved forward...*

Not a rejection. A step in the opposite direction. Chaynie's heart lifted. Finally, some good news after all those weeks of waiting around. She scanned the email for more information—her application had moved on to the referral stage of the hiring process. That was promising.

Even as she clicked to save the email, she knew that it was still early. There were certainly no guarantees for a successful outcome.

WHEN TUESDAY MORNING arrived, Chaynie requested a last-minute meeting with Mary to go over some details about the Valentine's event. None of them were pertinent—in fact, some of them weren't even issues at all, only made-up excuses to keep Mary occupied until her surprise party began.

Mary peered at her watch and grimaced. "We can't be late for the party," she reminded Chaynie from across the desk. "I was hoping to be there early to help with the preparations."

"I offered to help Doris, but she shooed me away. I think she wants to handle things herself. Don't worry. I only have a couple more points to go over. We'll make it in plenty of time." Chaynie had to elongate the points, fill up the time, hoping Mary wouldn't notice the minutes ticking by.

With three minutes to spare, Mary stood up and smoothed her skirt. "The rest can wait, I think. We should head to the conference room."

It was impossible to stop her, so Chaynie tried a different tactic, gathering her materials in slow motion, pretending she'd misplaced her books.

"I'll meet you there," Mary stated, heading toward the door.

Having failed at her task, Chaynie prayed that Doris's watch was running fast and maybe, just maybe, the group was prepared to issue the surprise a minute or two earlier than planned.

She joined Mary as she exited the office and headed two doors down to the conference room. Thankfully, Doris had thought ahead and closed the blinds, hiding their efforts. As they approached the door, Chaynie strained her ears for any signs of unpreparedness—chattering or shushing inside the room—but all she heard was silence.

"A closed door, how odd," Mary mumbled. "Did I get the date wrong? It *is* Tuesday, isn't it?"

"It is." Chaynie suppressed a giggle.

Mary placed her hand on the knob and twisted it as Chaynie held her breath. When Mary opened the door, a spirited wave of "Happy Birthday!" and "Surprise!" greeted her.

She stepped back in surprise, clasping her hands, her mouth agape. She scanned the room, her eyes wide. "What is this? What have you all done?"

Chaynie scanned the room, too, and noticed Sam, Britney, Mary's oldest daughter, and Greg as extra guests.

"A little birdie told us you had a birthday today," Lucille confessed from the corner of the room as Mary entered hesitantly with Chaynie following.

"And we decided to throw you a party," Doris added. "We hope you don't mind."

"Why on earth would I mind? Look at all you've done." Mary locked eyes with Doris. "Thank you, my friend." They hugged as the rest of the guests applauded.

From across the room, Chaynie watched Greg's tall frame in the corner as he clapped too. She hadn't expected to see him. *But of course he was included*, she thought. *Mary's his godmother.*

Greg had texted Chaynie a couple of times on Sunday afternoon. She'd ignored the first one then answered the second one with an excuse about being distracted by work and needing to return some calls. It was true—she *was* distracted with the upcoming Valentine's event, with the sequel to the children's book, and with a possible job opportunity in Virginia—ironically, she remembered later, that was Greg's alma mater.

When Greg's gaze found her across the conference room and they locked eyes, Chaynie felt it return, *the pang*. It was undeniable and even more distinct. Her excuses no longer worked—there was no horse ride, no cozy fireside to explain it away. Greg was merely standing in a corner across the room, looking over at her, and that alone had been enough to produce the warm sensation again.

Chaynie quickly busied herself with helping the ladies cut the cake, distribute plates, and pour sweet tea into paper cups. Chaynie was grateful to have a job to do. It brought her into the raucous, energetic party without having to be a real guest. She could maneuver around everyone, serving, helping, offering things, without having to participate fully.

"Hey," Greg said a few minutes later. He had moved in behind her as she added more paper napkins to the thinning stack.

"Oh. Hi." When she paused, they locked eyes again.

"My mom said to thank you... for the candle."

Yesterday, Chaynie had left work to sneak off to the ranch and hand Mrs. Peterson a scented candle and thank-you card. She had been invited inside but had explained that she was on a quick break and couldn't stay. She'd apologized to Mrs. Peterson for leaving so abruptly the other night.

"I'm glad she liked it," Chaynie told Greg. "I felt bad for running off the way I did. I'm sure I looked completely frazzled."

"Naw, Mama understood. Some things can't be helped."

So true, Chaynie thought and returned to her napkins.

"Are you the one who arranged all this?" Mary appeared at Chaynie's side.

"I wish I could take the credit, but it was Doris's idea," she admitted.

"Well, thanks just the same. It's lovely."

Greg had stepped back to give Mary room as she chattered on, and Chaynie noticed him tapping on his phone then slipping toward the door to leave. She found herself able to breathe again.

"WELL, THIS IS AN UNEXPECTED treat on a Friday afternoon!" Chaynie's mom brightened at the sight of her daughter entering her art classroom with a hesitant knock.

"I thought you might be in the mood for burgers." Chaynie scoped out the room to make sure she wasn't interrupting a student conference or class. She had attempted to coordinate her visit with her mother's lunch hour.

"It smells delicious. Better than the droopy leftover sandwich waiting for me in the lounge down the hall. Come. Sit."

Chaynie's mother cleared art supplies from a stiff wooden chair and shifted the seat closer to her desk.

The art room always remained in a state of organized chaos—empty easels standing at various angles in the center of the room, a stack of empty canvases waiting to be filled, baskets of art supplies gracing an entire bookshelf on one wall, an ongoing mural waiting on the opposite wall, scattered paint supplies and a well-used dust cloth lying wrinkled on the floor below. Then there was her mother's desk, which never contained an empty space. Stacked with paperwork and supplies and sticky note reminders, it was her mother's primary workspace. No matter how often she cleared and organized it, the desk always seemed permanently cluttered.

When Chaynie took her seat, her mother stacked papers on top of papers to make room for the bag of hamburgers on her desk.

"I feel like I haven't seen you all week." Her mother removed a yellow-paper-wrapped burger from the bag and handed it to Chaynie. "Even though we live together!"

"That's why I came. I wanted to catch up. Things have been crazy with the Valentine's event hovering. It's only four days away! I have no time to breathe."

Her mother nodded sympathetically and chewed on a french fry. "I can relate. When finals roll around, there is *so* much work to be done but not nearly enough time to complete it. I lose track of all time and meet myself coming and going. It suddenly becomes a two-person job, but I'm only one person!"

"Exactly." Chaynie folded the wrapper down to expose the top half of her burger. It bulged with cheese and onions and ketchup, her favorite combination. "So, I meant to tell you a couple of days ago... I got an email from the University of Virginia."

"About a job?" Her mother's eyes widened.

"Well, it's still far from being a yes, but it's not a no." She explained what the email said about the process and what to expect next.

"Honey, that's great. Fingers crossed."

Chaynie knew her mother meant it with her whole heart. But she also knew a part of her was sad at the thought of Chaynie leaving Morgan's Grove, because that was exactly how Chaynie felt too. Conflicted.

"So, tell me about your week." Chaynie took a sip of her soda.

"Not much to tell." Her mother shrugged and took another fry. "Student presentations, then some assessments and a couple of faculty meetings. But a break is coming soon, I hope. Things slow down during Valentine's week. Speaking of..."

Chaynie assumed her mother was going to inquire about the lawn event, how things were coming along. Instead, she said, "Mitch asked me to go to your Night Under the Stars."

"Did he?" Chaynie tempered her surprise, trying to gauge her mother's feelings first. "What did you say?"

"Well, he did it in a nonchalant, 'If you're going and I'm going, why don't we sit together?' sort of way. So, it's not a date or anything, which is good. Just two friends, sitting on the same blanket, maybe sharing some popcorn."

"That sounds nice. It's noncommittal and easygoing."

"So I told him yes, that I'd bring the blanket. He said he'd pay for the popcorn."

"Fair enough."

"Honey, I think it's a great idea, this event on the lawn. For everyone. For people like me, and like Mitch. I don't know what we are or if we'll ever become anything, but the thought of either staying at home on Valentine's, all alone, or being pressured to go to a restaurant with a man other than your father..." She stopped short, blinking away tears.

"Oh, Mom." Chaynie clutched her mother's hand. "I know what you mean."

Chaynie's mother sniffed. "So, anyway, this event of yours is the absolute perfect idea. I won't feel awkward with Mitch, and I won't be alone. It's the best of both worlds, something to look forward to this year."

Chaynie needed to hear that because during a hectic week of phone calls and to-do lists and fires to put out, she was reminded—again—of how special the event could potentially be to people, to the whole community. And that purpose would drive Chaynie through the rest of the coming days, up to the night of the event. It *wasn't* just a one-time promotion for the library. It was a chance for everyone to come together and be united, no matter their couple status. It could be a time for lonely people to stop feeling alone and for the Valentine's stigma to be broken—well, at least fractured a little.

CHAYNIE SHOOK TWO ASPIRIN into her palm and reached for the bottled water on her desk. She should've taken the medicine two hours ago, when the hint of a headache had first made its presence known. Then it wouldn't have developed into throbbing pain.

After chasing down the pills with two gulps of water, Chaynie capped the bottle and made a decision. The remaining items on her to-do list could be pushed to tomorrow morning, a Saturday, when she could work from home. At the moment, she was "good for nothing," as her father would often say after a long workday of his own, when all he wanted to do was lie around on the sofa and flip TV channels mindlessly. Add in a crackling fire, some fuzzy slippers, and a hot cocoa, and that image sounded like heaven to Chaynie.

Gathering her coat and laptop, she flicked off the light and closed her office door to hear a tapping sound coming from the alcove. As she moved closer and paused, she saw a large sheet covering the alcove's entire entrance, hiding all the progress inside. The drifting of soft indie guitar told her it was Greg behind the sheet, tapping away.

Normally, she would have sent Greg a playful text—*I'm on the other side! Come talk to me!* A minute later, he would have tipped back the sheet and grinned at her. They would have talked for a while about work, about how his office was coming along, or about nothing at all. He might have offered to walk her home, and she would've politely declined, not wanting to distract him from the alcove. She would have walked out the library door with a hint of a smile, having finished her day seeing his kind, handsome face.

Instead, Chaynie moved toward the staircase to exit the building and leave the tapping behind. When she grasped the library's front door handle, she felt hollow and unsatisfied, craving those lengthy talks she and Greg used to have. They hadn't even spoken since Mary's party, except for a brief text where he had sent a question about Pete. Momentum had been lost somehow in their friendship over the last few days. *Does Greg sense it too?*

Chaynie's hefty workload had become her legitimate distraction all week. That was the excuse she'd told herself and others, but it was more than that with Greg. Her awkward exit at the ranch followed by the university's email had forced Chaynie to peer again toward her future—a future which might not include the library or Morgan's Grove or her mother or Savannah. Or Greg. As she'd learned from past relationships, she had no reason to continue to nurture something that might soon disappear. Better to let it fade away on its own. It would be less painful when it came time for goodbyes.

Chapter Seventeen

"So, if you could arrive at five thirty, that would give us enough time to set up and find the best spot for you," Chaynie confirmed through the phone.

"That works for me," Amy agreed cheerfully.

Amy Howard was a soon-to-be graduate of UT whom Chaynie had contacted through the university's sign language department. It had occurred to her, on the walk to work that morning, that at least two Morgan's Grove residents might need the aid of an interpreter during the movie on the lawn. Even if they didn't attend, it would be wise of Chaynie to have Amy on standby in case an interpreter was needed.

"Great! Then it's all set. I'll see you tomorrow," Chaynie said. "Sorry again for the ridiculously short notice."

"It's no trouble. This will be great practice for me. I can even log some volunteer hours for this class I'm taking."

As they ended the call, Chaynie hoped Amy's signing would be as enthusiastic and bubbly as her personality over the phone.

"Next on the agenda..." Chaynie whispered aloud, taking another sip of coffee before moving on to her tablet. She had been the first person to enter the library that morning, eager to get started on her tasks for the day. Checking off items one by one was the only way to remove the stress of Valentine's Day—tomorrow.

Chaynie had already dealt with a major potential problem upon arriving at the office. Stan had called to say that the tenor in their quartet was sick with the flu. Rather than cancel, Stan had already contacted another singer friend of his who could hopefully step right in, do a couple of rehearsals, and be ready for the big night. Stan was just waiting on the call to see if the possible substitute would return his voicemail. Chaynie's first thought after hanging up with Stan was about those new flyers, which promised the quartet as a special addition to the Valentine's night. She couldn't bear having to tell the attendees that the flyer had been wrong and the quartet was a no-show.

Chaynie breathed deeply, preparing to check on her next major crisis, the weather. It had rained all day yesterday and into the night with some drizzle accompanying Chaynie on her walk to work that morning. She clicked on the local weather website, praying the forecast had changed in her favor since she'd last checked it a couple of hours ago, but things didn't look any more promising. Forty percent chance of rain, decreasing to twenty percent tomorrow, the big day. Chaynie had to face it—the Valentine's event might have to take place *inside* the library. She would need to speak with Greg about his contingency plan.

Chaynie's office phone rang, jarring her thoughts. Hardly anyone contacted her by landline anymore. Most people used her cell number.

"What now?" she mumbled before picking up the receiver. "This is Chaynie Mayfield."

"Chaynie! Gail Waters here."

Waters. Chaynie's mind went blank for a split second until she placed the name in the right context. Dr. Waters, her beloved professor from UT. Chaynie hadn't spoken to her in ages, years in fact.

"Dr. Waters, how nice to hear from you!"

"It's been a long time. How have you been?"

"I've been well." Chaynie ran through the quick summary of her life since her master's graduation—working in Austin at a couple of libraries as an assistant, then moving back to Morgan's Grove for her current position.

"Well, I'll get right to the point," Dr. Waters said. "I got a call a few minutes ago from the library director at the University of Virginia."

Chaynie took in a quick breath. Suddenly, the call made perfect sense. She'd totally forgotten that she had used Dr. Waters' name, one of a long list, as a reference on all her applications. So, the process *had* gotten that far after all.

"I gave you a glowing referral," Dr. Waters assured her. "And you won't believe this, but as I was speaking with the director, I realized we knew each other. We both attended UT back in the eighties. In fact, she lived across the hall from me at the dorm!"

"Small world!"

"Indeed. We spent some time catching up, but then we moved the focus back to you. And I have it on good authority that you'll be receiving a call very soon for an interview."

Chaynie's heart jumped, but she couldn't tell if it was from elation or from fear. "Really?"

"Really. I'm calling to give you a heads-up. Between you and me, I think you're a shoo-in for the position."

"Well, thank you so much. That's just... I don't know what to say."

"You deserve it. You were one of the most diligent students I ever had, and Virginia would be lucky to have you. I wish you all the best."

Chaynie ended the call after another thank-you, set down the receiver, and stared at the gray stapler on her desk.

An interview. In Virginia. She would obviously have to travel there—or perhaps a video conference would suffice. She hadn't prepared herself for *this* stage of the process. Up until then, getting a job outside Morgan's Grove had been some wispy fantasy of someday. But it was looking more and more like someday could be someday soon.

RAIN PATTERED ON CHAYNIE'S umbrella, creating a rhythm that would normally be soothing, but that day, the sound was nothing short of ominous. Those innocent raindrops had the power to change a long-awaited Valentine's Day, a hundred hours of preparation and work and crossed fingers behind it. But as the day wore on, she didn't have much hope left. Even if the rain decided to stop altogether by the afternoon, there was still the strong possibility that the lawn would be too soaked to enjoy the movie on the lawn tomorrow night. *Squish*, Chaynie heard in her head, picturing the scene of chair legs sinking down into the mud or damp blankets soaking people's clothing straight through.

She paused in front of the deli behind the library, hoping for a quick takeout of a sandwich and soup, comfort food that she could eat at her desk before launching into the rest of her busy day.

Just as she ducked underneath the green-and-white-striped awning and folded up her dripping umbrella, Chaynie's cell rang inside her pocket. She pulled out the phone and saw Savannah's name on the screen.

"Hey." She stepped aside under the awning to give room to the soaked, hunched-over couple opening the deli door beside her.

"I've done something," Savannah whispered through the phone.

Savannah's tendency, since childhood, was to be melodramatic whenever she announced a piece of news. So, instead of instantly assuming Savannah had committed some high crime, Chaynie half-smiled and asked, "Something good or bad?"

"I can't tell yet."

Chaynie shook her head and chuckled. "Where are you?"

"At school. Lunch break. This is the first chance I've had to phone you."

"Well, go on. Spit it out," she urged.

"Okay. So, this morning I got a sub during study hall and drove to Greg's parents' ranch. I needed to bring them some paperwork for the sale, and Greg happened to be there."

Chaynie raised her eyebrows, unsure of where the story was going.

"Anyway, so Greg and I were both leaving at the same time, after his parents signed the documents, and as I was standing on the porch with him, making chitchat, I got bold."

"What do you mean?" Chaynie watched Bicycle Bob roll past her with a wet wave.

"I asked him to the Valentine's movie night! Sort of. I asked if he was going, and he said yes. I told him I was going, too, and that if he needed to share a blanket, I had one available."

That *was* bold. Even though it was no surprise that Savannah was attracted to Greg, Savannah had spent very little time with Greg overall. They barely knew each other. In fact, Savannah hadn't brought his name up to Chaynie at all in the last two weeks, so Chaynie had assumed she'd given up or lost interest—or moved on to Lucas, instead. Apparently not.

"What did Greg say?"

"He gave me a polite non-answer. He said that he'd be working most of the night, setting up early, helping out with the event, checking on the projector and such, but that if he had a break, he *might* take me up on it. That's still good, right? A 'might'?"

"So, it wasn't a no."

"Exactly. It wasn't a no."

Chaynie could hear the hope inside her best friend's voice and was suddenly grateful that she was hearing the news over the phone and not in person. Because she wasn't entirely confident that her facial expression could've matched Savannah's enthusiasm.

"Listen, sorry, I'm late to pick up a deli order. Can we talk more about this tonight?"

"Sure! I just had to tell you the news. The maybe-good news."

Chaynie ended the call then let out an audible sigh. In truth, she hadn't even placed her deli order yet. She'd planned to go inside and order in person after seeing the daily soup specials. But if she had stayed on the line any longer, Savannah would've seen right through her, even over the phone, and start asking questions—"Why aren't you happier about this? Do you think I made a mistake, asking him? Maybe he's not interested in me?"—questions Chaynie wasn't sure she could truthfully answer.

Suddenly, Chaynie craved the quiet of her office. She needed some silence to process the two recent calls from Dr. Waters and from Savannah, which had each produced unexpected developments on two fronts: a possible job and a possible relationship. Well, if she could call the quick, sporadic conversations between Greg and Savannah a relationship. But if things moved forward with Virginia and Chaynie ended up leaving Morgan's Grove and disappearing from the equation, she had no idea what might happen between Savannah and Greg in her absence. Anything was possible.

After rushing through the lunch line then scarfing down her sandwich and soup at the office, Chaynie stared hard at the rain still beating relentlessly on the window. She stood from her seat, drew out her phone, and texted Greg. He was the only one to speak with about moving the event indoors tomorrow night, if it still came to that.

Still raining. Looks like we might have to move the projector inside tomorrow? Need your input.

She sent the text and waited for his reply. Greg was usually prompt, so she wouldn't have to wait long. Chaynie folded her arms across her chest and focused on the town square below, a beautiful image of rain-glossed sidewalks, dark-gray skies, streetlights tricked into thinking it was evening and casting their eerie glow on raindrops falling in perfect sequence. It was hard to be upset with Mother Nature when she presented such a serene and peaceful scene.

A tap at her office door made Chaynie whirl around.

Greg poked his head in then widened the door. "Got your text."

Chaynie moved from the window and met him in the center of the room.

"They've been pretty formal lately," Greg noted.

"What have?" Chaynie scrunched her eyebrows.

"Your texts." He turned his screen to view it. "'... still raining, need your input...' Matter-of-fact. Businesslike."

Greg lowered his phone, shook his head, then locked eyes with her. "Chaynie, have I done something? We've barely spoken in days, and whenever we do, it's this." He raised the phone again. "You keep on... you avoid my texts, saying you're distracted... you're busy, but I don't buy it. There's gotta be another reason." He ran a hand through his dark hair and diverted his stare toward her desk.

Chaynie had never seen him agitated, emotional.

Greg returned his gaze, his blue eyes settling on her. "I'm not sure what's changed or why it happened, but there's a distance with us. Tell me I'm not crazy. Why are you backing away?"

She couldn't hide behind texts or excuses anymore. Chaynie reached for a nearby chair and plunked down. Greg took the one beside her, and their knees touched as he sat.

This is Greg, she reminded herself. *I* have *treated him like a stranger lately, blowing him off, ignoring him. He deserves better than that. He deserves the truth.*

"I have been distant. But what I told you *is* true—I have been insanely busy. There've been all these glitches and problems with the Valentine's event. The weather, for one thing, and also the tenor in the barbershop quartet fell sick with the flu, and Stan's trying to find a replacement."

"Why didn't you tell me?"

"I'm not proud of it, but I tend to shut people out sometimes when I feel overwhelmed. I guess I need to handle it myself, not lean on anyone. Maybe I think I'm being weak if I ask for help."

Greg nodded as though he understood.

"But it's more than just the Valentine's event," she confessed. "You were right. I have been backing away from you, from Morgan's Grove, even from my mom."

"Why?"

"Remember when I told you a few weeks ago that I'd sent applications to other libraries?"

"Yeah."

"Well, one of them might actually pan out. A week ago, I got an email that my application was being processed. And this morning, I got a call from my former UT professor. She's been contacted for a referral. She says an interview is imminent and that I have a good chance of getting the job."

"Oh."

Chaynie had expected more than just "Oh." At the least, an obligatory "Congratulations." But Greg's expression still held the same look of confusion.

"The position is at the University of Virginia," she continued.

At that, he raised his eyebrows slightly. "My alma mater."

"I haven't told anyone yet about the professor's call, not even my mom. I don't know if this will work out or not. I'm sure they have dozens of applicants more qualified than I am, but there's a chance—"

"That you might be leaving."

"And maybe, without realizing it, I've been mentally preparing myself. You know, slowly detaching?"

"I get it," Greg said. "But this is what you wanted, right? A job as head librarian in a big university?"

"Yes, it was. I mean *is*. This was always my plan. Eventually."

"I'm glad you told me. I was starting to think you were avoiding me on purpose." Greg stood up and rubbed his hands together. "Listen, I'd better let you get back to work, but lean on me if you need to. You shouldn't have to handle this event—or anything else—alone."

Chaynie stood, too, and placed a hand on Greg's arm. "I'm sorry things got weird with us. I didn't mean for them to." Chaynie removed her hand and folded her arms again.

"I understand. Listen, I've got a quick meeting with the guys in a minute," Greg added. "The ceiling restoration begins on the north side the day after tomorrow, and there's still prep work to do. But I'll be free later this afternoon to fill in the gaps, help you out with the odd jobs, whatever you need. And about the rain, no worries. If we're forced inside, we'll make the best of it. Pete and I have already talked about our options. I called him this morning."

That's so Greg, Chaynie thought, *anticipating troubles before they arise, finding a calm way around them, taking care of things before I even have to ask.*

"Thanks. For everything. I mean it, Greg. These last few weeks have been... special."

"Yeah. They have."

With that, Greg disappeared behind the door, leaving Chaynie alone with her thoughts, which seemed even more muddled than before Greg had entered the room.

"DID YOU WANT THESE candles wrapped in tissue?" Mary asked.

Chaynie could smell their strong vanilla scent from a few feet away. "Yes. There should be some extra tissue paper in that bag." She pointed beside Mary.

They stood together at the circulation desk, finishing up what should have been Britney's duties—sorting through the door prizes and making sure they were organized, catalogued, and wrapped in appealing colors and textures. Britney had phoned in sick that morning with a migraine.

Chaynie hadn't expected to be so relaxed on the day before the big event, especially after the hectic morning she'd experienced. But surprisingly, after her cathartic talk with Greg, nearly everything else had fallen into place. Chaynie had spent the rest of the afternoon touching base with all the participants, from the food vendors around town to Pete at his movie warehouse to the two high school students who'd agreed to help run the popcorn and cotton candy machines and, finally, to Stan, who'd confirmed that the quartet with their substitute member would indeed be ready to perform.

Mary reached for the bag, but her hand froze in midair. "Look at that," she whispered.

"Look at what?" Chaynie continued tying the pink ribbon on her package, only half-listening.

"Here! This!"

Chaynie shifted her attention to Mary, who was pointing toward an empty space on the counter.

Confused, Chaynie squinted. "I don't see—" Then she realized what Mary was pointing toward. The space wasn't empty. It was reflecting something. Chaynie watched the sunlight streaming down through the stained glass window.

"It can't be." Until that moment, Chaynie had given up all hope of seeing even a single ray of sunshine. She abandoned her post and rushed outside through the library's front door to the lawn, where the long shadows and bright sky confirmed it. The rain clouds had finally taken their leave.

Mary had followed her outside, and together, they looked skyward and saw a peerless blue above with only a few wisps of clouds remaining. The sun had emerged.

Chaynie found her phone and refreshed the forecast, which verified her hopes for sunny skies through tomorrow.

"Does this mean what I think it means?" Mary asked.

"I don't want to get my hopes too high, but yes. I'm thinking our Under the Stars night can happen on the lawn after all."

"I think you're right," someone said from behind.

Chaynie twisted her neck to see Greg, head tilted, soaking up the sun.

"You did this, I'm sure," Chaynie teased.

"What? Made the clouds melt away and the sun beat down? Sure, I'll take credit for that, if you want me to."

"You waited long enough to make it happen," Mary chided then returned to the library and her candles.

"What about the lawn?" Chaynie wondered. "Even with the sun coming out, the grass could still be too damp for tomorrow."

"Sam made the suggestion of tarps. He's got access to some huge ones, and we could lay them out tomorrow afternoon if we need them. Blankets and chairs would go on top, problem solved."

"This is really happening, all of it." Chaynie felt the original surge of excitement from when she and Greg had brainstormed the idea weeks before.

"Yep. And now we can finally string the lights. Sam and I were waiting on the weather."

"They're up in storage," Chaynie confirmed. "I'll show you."

She led Greg upstairs to the storage closet then rummaged around to find the large bulbs of string lights she'd ordered from an online party company. When she and Savannah had left the restaurant in Austin the week before, Chaynie had noticed the gorgeous bulbs strung outside, tree to tree, and had a sudden vision of them for the library lawn—a soft way to light the entire venue—festive, cheerful, and even a bit romantic.

Chaynie had decided to go online and purchase plenty of lights, the best quality, presuming the lawn event would become an annual one if Valentine's Day went well. She had even considered pitching Mary some sort of "Arts on the Lawn" idea involving poetry readings or music events, craft festivals or more movie nights, each hosted by the library. Of course, Chaynie might not *be* in Morgan's Grove to facilitate those events in the long term.

"Here they are!" Chaynie found the three plastic-wrapped packages on a top shelf and reached for them.

She was tall but not *that* tall, and it took Greg's extra few inches of height to lean in behind her and grab them. She helped lower them down and clutched one of the packages to her chest as Greg took two in his arms.

"Tight space in here." The painted children's chairs were still taking up most of the floor space, leaving very little room for anything else, including people in search of lights. She and Greg stood face-to-face, and she could feel his minty breath on her cheeks.

"Yeah." He smiled awkwardly then started for the door as Chaynie followed.

BY THE DAY'S END, CHAYNIE had finished everything on her list and actually left the library earlier than usual. She needed a long, hot bath and a good night's sleep.

When Chaynie pushed open the door to her mom's house, a delicious scent hit her senses. At first, she couldn't place it, but it was clear that her mother had been cooking. It wasn't takeout or a fast, thrown-together pasta meal. This food was delicate and rich and slow cooked.

Roast beef, Chaynie realized. Her favorite.

Max stretched on the living room floor as Chaynie entered, removing her light jacket and setting down her bag.

"Hey, boy! How was your day?"

He responded with a meow and followed her into the kitchen, where her mother stood ladling golden potatoes into a ceramic bowl.

"This smells incredible!" Chaynie moved closer and kissed her mother's cheek. "What made you go to all this trouble?"

Her mother paused her ladling to look her daughter in the eye. "You! I know how hard you've worked on this Valentine's project, and I thought you deserved a hearty meal. I stole away from school at lunchtime to pop the roast into the oven so it could be ready in time. I have all your favorites—Yukon Gold potatoes, carrots, green beans—and the rolls are in the oven."

On cue, the oven timer beeped, and Chaynie stepped in to retrieve them with a nearby oven mitt.

"You don't know how much I needed some comfort food. Thank you! This will put me right to sleep."

"Well, good. Because sleep is what you need after all these weeks. How's the progress coming along at the library?"

Chaynie brought the rolls to the counter and filled her mother in on all the bustling activity of the day, including the positive change in the weather.

"I'm so glad, honey. Sounds like everything will be perfect for the big day."

"Let's hope so!"

It only took a few minutes for Chaynie to set the dining table and a couple of minutes for the plates to be piled high with steaming mounds of gravy-coated beef, golden round potatoes, dark green beans, and buttered rolls. The roast was every bit as delicious as it had smelled earlier. The meat fell apart when Chaynie's fork touched it then melted in her mouth the moment it hit her tongue.

She and her mother chatted about work in between bites, and before long, it was time for dessert—a butterscotch pie Chaynie's mother presented at the end of the meal.

"When did you have time for this?" Chaynie wondered.

"Oh, it was easy to whip up after school. Then it chilled in the fridge while we ate the meal."

Her mother cut slices and handed a plate over to Chaynie. Settling into her chair again, her mother asked how things were going with Greg.

"Where did that come from?" Chaynie wondered.

"Curiosity. You haven't brought him up lately, so I've stayed quiet. But two weekends ago, you darted out of this house on a mysterious mission to see him—boots required, if I recall—and you were gone all day! Next thing I knew, Savannah was knocking at the door, saying she was expecting you for dinner, and I didn't know where you were or what to tell her. Even afterward, you never explained. Were you with Greg all that time?"

Chaynie set her fork down then leaned back in her chair. She was surprised her mother hadn't brought up the topic well before then. "Yeah, Greg had saddled up his horses that day, and we went for this long ride. His parents' ranch, where he grew up, is beautiful. It has all these hills and valleys and streams." She could picture it all again in her mind's eye. "And then his mom insisted on my staying for dinner. I couldn't say no. And after that, it was on to dessert, and before I knew it, I was late to meet Savannah."

Her mother set down her fork too. "You know what that sounds like."

"A date. But it wasn't."

"Would that be so bad, a date with Greg?"

"I might've given you a different answer yesterday. But today? Dating him—dating *any*one—is not a good idea." Chaynie took a sip of tea then continued, wishing the entire subject could've been avoided. Tonight was about letting go of stresses, not inviting more. "I didn't have time this morning to text you about some news. A professor I had for a few classes at UT called and said that Virginia had contacted her about my application."

"A referral?"

"A glowing one, apparently. Dr. Waters thinks I'll be called for an interview soon."

"That's amazing news, honey."

"It's what I've wanted for so long, and it's almost right in front of me. But this job possibility colors everything, even with Greg. Especially with Greg. If I'm honest, that day at the ranch with him was magical. In fact, as we were sitting at the fireside, eating cobbler that night..." She took in a breath before saying the words aloud. "Mom, I felt something for him. Beyond friendship, beyond anything I expected. It caught me by surprise. Or maybe it didn't."

"It sounds like your heart talking. And you're starting to pay attention."

"Well, my heart has terrible timing, then. There's the potential Virginia position standing in the way. Plus, Savannah still has a crush on Greg. He's even 'maybe' agreed to sit with her during the movie tomorrow. And besides, I have *no* idea how Greg feels about me."

"Does he know about Virginia?"

"I told him today."

"What did he say?"

"He said, 'Oh.'"

"Oh? That's all?"

"That's all, like he didn't mind either way if I stayed or went. For all I know, he sees me as someone from high school he's gotten to know better, strictly as a friend. I mean, we've only really known each other for a handful of weeks."

"You've just rattled off some very legitimate reasons not to get involved with Greg. In fact, you've laid out quite a strong case against him, but what's the case *for* him?"

Chaynie tilted her head. "What do you mean?"

"You've spent all this time figuring out why it wouldn't work, but have you ever tried to figure out why it might work? Have you ever gone in the other direction—wondered what it would be like, taking that risk, opening up to him, seeing if there's something there? Even with this 'terrible' timing? You can't always sit around and wait for things to happen *to* you. You have to make them happen."

Chaynie shifted in her seat and smoothed a wrinkle on the table-cloth, not sure if she wanted to hear her mother's advice. It was too close to a truth she'd been pushing away for weeks. But there it was, at the table, on display as vividly as the half-eaten piece of pie in front of her.

"As a little girl, you were always so structured," her mother continued, her voice softening, wistful. "Completely organized and detailed. You even cataloged all your books. Remember that? You gave them reviews, put them in alphabetical order on the shelves."

Chaynie snickered. "I remember."

"You also loved to make to-do lists and check them off. I think it helped you feel safe, somehow, to keep order in your life, to stay in control. In many ways, you're still doing that—holding this rigid, logical view of the world and how it should be. This isn't a criticism. In fact, looking through that sort of lens makes you good at your job. It's in your librarian's skill set. But when it comes to the heart, I think you have to approach things a different way. From an emotional angle, not a logical one." She paused, waiting for Chaynie to make eye contact again, then added gently, "In this case, with Greg, maybe it's time to throw out your list and stop playing it safe. What's your heart *really* telling you?"

Chaynie couldn't answer because she didn't know. Maybe she wasn't ready to know. She nodded to let her mother understand she'd heard, but Chaynie needed time to let her mother's words sink in, swirl around in her head, permeate her heart—something that couldn't possibly happen over a quick dessert of butterscotch pie.

Chapter Eighteen

Chaynie pivoted in front of her full-length bedroom mirror to get the full effect of her new silky blouse, which swished along with her movements. A special occasion deserved a special outfit.

A few days ago, when she'd still had time on her hands, she had decided to go all out for Valentine's and buy a new cherry-red blouse at Mindy's boutique for the occasion. It was more expensive than she usually paid for clothes, but she wanted to feel the part—cheerful, feminine, Valentiney. She compromised by wearing jeans with the blouse so she could be comfortable, anticipating all the running around she would be doing in preparation for the day's big event.

Chaynie shook her wrists at her sides and blew out a sigh. February fourteenth, Valentine's, the day she had dreaded for so many months. But now that it was happening, now that she held such responsibility for everyone *else's* Valentine's experience because of the movie event, the focus had shifted off of her dateless state and onto other people.

Staring into the mirror, she suddenly imagined her dad, hands square on her shoulders as he stood behind her, giving her a pep talk, just like he had whenever she was about to deliver lines in a school play or participate in the spelling bee or head off for her first year at college.

You can do this. You're smart and capable. You can handle anything, and I'll be rooting for you, all the way. He gave her the same speech every single time.

Tears stung Chaynie's eyes. "I miss you, Daddy," she told the mirror. "I wish you were here."

His image faded from her mind's eye as she wiped her cheek. He *was* there, in her thoughts, in her memory, and he wouldn't want her sadness over his absence to taint the day.

It was time to go.

THE BUSY MORNING BREEZED by, as busy mornings tended to do. Chaynie had first met with Sam, Britney, and Mary to finalize their duties. Mary would stay at her post as librarian so the library would still run smoothly, like a usual business day. Britney would finish decorating the inside of the library with paper hearts and Cupids. Sam would test the hanging outside lights then set down the tarps on the lawn. And Chaynie would oversee everything, fill in the gaps, put out potential fires that might arise, answer calls, and check on the overall progress at each station.

Greg had given his renovation crew the day off but had paid a couple of them overtime to help out with the screen and any other heavy lifting Chaynie required. She had seen him around the fringes of the library and lawn, helping out with Sam, but she hadn't spoken to him yet. By midmorning, Greg found time for a break and joined her on the lawn.

He noticed her blouse. "You're looking festive in red."

"You too." She pointed toward the dark-crimson sweater he wore.

"Unintentional color pick. I grabbed the first thing I saw from the closet."

"Irony?"

"Coincidence." Greg peered toward the sky. "I guess you got your miracle—a sunny day."

Chaynie gazed upward too. "And the temperature is perfect." The highs were supposed to nudge up toward seventy degrees. "Two days ago, I was convinced we'd have to move everything indoors because of the rain. What a pain that would've been."

"But it all worked out in the end."

Chaynie hoped the same could be said for the loose ends and question marks recently popping up in her own life.

"So, I know how busy you are, but do you think we could grab a minute to talk?" Greg squinted from the sun's brightness. "There was still something I needed to say—"

A couple of sharp honks yanked their attention toward the street. Pete, driving up in his truck and trailer, slowed to a stop on the street near the library, the spot Chaynie had instructed him about yesterday on the phone.

"He's early." Chaynie looked at Greg. "I'm sorry. This is a crazy day. Do you think it can wait?"

"Yeah, it'll have to," he agreed, following her toward Pete's vehicle.

The Morgan's Grove police had given special permission to Chaynie for her vehicles to park on the street that day, which made this important part of the process that much easier.

Pete edged out of the truck and shook Greg's hand then leaned in for a brief hug from Chaynie. "The big day is here, eh?"

"It is! I'm so excited to see the main attraction, the giant screen on the library's wall."

"Well, don't worry about a thing. We'll take care of it. Won't we, Greg?" Pete slapped a hand onto Greg's shoulder.

"Absolutely. I've texted my crew, and they're headed over here. We'll get this set up in no time."

"And you're staying, right?" Chaynie asked Pete. "For the movie. Free popcorn, free snacks, whatever you want. You're our guest tonight."

"Sounds good. Better than my original plan, drinking a beer at home alone, flipping TV channels." Pete turned toward Greg. "Ready to get this thing done?"

"Let's do it."

Chaynie had planned to stick around and watch, curious about how the whole process might work, but her priorities shifted instantly with the ring of her cell phone.

Walking toward the library to avoid the clatter of the trailer doors being opened, Chaynie stared at her phone's screen. *Unknown number.* On any other day, on any other occasion, Chaynie would've ignored the call, but today, she felt pressured to answer it. It could be Valentine related.

"Miss Mayfield?" the caller asked.

"Yes?"

"I'm Mandy Wright, the secretary for Judith Banks, library director at the University of Virginia."

Heat flushed Chaynie's cheeks as she entered the library, her heart beating faster. *This is it. This is the call.*

"Dr. Banks would like to speak to you regarding your application. Do you have a moment?"

"Yes. Yes, I do."

Chaynie noticed Mary at the circulation desk, busy answering a patron's question, then made her way upstairs. She needed privacy for this call, and her office was the perfect place.

"Please hold. I'll put Dr. Banks through," Mandy told her.

That would give Chaynie enough time to dart into her office, close the door, and nudge her breathing back to a normal pace after climbing the stairs. On her way there, Chaynie's attention was pulled for a split second toward the alcove—the sheet was still covering the tree deep inside the Children's Corner. *When will it finally be finished?* she wondered as she scurried to her office.

Even receiving yesterday's heads-up from her professor, Chaynie still wasn't prepared for the call. After locking the door, she walked toward her desk, trying to shift gears from event planner at a small hometown library to potential employee of the enormous and prestigious university library. She cleared her throat, planning to slow her speech with Dr. Banks. Chaynie had a tendency to speak quickly or ramble when she got nervous.

The classical music piping through Chaynie's phone came to an abrupt halt, and a low, husky female voice asked, "Am I speaking with Miss Mayfield?"

"Yes, ma'am. This is she. Call me Chaynie."

"Chaynie. My name is Judith Banks, director of the University of Virginia's library system. I have your application and CV in front of me here. I've spoken with some of your references over the past two days, and I must say, they all give glowing recommendations of your work ethic, your library skills, and your education."

Chaynie lowered herself into her desk chair. "Thank you."

"I'd like to schedule an interview with you for the position of Teaching and Learning Librarian..."

Chaynie listened as Dr. Banks rattled off the details and duties that Chaynie was already familiar with—she had read about them online before she'd applied—and nodded, as though Dr. Banks could see her through the phone.

"How does next week sound for an interview?" Dr. Banks asked. "Wednesday afternoon, perhaps? The college could pay for the plane ride here, but you'd be responsible for the trip back to... Morgan's Grove?"

"Morgan's Grove, that's right." Chaynie's brain suddenly went fuzzy as she was handed a specific date for a specific interview. It was no longer a maybe. The interview was a sure thing—what she'd been hoping for. *Why am I not elated? Smiling? Breathless? Why am I hesitating?*

"Miss Mayfield? Are we still connected?"

"Oh. Yes, ma'am. I'm sorry. I was just flipping through my work calendar to see if Wednesday would be clear."

"And is it?"

The robotic words spilled from Chaynie's mouth almost without her consent. "Yes. It is."

"Wednesday, then. I'll email you the flight details after we hang up. We have a student intern who can meet you at the airport and drive you to the university. How does that sound?"

"Perfect. Thank you."

After they said their goodbyes, Chaynie clicked off the call and set down the phone. She didn't feel happy or frightened, giddy or nervous. She only felt numb.

A tap at the door brought her back into the moment, and she remembered she'd locked the door. She pushed out of the chair with some effort then went to see who the knock belonged to. Britney stood on the other side.

"So sorry to bother you, Chaynie, but I had a couple of last-minute questions about the door prizes and how you wanted them arranged. Do you have a sec to come look at them?"

Grateful for the distraction, Chaynie grabbed her phone from the desk. "Sure. Let's go."

Chapter Nineteen

Since the moment Britney had pulled her away from the office, Chaynie had moved from point to point, inside and out of the library, checking details, answering questions, and making significant progress on her list. In the bluster of things, she'd only snagged a quick minute to text her mom and Savannah about the interview, saying she would provide details later.

After that, Chaynie spent at least half an hour pairing up Tom and Jack, the student volunteers, with the rental guy who had delivered the popcorn and cotton candy machines. The young men seemed capable of following the man's instructions, so Chaynie left them to it and moved to the next item on her agenda.

By midafternoon, Chaynie had decided it was time for a quick break for a swig of bottled water she'd kept behind the circulation desk. With her free hand, she checked the time—only a couple of hours away from guests arriving. Chaynie had opened the event early enough that the participants would have daylight hours to enter the drawing for door prizes, mingle a bit inside the library, then choose food from the vendor tables, find a place on the lawn, and settle in. February in Texas meant sunset would occur around six o'clock, which was when the movie would begin.

Her phone pinged with a text from Greg. *Screen is up. Wanna come see?*

Smiling, she capped the bottle and walked outside to the lawn, already buzzing with activity. Sam had finished laying down tarps and was already placing a few chairs for those who might prefer them over blankets. The men from the barbershop quartet were setting up their microphones and a makeshift stage near the library's wall. Britney was at a nearby table, fluffing up the tissue paper of a door prize gift bag.

"Look at that!" Chaynie shielded her eyes from the sun as she joined Greg in the middle of the lawn. She stared up at their handiwork—an enormous white screen, perfectly centered on the library's side wall.

"It's huge! Bigger than I'd imagined. It's hanging from the roof, right?"

"Yeah, it took four of us to get it secured, but trust me, it is. A tornado couldn't blow it away. Well, okay, maybe a tornado, but that's not in the forecast, thankfully. Pete's already rigged up the projector and done a sound check. As we get closer to dusk, he can test the picture on the screen."

"This will be amazing." Chaynie lowered her hand and heard her stomach grumble so loudly she wondered if Greg heard it too. "Guess I'm a little hungry. No time to eat today."

"Well, we can fix that. My office is close by. Let's take a break and go raid my new fridge. Besides, you haven't seen the finished product. The office furniture arrived last week. I want you to see it."

"I don't think there's time."

"Chay, everything is under control. C'mon. Five minutes? You deserve a break, and you need to eat. Your mom would back me up on this."

"Manipulation and guilt tactics? That's not your style, Greg Peterson."

"But are they working?"

"Well, yes, but I can *only* spare five minutes."

"I swear."

They walked across the street to Greg's new office, where he unlocked the door then swung it open to let Chaynie inside first.

"Wow. I can't believe this place." Chaynie swiveled around to view the entire space as Greg flicked on the light. "It's gorgeous. All of it. The colors, the furniture. It's very professional."

"So, you approve?" Greg walked past her, toward a mini fridge discreetly wedged into a back corner.

"More than approve. I'm incredibly impressed."

Greg opened the door and drew out two cans. "Coke or Pibb?"

"Pibb. Always."

He replaced the Coke and brought out another Mr. Pibb. "My favorite too." He handed her a cold can.

She popped the tab open and took a long, refreshing drink. It hit the spot.

"I found this too." He gave her an energy bar. "Consider it lunch."

Chaynie accepted the bar then set down her drink and peeled open the package. She leaned against the nearby desk.

"Anything wrong?" he asked. "I mean, today is stressful—it's all on your shoulders—but you seem... I don't know. Distracted by something else."

How can he possibly see it, this anxiety over my job interview? Is it written on my face?

Chaynie could easily give him the fake all-is-well answer, but maybe it *would* help to get it out in the open, off her chest. Maybe she could focus more easily on the Valentine's event if she unburdened herself to Greg.

"You're right," she confessed, playing with the bit of wrapper she'd peeled away. "I got a call this afternoon, from Virginia, about my application. They've scheduled an interview."

Greg raised his eyebrows. "That's big. It's really happening, then."

"I guess so."

"How do you feel about it?"

"That's the weird thing. I thought I would be ecstatic. I mean, weeks ago, when I applied for all these positions, I couldn't wait to get a call like this, but now..."

"What's changed?" Greg set down his can and shifted his weight.

Chaynie hadn't yet sorted things out internally past that point, so she couldn't answer his question accurately. "I have some mixed feelings, I guess. There hasn't been a minute to let it sink in. The timing of the call was unexpected."

Greg stared at the floor, silent. Chaynie had hoped for some reassurance from him, some input about the situation, some clarity, but all she expected was another "Oh."

"What are you thinking?" she asked.

Greg's gaze met hers as he gave a gentle shrug. "I've got mixed feelings too. It's why I tried to talk to you earlier. Chaynie, I want you to be happy. I want you to have the career you've been waiting for, but Virginia... it's so far from Morgan's Grove. Is there a chance for a closer library, maybe in Texas?"

Chaynie shook her head. "I've already gotten rejections from my applications in Texas. There are more to try, I guess, but I need to give this interview a chance first. See what comes next with Virginia. It's worth exploring, isn't it?"

Greg frowned and took a step backward, rubbing his face with his palm. He seemed out of sorts. "I have no right to say this, but here goes. I think you and I have been building something the last few weeks. We haven't talked about it or defined anything, but I feel it between us, and a huge part of me wants to say this incredibly selfish thing to you."

"What's that?"

"Stay. I want you to stay in Texas, to stay in Morgan's Grove. But at the same time, I don't want you to sacrifice your dreams, your career. If Virginia is what you really want..." He gave a small, frustrated sigh and shook his head. "I don't know what I'm saying. This has caught me off guard."

Both their cell phones chimed at the same time with a text message.

Greg glanced at his screen. "Pete."

"He's texting me too. I guess our break is over."

"Can we talk about this later? The interview and... some other stuff?"

"Sure. I won't leave until next Wednesday. We'll have plenty of time."

She could tell her answer didn't satisfy him—Greg wore the same discontented expression as when she'd first told him about the interview, and part of her regretted saying anything at all. Because now, with his reaction, she was more confused than ever.

AFTER ANSWERING PETE'S questions and checking on the student volunteers again, Chaynie realized something. She had told her mother, Savannah, and Greg about the interview but not the person who would be most affected. It was time to tell Mary.

Chaynie took a chance that things at the library wouldn't fall apart without her presence for the next few minutes and decided to find Mary, who was upstairs in her office on a rare break.

She tapped on the open door and caught Mary's eye. "May I come in?"

"Certainly." Mary pointed toward the chair across from her desk after Chaynie shut the door. "Is anything wrong? With the event details, I mean?"

"No, no," Chaynie assured her, taking a seat. "Everything is set up, and the only thing we're waiting on are the attendees. It's all gone quite smoothly, in the end."

"Well, that's a tribute to you. I'm so proud of all you've done for today's event. When I handed you that assignment weeks ago, I never dreamed it would become this big, this epic. Surely the entire town will turn out for it!"

"I'm not sure we have quite enough lawn for that, but I do hope we have a very strong turnout. And it's been a group effort. Sam, Britney, Greg, and Pete—they've all done so much to help. I could never have done all this on my own."

"We have a strong, committed team here."

Chaynie swallowed hard. *How can I tell Mary that I plan on breaking up the team by leaving?*

"Well, that's what I needed to talk to you about. This isn't the best timing, but I wanted you to hear it from me first."

Chaynie started at the beginning, telling Mary about the applications she'd sent in early January then explaining that she loved Morgan's Grove, adored the library, but was eager to spread her wings and find a head-librarian position. She recognized, halfway through, that she was talking too fast, but she continued on. Before she could lose her nerve, Chaynie told Mary about the interview in Virginia.

When she was finished, Chaynie breathed in and studied Mary's expression, which was stoic. Mary was rarely stoic.

"I probably should have told you weeks ago," Chaynie confessed. "About the applications. I wasn't purposely trying to hide my situation, but I couldn't be sure anything would pan out, so I waited until—"

"Until you got a call for an interview."

"Precisely."

Mary's expression had softened, but Chaynie still couldn't tell what Mary was thinking.

"Are you... upset with me? For trying to leave?"

That was when Mary finally smiled—a warm, genuine smile that told Chaynie she wasn't upset in the least. Mary leaned in toward the desk and clasped her hands, looking Chaynie in the eye. "Of course I'm not upset. I was processing your news. I understand your desire to branch out, use your skills and your training. Chaynie, you deserve to be the head librarian, not some assistant for the rest of your life. I've been grateful you've stayed on as long as you have."

This was going better than Chaynie had expected.

"But..." Mary shook her head. "I'm afraid I've been keeping something from you too. As you know, I've recently had a birthday. A big one. *Seventy.*" She drew out every syllable of the word in hushed, overdramatic tones. "I usually don't put stock in numbers. 'Age is just a frame of mind,' I've always said, but this particular birthday has hit me in an unexpected way. I've been mulling this over for a couple of years, actually, but suddenly, with seventy, it's upon me."

"What's upon you?"

Mary unclasped her hands and tapped her painted fingernail on the desk. "I wasn't going to announce this until next week, at our Monday staff meeting. I wanted to give your Valentine's event the spotlight it deserved and not spoil it with my own news, but, here goes. I've made the decision to retire."

"Retire?"

"Can you believe the timing? It's positively eerie."

"I had no idea you were thinking of retiring. Are you sure about it?"

"I've been incredibly stubborn, Chaynie. I've fought the idea for so long, always worried that I would be lonely or bored or would feel my age when retirement rolled around. That I would become *old*. But I've been chatting with some of the Sassy Ladies, and they've been so encouraging. Most all of them are retired, and they highly recommend it. They love being retired, the freedom it offers. No more being chained to duties and desks. The ladies gave me all sorts of ideas about travel and hobbies, committees I could be on, volunteer work I could do around town. I would finally have *time* for those things if I retire. Speaking with them has changed my entire perspective. I'll stay at the library for about a month, but then I'm leaving. For good."

Chaynie could see the emotion in Mary's eyes as she spoke those last two words—how final they must sound to her, saying them aloud.

Mary drew in a breath then continued. "This will probably throw a wrench in things for you, considering your interview, but you were the first—and only—person I thought of to fill the slot, taking over as head librarian here. I wasn't even going to advertise the position. You're more than qualified and capable. I could trust you, Chaynie. I could leave this cherished library in your hands and walk away with total peace of mind. You know this place as well as I do, inside and out, and more than anything else, you *love* this place as much as I do. You've loved it since you were a little girl."

"That's true," Chaynie whispered, still reeling from the turn of events.

"So. What do you say? Is Morgan's Grove Library in the running? Would you consider taking this position? It's not as prestigious as working for a huge university, and not nearly as challenging, but this library has its own charms. I'd be willing to negotiate salary and benefits, though I'm not sure we could match the competition. The job is yours, here and now, if you want it."

"I don't know what to say," Chaynie fumbled. She rose to her feet, suddenly remembering the pressing duties that awaited her downstairs. The clock was ticking, and she couldn't possibly respond to Mary's news with a thoughtful answer. "This is the absolute last thing I expected when I walked into your office."

Mary stood, too, then rounded her desk, meeting Chaynie on the other side.

"I've caught you off guard," Mary admitted. "I'm sorry. I wasn't going to tell you, today of all days, but then you came to me, and... well, I had to let you know that you have options." She clasped Chaynie's arms and peered up into her face. "Listen, there's no rush. I don't need an immediate answer. Get through today, consider what I've said, and maybe we can talk about it after the weekend. Okay?"

"Thank you for thinking of me. I'm so honored."

"Everything I said was true." She removed her grasp. "When you make this decision, do me one favor."

"What's that?"

"Use your head, but listen to your heart a little too."

Exactly what her mother had told her last night.

"I will. I promise."

Chapter Twenty

"Chay, this crowd! It's not even four o' clock yet!" her mother whispered.

"I know. I wasn't expecting anyone for another half hour."

They stood at the corner of the library's lawn, watching about two dozen people wandering around, some getting food, some spreading out blankets, some standing and chattering.

"School just let out," Chaynie mused. "And I'm sure you told everyone in sight about the event. Are these teachers and students?"

"Mostly. I recognize a lot of them. But, hey, they're drawing interest from the rest of the square. Look!" She pointed across the street to a couple of people paused outside a shop, staring toward the library. "Trust me. Curiosity will bring people in too. This is going to be great!" She turned back to Chaynie. "I meant to ask earlier—are you excited about the interview?"

"Excited is too strong a word. And there have been a couple of... developments."

"Do tell."

"It's too much to get into right now, but I promise you'll know everything tonight, after the movie."

"Sounds mysterious. I can't believe you're leaving me hanging!"

"I'm so cruel. Go have a great time with Mitch tonight. Are you still glad you said yes to him?"

"Very. I feel calm and comfortable, and that's all I hoped for tonight."

Chaynie side-hugged her mother then watched her join Mitch on his blanket, where he had secured the corners with a couple of rocks. Chaynie knew her mother appreciated those tiny gestures, the way he took care of her, thought of her first. Watching her mother beam at him as she approached the blanket, Chaynie could easily see things progressing between them, possibly swiftly after tonight.

Chaynie's attention drifted over to another blanket, where she recognized Savannah talking to a guy. But it wasn't Greg. It was Lucas.

Almost by telepathy, Savannah looked up to see Chaynie, who crooked her finger in a come-here gesture. Savannah whispered to Lucas then came jogging over to Chaynie.

"Are you sharing a blanket? With him?" Chaynie asked.

"Yes and yes. Lucas found me during second period this morning and asked if I was coming to the library event. Then he asked me to share his blanket, and I said yes."

"What about Greg?"

Savannah rolled her eyes. "We both know that's dead in the water. I never had a chance with him."

"What do you mean?"

"Well, I got real with myself today. I remembered the *very few* encounters I've ever had with Greg, and they were formal at best. He was nice to me, but let's face it. There's no spark, not on his end, at least. He was only being polite. He's just not into me, and I've accepted it. Why keep chasing someone who doesn't want you back? It's exhausting. Besides, I have it on good authority that Greg is interested in someone else. A certain librarian—tall, sophisticated, well-read."

"Stop it." Chaynie play-slapped Savannah's arm.

"No, I'm serious. A few minutes ago, when I first got here, I saw Greg staring intensely at someone across the lawn. I followed his eyeline, and *you* were the someone. It wasn't a creepy stare. It was this sweet, lingering gaze, like a scene out of a Jane Austen novel. Then he looked away, probably thinking nobody saw him. But I did, and that's when I knew for sure. He's into *you*. C'mon, what's the real scoop with you two?"

"Nothing. I mean, we've been hanging out *as friends*," she emphasized. "But if I'm honest, then okay, yes. I think something's been happening between us. I guess I was in denial." Chaynie winced. "Are you mad? I mean, this is weird, right? Liking the same guy?"

"Well, technically, you're the only one liking him now. I've moved on." She nodded toward Lucas, who had wandered to The Pit's table and was selecting a Mississippi Mud.

Relieved, Chaynie told her, "I'm glad things aren't awkward between us."

"They never were. I was in denial, too, about Greg. I kept thinking he'd come around, but he never did. And besides, Lucas keeps hovering around my classroom, asking questions that anybody else could answer, coming up with excuses to talk to me. It's sweet. I mean, he's, like, five years younger than me, but..." She rose up on her tiptoes to whisper, "I think I might be falling for him," then lowered herself again.

"I'm happy for you, Savannah."

"The question is, what are *you* gonna do? About Greg? About the interview?"

"I've been pushing it away all day, using the Valentine's event to avoid it, but I can't keep hiding forever."

"You'll make all the right decisions in the end." Savannah squeezed Chaynie's elbow. "Happy Valentine's!"

"You too." Chaynie smiled as she watched her friend rejoin Lucas on their blanket.

THIS IS IT. The evening Chaynie had fretted over and planned for was finally here. Chaynie stood at the edge of the library's wall, listening to Britney call out the name of the final door-prize winner. The quartet had set up their own sound system, so Britney had been using their microphone to talk to the crowd while Amy interpreted through sign language from a nearby seat.

Chaynie scanned the audience with her eyes—over two hundred attendees, at least. Double what she'd anticipated. They had spilled over into the street with their blankets and chairs, and Sam had to scramble to find extras. "A good problem to have," her dad would've said.

Pete stood at his post with the projector ready to roll. The vendors had nearly sold out of all their food and had taken their places on the lawn to enjoy the movie. Just as Chaynie and Greg had envisioned weeks ago, the night was for everyone—children, couples, singles, young people, older people, and even pets. Every possible age group and status was represented, a true community gathering. And under the glow of the hanging lights draped from tree to tree, Chaynie saw what she'd hoped for on people's faces, happiness. They were glad to be there, at this place, on this night, and so was Chaynie.

Dusk had fallen on Morgan's Grove, and a dark sky lay over the town, punctuated with shimmering stars. Cobalt-blue tones gave the skyline a beautiful glow as the sun continued to set. Chaynie closed her eyes and let the cool air touch her cheeks. She couldn't have asked for a more perfect evening.

She opened her eyes to notice that one thing was missing. She hadn't seen Greg in at least an hour, when he'd been chatting with Pete near the projector. Chaynie scanned the crowd again, trying to find his familiar image. She saw his parents sitting in chairs with Buddy at their feet, but no sign of Greg.

"It's time to hand the mic over to the creator and organizer of this event, Chaynie Mayfield!"

Chaynie's attention snapped toward Britney, who was awaiting her on the stage.

The audience was clapping, all eyes on Chaynie. She tucked a wavy lock of hair behind her ear and walked toward Britney, taking the microphone with a whispered "Thanks."

She wasn't normally afraid of public speaking, but suddenly, Chaynie became flustered. When she noticed the entire group of Sassy Ladies in the front row, she relaxed. These people were in her corner—glad to be there, excited for a fun evening. She had nothing to be nervous about.

Chaynie cleared her throat and spoke into the microphone, gauging its volume. "I want to thank everyone for coming out tonight. It's a special evening where we celebrate all kinds of love. That's the purpose of tonight's event, to enjoy each other's company and to experience fellowship, food, and a classic film. I hope you have a wonderful time. Happy Valentine's!"

The applause started up again, with a couple of sharp whistles coming from the direction of Savannah's blanket.

"To kick off this magical night, here's our beloved Morgan's Grove quartet to sing a *Music Man* medley. Please help me welcome our very own award-winning foursome, Then and Now!"

The crowd went wild as Chaynie secured the microphone onto the stand and stood aside for the quartet to approach the stage. She walked away, back into the darkness, and watched the quartet bow and wave as the crowd continued to cheer. Finally, the clapping died down, and Stan blew the pitch pipe for the first chord of "Lida Rose."

Chaynie returned to her place on the sidelines with nothing left to do. No calls to make, no one to check on, no to-do list to consult. All she had to do was enjoy the results of her efforts. She hadn't even thought of what to do past that point. Her mother had offered space on her blanket with Mitch, but three was a crowd, so Chaynie had planned to find an empty space somewhere in the back row when the movie began.

The quartet moved smoothly into another song, and Chaynie swayed to the easy rhythm, her arms crossed at her chest. Near the front row, she spied a little boy, maybe four years old, mesmerized by the quartet, clapping along.

More than the event, more than the quartet or the movie or the food, Chaynie decided something else had made that evening special. It was Morgan's Grove itself. She was staring at the heart of the town, its people, all in one place, folks she'd known her entire life—teachers and pastors, store owners and coworkers, family and friends.

Her eyes wandered toward Savannah, singing along with the quartet, then to her mother, bobbing her head in rhythm to the music. *This* was home, these people, this town, this library—right here, right now—and it always had been.

Chaynie thought she'd clicked off her phone, but she felt it vibrate in her pocket. She stepped backward, toward the library and away from the crowd, and saw a text from Greg. *I have a surprise. Upstairs in the library.*

Chaynie heard the intro music of the film play as the strong light emanated from Pete's projector in the distance. The crowd was still, settled in, ready to watch.

She tapped out a response to Greg. *Coming now.*

By the time she reached the second floor on foot, the movie's familiar music still lingering in her ears, Chaynie had guessed Greg's surprise. He was finished with the alcove.

She looked toward the Children's Corner and saw Greg standing at its entrance. He wore a wide smile, which grew wider as she approached.

"I didn't think you'd mind being pulled away for a bit," he said. "Everything going well downstairs?"

"Everything is *perfect*. So, what's this surprise of yours?"

Greg stepped aside and let Chaynie walk into the dark space.

"Here, let me get the lights."

He pressed a button nearby, and suddenly, the finished tree came to life, glowing with tiny fairy lights all over its branches. Chaynie's mouth fell open as she moved toward the tree, taking it all in. The tree trunk was enormous in scale, and the new branches dangled delicate green leaves illuminated by the soft glow of light.

"I can't take my eyes off it," she told Greg, realizing the level of intricate detail he had added to the trunk since she'd last seen it—the lushness of the branches, the symmetry of the leaves draping downward. "It's exactly what I pictured in my head. You brought it to life."

Greg stepped in behind her, and though they weren't touching, she could feel the warmth of his presence inches away.

"And there's something else. I'll need the overhead light for this."

As Greg reached over to flick it on, Chaynie's focus was pulled downward, away from the twinkling branches. Her reading chair came into view, but it wasn't the original chair. It was taller, grander. The wood was carved and detailed, and the seat held a purple velour cushion.

Chaynie moved forward to touch the arm.

"It's your new chair. Dad and I have been working on it in his shed for the past few weeks."

She noticed the carvings of vines and branches and grapes to match the forest theme. "It's almost like a throne."

"That's what we were going for. You can be the queen of the Book Forest."

Chaynie pivoted away from the chair to see Greg. "I don't know what to say. It's so beautiful. I never expected..." She knew she was rambling, and she felt sudden, surprising tears stinging her eyes. Perhaps the weight of the entire day had settled on her at once. It was all too much. "You've been so good to me, and I..."

"Hey, no tears. I wasn't trying to make you cry." Greg raised his hand to wipe the corner of her eye with a tender touch. His hand lingered near her face as he stroked her cheek.

"It's the best gift. So thoughtful. I don't deserve it."

"Sure you do. In fact, you deserve one more thing."

Chaynie sniffed back her tears. "What are you talking about? This is enough, more than enough."

Greg removed his hand from her cheek and produced a small gold box from his pocket.

"Open it."

Chaynie lifted the box and raised the lid slowly. Inside, on a velvety pillow, sat a silver circle of jewelry. Chaynie drew the chain out with her fingertips. "A bracelet," she whispered.

"And something else."

Chaynie looked closer and saw a silver piece dangling at the end of the chain.

"A charm bracelet," she said.

On Valentine's Day. The connection struck her instantly—the vivid memory of all those other charms, all those other Valentine's Days.

She gazed up into Greg's face, and she knew. "It was you. All those years ago in school. A new charm every Valentine's Day for—"

"For five years," Greg confirmed. "It was me."

"But I thought... I mean, Dean Reynolds told me *he* was the one giving me the charms. That jerk. He took all the credit! But you were my secret admirer all along."

"I still am. Well, not so secret anymore."

He opened the clasp and dangled the bracelet over her wrist.

Chaynie went backward in her mind, picturing a shy, young Greg shopping for the perfect charm, wrapping it, then sneaking into the classroom to place it on her chair. Every year.

"But why? I mean, we barely knew each other in school. Why me?"

Greg secured the clasp then pushed his hand into his jeans pocket. "Well, that first Valentine's, you were the new kid. Your dad had moved you to Morgan's Grove, and you didn't know anyone, and I saw the way the other girls treated you."

Chaynie nodded. "That was a tough year."

"Some were mean, but mostly, they kept their distance, didn't include you. I understood how that felt, so I thought I'd give you a present to cheer you up and to give the other girls something to talk about."

"But why the years after that? By the next year, the girls had warmed up to me, and I had made friends. I wasn't the new girl anymore, but the charms kept coming."

"I liked how the first charm made you happy. So I kept getting them." He pointed toward Chaynie's wrist. "This charm is an open book. I thought it could represent your love for books, obviously, but also your open future. It can be whatever you want it to be. You get to write your own story."

A sudden, comforting warmth flooded Chaynie's entire body as she stood, charm bracelet on her wrist, peering up at this man, the most caring man she'd ever known, aside from her father. He was a good man, inside and out, and most importantly, someone she could trust with her entire heart. On this Valentine's Day and every day after.

She stepped closer and moved her hands to touch his chest. "Ask me again," she whispered, hoping he understood.

Greg clasped his hands around her waist. "Stay."

Chaynie's answer was in the form of a kiss. She leaned in and pressed her lips to his, feeling their warmth and softness. Greg responded, touching her neck and hair, drawing her closer, kissing her deeper. When Chaynie backed away slightly, head spinning, heart thumping, she smiled as Greg stroked her shoulder.

"I'm not going anywhere," she assured him. "This is home. The library, my friends, my mother, they're all right here. And so are you."

Greg leaned in for another kiss, and it was every bit as magical and dizzying for Chaynie as the first one.

When they parted, Chaynie touched his lips and traced his smile. "Thank you for my present. And for the beautiful tree."

"You're welcome. Happy Valentine's."

Chaynie started to lean in again, but something drew her attention away. She heard the energetic beginning notes of "Ya Got Trouble" piped in from the movie below and remembered the event going on without them. Although a huge part of her wanted to stay in the alcove with Greg and linger in the afterglow of their kisses, she knew that many more were to come, especially on a romantic Valentine's night. She felt a strong pull to join the rest of the town and enjoy the special night she and Greg had worked so hard to create.

"Let's go join the others. You *have* to watch this song. It's a classic." She grasped his hand and led him out of the alcove.

Outside, the moviegoers seemed enthralled by Robert Preston's lighthearted but dire warning about the town needing to form a band... or else! Even the children on the lawn, many eating popcorn or cotton candy, were glued to the sight.

As she walked toward the crowd, Chaynie switched places with Greg, and he led her to his blanket set up on the outskirts of the lawn, likely to give everyone else the best spots. *So Greg of him.*

They settled onto the blanket, and Chaynie rested against Greg's chest as he wrapped his arms around her. She held his hands and felt the new charm bracelet brush against her skin. Never could she have imagined how this Valentine's night would end—watching a favorite film in the comforting arms of a brand-new love, under a canopy of stars, and surrounded by people she adored. Chaynie was exactly where she was meant to be.

Mississippi Mud Recipe

~ <u>First layer (brownie)</u>

In a mixer, cream together:

2 cups sugar

2 sticks softened butter

4 eggs

Then add:

1 ⅓ cups natural unsweetened cocoa

1 ½ cups flour

¼ teaspoon salt

2 teaspoons vanilla

Pour into a glass cake pan (greased with butter) and bake:

350 degrees for 30 minutes

<u>Second Layer (marshmallow)</u>

Remove pan from oven and spread 16 ounces of marshmallow cream over the brownie layer.

<u>Third Layer (fudge frosting)</u>

In a saucepan, over medium to medium-high heat, mix:

1 cup sugar

½ cup natural unsweetened cocoa

1 ½ sticks butter

½ cup skim milk

2 tablespoons Karo light corn syrup

dash of salt

Then:

Bring it to a boil.

Stir 3 minutes (while boiling).

Remove from heat.

Finally, pour the mixture into a mixer and add:

2 teaspoons vanilla

4 ½ cups powdered sugar

(Add a little more sugar to reach desired frosting consistency.)

Pour the frosting over the marshmallow layer in long continuous pours to mostly cover the second layer. The marshmallows will bubble up through the fudge frosting to give a unique texture and appearance.

Acknowledgements

To my entire extended family, whose support and encouragement mean everything.

To beloved family members who are no longer with me and have made their exit to heaven: Daddy, Maw, Pa-Paw, Grammy, Pappy, and Mark. They would have been so supportive of this new book and series. I miss them every day.

To all those friends who have been my cheerleaders along the way: Augusta Malvagno, Linda Bratcher, Becky Bray, Karen Peterson, Michelle Cotter, Doris Lininger, Sue Willis, Sheree Webb, Deanna Markham, Stephen and Laurie Stine, Carla Krae, Rebecca Sanders, Rae Champagne, Brittni Tracy, Leigh Ann Olejnik, and Silvana Vierkant-Waller, as well as my beloved Commando sisters.

Special thanks to my publisher, Lynn McNamee, whose professionalism, knowledge, and ambition have helped create an amazing publishing company that produces high-quality books. I'm honored to be on board with Red Adept.

Also special thanks to my line editor, Amanda Kruse. Her careful input and guidance has heightened the quality of this book. She made the editing experience informative and enjoyable.

To the entire Red Adept team, but especially Erica Lucke Dean, Streetlight Graphics (particularly Glendon Haddix), and all the proofreaders and formatters. This novel is what it is because of your diligence and dedication and talents. I'm so grateful to you. And I *love* my cover.

To Clint Jones at Motophoto for my author photo.

Finally, all thanks to God, who makes everything in this life worthwhile. He is the Source.

Also by Traci Borum

Chilton Crosse
Painting the Moon
Finding the Rainbow
Seeking the Star
Savoring the Seasons

Morgan's Grove
Love Starts Here
Meet You Under the Stars

Standalone
The Chilton Crosse Collection #1

Watch for more at writerscorner-traci.blogspot.com.

About the Author

Traci Borum is an insatiable bookworm whose first love is fiction. As a little girl, she became mesmerized with books—with the textures, the smells, and most especially, the worlds created between the pages. Years later, she discovered she could create her *own* worlds by writing. She's been scribbling away ever since, writing bits of poetry, articles, and especially fiction.

Traci has been a Creative Writing teacher at a community college for the past ten years. She's a native Texan and an Anglophile at heart. She owns two "British" dogs—a Corgi and a Sheltie—and she's completely addicted to Masterpiece Theater (must be those dreamy British accents!). More than anything, she treasures the friendships in her life and adores her supportive family.

Read more at writerscorner-traci.blogspot.com.

About the Publisher

Dear Reader,

We hope you enjoyed this book. Please consider leaving a review on your favorite book site.

Visit https://RedAdeptPublishing.com to see our entire catalogue.

Don't forget to subscribe to our monthly newsletter to be notified of future releases and special sales.

9 781948 051620